ON THE BRINK

COMPLETE BOXED SET

ERIKA RHYS

For Christina Ross, in appreciation of friendship, encouragement, and inspiration.

For Teresa Woroniecka, in gratitude for unwavering friendship and support.

Copyright and Legal Notice:

This publication is protected under the US Copyright Act of 1976 and all other applicable international, federal, state and local laws, and all rights are reserved, including resale rights.

Any trademarks, service marks, product names or named features are assumed to be the property of their respective owners, and are used only for reference. There is no implied endorsement if we use one of these terms. No part of this book may be reproduced in any form by any electronic or mechanical means (including photocopying, recording, or information storage and retrieval) without permission in writing from the author.

First ebook edition © 2013.

Disclaimer:

This is a work of fiction. Any similarity to persons living or dead (unless explicitly noted) is merely coincidental. Copyright © 2013 Erika Rhys. All rights reserved worldwide.

ALSO BY ERIKA RHYS

Heir of the Hamptons

The Gentlemen's Club, vol. 1

The Gentlemen's Club, vol. 2

The Gentlemen's Club, vol. 3

Over the Edge, vol. 1

Over the Edge, vol. 2

On the Brink, vol. 1

On the Brink, vol. 2

On the Brink, vol. 3

ON THE BRINK, VOL. 1

1

Boston, MA

"Nope. No Juliana West in the university payroll system. You have to fill out a W-4 form and make sure your department has filed the necessary paperwork."

Hunched toad-like behind her dingy monitor, the payroll office employee glared at me and tapped a few final keystrokes with her chipped red talons. Through oversized glasses, her magnified, bulging eyes communicated a surprising degree of ire. After all, I had submitted the paperwork in question.

Twice.

I told her so.

"I have no record of that. You'll need to submit again. Sorry."

Her tone said that she wasn't sorry at all, so I turned and left the Tremont University payroll office with my shoulders slumped, and my eyes burning with unshed tears. Frustration and despair threatened to overwhelm me.

I needed rent money in two weeks, and the odds of getting it were rapidly approaching zero.

For two stressful months, I'd managed to survive without a paycheck, but time was running out. I would resubmit my employment paperwork to the university, but there was little hope that it would get through their labyrinthine payment system before the rent was due. My bank account was empty, and my credit card was maxed.

Since graduating in May, I'd applied for dozens of jobs, and signed up with every temp agency in town. A few times, I'd made it to the interview stage. But someone else inevitably got the job. At this point, I was exhausted and worried. The economy was weak, and young, less-experienced people—like me—had difficulty finding work.

For the moment, what I had was a part-time teaching gig at Tremont for the fall semester. I was grateful that I wasn't completely unemployed, but the Tremont job had yet to pay me, thanks to a succession of paperwork screw-ups. I was broke, and after today's depressing visit to the payroll office, I was concerned that I might not see a paycheck anytime soon.

And then what?

I'd borrowed last month's rent from Duncan—my best friend and roommate—but at this point we were pretty much penniless. In a heartbeat, our unsympathetic landlord would evict us from our drafty little Somerville apartment, and it would be my fault. Most recent graduates would get help from their parents, but that wasn't an option for us; Duncan's parents were dead, and if my DNA donors had a nickel to share with anyone, it sure as hell wouldn't be me.

I pulled my phone from my briefcase and called Duncan.

"Hey Jules—any luck getting paid?" His baritone voice sounded concerned.

"No. The Tremont payroll hags lost my paperwork again. It's probably buried somewhere in their shithole of an office, wedged between a broken pencil sharpener and a ceramic frog. I'll resubmit, but we can't be sure that my check will show up before next month's rent is due. Bottom line, Dunc, I've got to find another job. Any job —and fast."

Duncan sighed. "Unbelievable. I've asked for more hours, but no shifts have opened up yet. I'll post my Nikon on eBay. It should sell for enough money to cover the rent."

When he offered to sell something that I knew was so dear to him, I felt a wave of affection for Duncan. He always had my back. But I couldn't let him sell the Nikon. He'd saved for months to buy it. It was the best camera he'd ever owned, and photography was his passion.

"Hold off for a couple days, OK? One of my co-workers mentioned that transcription services pay well—if you can type fast enough. If that doesn't work out, I'll try the temp agencies again. And I'll keep fighting with the Tremont payroll office."

"Remind me never to graduate in a crap economy," Duncan said. "Or to major in art."

"Never again," I agreed. "I never thought that I'd say this, but I'm now glad that I minored in business. If my painting career doesn't take off soon, I'm going to quit teaching art and look for a full-time commercial design job. Either that, or I'll go to business school and at least stand some chance in hell of getting a job."

Several hours and a dozen phone calls later, an agency called Perfect Transcripts offered me the opportunity of work, but only if I could type 60 words per minute and pass a transcription test. The woman with whom I spoke—a Ms. Klein—scheduled me to take the test at 4 p.m. After I hung up the phone, I immediately texted Duncan.

Job interview at 4!!! Wish me luck.

A moment later, my phone chimed.

Yaaay! Fingers crossed. Knock their socks off!!!

I quickly decided what to wear. Given my limited wardrobe, it certainly wasn't difficult. I owned a single black business suit—a lucky find at Filene's Basement—that I paired with an ivory silk blouse and faux pearls. I wore my hair up instead of down, and glasses in lieu of my usual contacts. Light foundation and a touch of eyeliner helped to complete a look that was professional. I checked myself in the mirror and stuck out my tongue at my reflection.

Though people sometimes told me that I was beautiful, I didn't see it. My dark hair, thick and wavy, seemed perpetually out of control, and my skin, though smooth and unblemished, always looked too pale for my taste. My eyes—green, expressive, and long-lashed—were the one aspect of my appearance that I liked.

Shoes were an issue. My one pair of good black heels had done way too much time on the dance floor and they looked more than a little shabby. I tore through the contents of the bathroom closet and turned up a grungy container of desiccated brown polish, but didn't find any black.

And then an idea struck.

I raced to the kitchen, grabbed a handful of junk flyers from the recycling bin, and then ran to the tiny room that functioned as my painting studio. There, I tossed the flyers in the center of the floor, placed the offending heels on the flyers, shook a can of fast-drying black spray paint, and sprayed my shoes until they gleamed almost as if they were new. I opened the studio window to get rid of the paint fumes, congratulated myself on a job well done, and checked the time. Twenty minutes to spare. I needed to get a move on.

I left the heels to dry and checked the contents of my briefcase. Two forms of ID, several copies of my resume, keys, cash, phone. I retrieved the freshly black heels, shoved my feet into them, and crossed my fingers that the paint fumes would wear off before I arrived at the agency.

2

I exited the Red Line subway at Kendall Square and emerged into the warm sunlight and crisp air of a perfect fall day. Next to MIT and the Charles River, the cityscape of modern office towers housed biotech and other technology businesses. I walked for several blocks, until I reached Manning Tower, where Perfect Transcripts was located.

Sheathed in dark glass, Manning Tower reflected bright flashes of the descending October sun. I passed through the revolving doors into a gloomy atrium, its expanse of steel and dark glass interrupted by a security desk and a bank of elevators.

I glanced at my watch, realized that I was early, and decided that I should wait downstairs in the atrium for ten minutes or so. I found a bench to one side of the doors, sat down, and rested my briefcase at my feet.

A tall businessman in a dark suit emerged from one of the elevators, and walked briskly toward the security desk, not twenty feet away from where I sat. As he came closer, I nearly knocked over my briefcase. In my entire life, I'd never seen a more striking man.

He was tall and lean, and his dark blue eyes contrasted with his olive skin. Tousled black hair and a touch of stubble framed his chiseled features. His flawlessly fitted suit complimented his broad shoulders and narrow hips. This guy had it all. Beauty and masculinity in ideal proportion, accompanied by an air of supreme confidence unusual in such a young man—he didn't look a day over thirty.

He finished his conversation with the security guard, turned, and strode toward the doors—and toward me. For a split second, our eyes met, and his intense, dark gaze seared through me to my toes. I felt myself flush, and my imagination spiraled through a series of unlikely images, mostly X-rated. Then the doors closed behind him, and he was gone.

I watched him walk to the curb and get into a waiting limousine. Based on the limo—and the air of unselfconscious authority—he was probably a high-flying business executive. Since it appeared as if he knew the security guard, he probably had offices in the building.

I checked the time, and realized that I needed to focus. Now wasn't the time to indulge in fantasy, though God knows indulging in one with *that* man would have been festive in a different location and at another time.

Now, I needed to get to my interview, ace the typing test, and land this job, which I desperately needed. I got up, walked to the security desk, signed in, and took the elevator to the fourth floor.

The front office of Perfect Transcripts was generically professional with industrial carpet and off-white walls that were decorated with framed prints of New England landscapes. Under a print of a red-and-white lighthouse, an enormously fat, expensively dressed woman sat in an oversized swivel chair. A large monitor rested on her expansive glass-topped desk, flanked by a pair of fake plants and a dog bed. A Toy Maltese leapt from under the desk. Yip...yip-yip-yip...yip!

"Good afternoon," I said. "I'm Juliana West. I have an appointment with Ms. Klein to take a transcription test."

"Moxie!" the woman yelled. "Get in here." She turned to the dog and lowered her voice. "Dolce, shut up. Mama's right here." She extended her plump hand to me. "Berta Klein. I own Perfect Transcripts. Just call me Berta."

We shook hands. "You'll take the test with Moxie Palermo," Berta said. "Moxie's the office manager."

A thirtyish woman entered from a hallway to the left of Berta's desk. Tall and skeletally thin, with short, curly auburn hair, she was dressed eccentrically in a man's navy blazer over a short houndstooth skirt and bright yellow tights.

"Moxie, this is Juliana West," Berta said. "She's here to take the transcription test."

"Perfect! Why don't we get started?"

I followed her down a long hallway, and listened to her while she spoke. "It's just a short transcription job to test your speed and accuracy. If you type quickly and accurately, you'll be fine. The transcription area is here in the back." She lowered her voice to a whisper, and added, "Keep away from Dolce. He may be Berta's pride and joy, but mark my words, there's nothing sweet about that dog. That little shit bites."

The transcription area turned out to be a large, windowless room with workstations set up around the perimeter. The fluorescent-lit space could have used a fresh coat of paint, and its dingy walls were sparsely decorated with faded motivational posters. "Winners never quit and quitters never win—Vince Lombardi" read one. "You can have RESULTS or EXCUSES not both. Which one do YOU CHOOSE?" trumpeted another.

I choose a well-paying job, I thought.

Several women of varied ages and a lone man occupied the workstations, all wearing headphones and typing. Another woman, dressed in a faded but clean yellow blouse and a brown tweed skirt, was on her hands and knees, patting the floor around her with one hand.

"What in God's name are you doing down there, Luanne?" Moxie asked irritably. "Please don't tell me you're still searching for your missing earring. If it was here, we would have found it when I helped you look earlier."

Luanne clambered to her feet with some difficulty. Tall, angular, and sixtyish, with large hands and chapped, reddened skin, she wore oversized glasses with thick lenses, connected to a chain around her neck. The overall effect was that of a man in badly done drag, minus the lipstick. Even her hair reminded me of Jack Lemmon's wig in *Some Like it Hot*.

"But I'm positive I lost it right here," she said plaintively. "My daughter gave me those earrings for Christmas, and they're real 14-carat gold." Behind the thick glasses, her eyes were red-rimmed and watery, and it occurred to me that her vision might not be very good.

"Mind if I take a quick look?" I asked.

Moxie shrugged.

I picked up Luanne's desk lamp, angled its light underneath her desk, and swept the beam of light around. Something metallic glinted next to one of the back legs of the desk. I got down on my knees and crawled underneath the desk to retrieve it—a small gold ball earring. I extracted myself from under the desk, got to my feet, and handed it to Luanne.

"Is this it?" I asked.

"Bless you, sweetie. It is. Thank you for finding it." She threw a glare at Moxie. "I knew it was here."

Moxie rolled her eyes. "I'm glad your earring turned up, Luanne." She turned back to me. "Let's get on with the transcription test." She motioned at an unoccupied workstation.

"Here are some headphones. The test is five minutes of audio from a meeting. Accuracy is the top priority; speed is the second. I'll be working at that workstation over there. Come and get me when you're done."

I thanked Moxie and started the test. Half an hour later, I was done. I wasn't sure if I'd gotten everything right, but it was the best that I could do. I went over to Moxie's station and cleared my throat.

"Done already?" she said. "Berta's going to hire you for sure."

"I couldn't figure out a few spots where people were talking over each other, but the rest should be OK."

Moxie printed the transcript, looked over the printout, and motioned for me to follow her. She led the way back to the front office.

"She's a keeper, Berta. Accurate and fairly fast for a newbie."

Berta grabbed the transcript, gave it a quick glance, and nodded in agreement.

"Ten dollars an hour, unless it's medical or legal. Then it's twelve. If you work six hours or more, you get a thirty-minute paid break. Moxie, have Juliana put her hours on next week's schedule. Juliana, you can do the paperwork when you come in for your first shift. Just remember to bring a photo ID."

I contained my relief long enough to sign up for as many hours as I could fit around my teaching schedule. The moment the elevator doors closed behind me, I thrust my fists in the air in a silent whoop of joy. I'd finally done it. I'd found a job. Filled with excitement and relief, I reached into my briefcase, retrieved my phone, and texted Duncan.

Got the job!!!

3

Several subway stops and a fifteen-minute walk later, I reached the apartment that I shared with Duncan. I let myself in, kicked off my freshly spray-painted ghetto heels, and closed the door, glad to be home. The apartment was cramped and drafty, but at least now I could pay for it. Located on the top floor of a bright blue Victorian with white trim, it was conveniently close to the Davis Square subway station.

In addition to a kitchen, living room, and two small bedrooms, the apartment included a tiny, unheated room that served as my painting studio. Although the ancient kitchen lacked a dishwasher, and the bathroom was so tight, it barely permitted turning around, I loved the battered but beautiful dark hardwood floors and the creaky wooden pane windows that admitted generous patches of sunlight, filtered by the surrounding trees. When we first moved in, Duncan and I had painted the apartment in warm, inviting colors and furnished it with an eclectic mix of items purchased from thrift stores and IKEA, which created a cozy, funky atmosphere.

I changed into pajama bottoms and a T-shirt, made myself a tomato and cheese sandwich, poured a glass of water, and headed for the couch. After a few minutes of channel surfing, I settled on a

Masterpiece Theatre production of Jane Eyre. After my emotional roller coaster of a day, what I needed right now was to lose myself in another time and place.

Later, I was awakened by the rattle of Duncan's key in the lock. I sat up, stretched, and yawned, surprised that I had fallen asleep.

"Let's celebrate!" Duncan said, and held up a bottle of champagne. Tall and slender, with a thick shock of blond hair and blue-gray eyes, he always insisted on recognizing every victory in my life, however small.

I smiled at him with affection. "Champagne, Dunc? You spoil me. Not that I'm complaining, of course." I got up from the couch. "I'll get the glasses." I padded into the kitchen and returned with two champagne flutes. With fluid motions acquired during his years of waiting tables and tending bar, Duncan popped the cork and filled our glasses.

"To new jobs and paychecks!"

"New jobs and paid rent," I answered. I touched my glass to his, and then drained it. "Thank goodness for this job. Who knows when Tremont will get my paperwork sorted out?"

"It's just a matter of time," Duncan said. "But it's still an unnecessary pain in the ass."

Throughout the stress of the past few months, Duncan had been my rock. He was always there for me.

"Right now, I'm just grateful that I have a second job. Neither of my jobs is ideal, but at least I'm employed, and I have you—the perfect friend and roomie."

"You're tipsy," Duncan laughed. "No one's perfect."

"You are. Except, of course, when you hog the TV remote. In that respect, you're a standard-issue imperfect American male." I held out my empty glass. "More, please."

"Like you never grab the remote? Get real. Anyway, tell me more about your new job," Duncan said as he poured. "I need details."

"It's at a transcription agency in Kendall Square. Perfect Transcripts. My fellow inmates look to be a varied collection of oddballs and outcasts, but they seem nice. I think I'm going to like the office manager, Moxie. I can tell that she has a sense of humor. The boss, Berta, is a piece of work. She keeps a neurotic, yappy toy Maltese named Dolce next to her desk."

"Dolce?" Duncan sputtered. "Isn't that Italian for sweet, like the movie *La Dolce Vita*? That's sooo wrong."

"Tell me about it. Moxie Palermo—the office manager—warned me that Dolce's a biter."

Duncan narrowed his eyes at me. "I see rabies shots in your future."

"I see scars on my ankles."

"I see shit in your shoes."

"If he does that, I see me shoving that dog's nose in it."

"You know what's worse?"

"Nothing can be worse."

"You're wrong. I bet that dog's a serial humper. I can see him humping your leg."

My eyes popped in disgust. "If that dog humps my leg, I swear to God I'll bite him in the ass."

"Cookie, at this point in your life, you need a good humping. Take what you can get."

We cackled at that and, fueled by relief and champagne, we continued our bantering, as carefree and as silly as only best friends can be. After a particularly gut-busting laugh, I clutched my aching sides and begged for mercy.

"Stop...I can't...can't laugh any more. You're killing me." I took a deep breath and wiped my eyes.

"So, when do you start this high-risk job, anyway?" Duncan asked.

"Tomorrow at five. Between evenings and Saturdays, I'll have the rent by the first. Then I'll start to pay you back and catch up on other bills." I stopped short when I remembered the handsome businessman at Manning Tower. "Oh, my God, I can't believe I didn't tell you. I spotted a really dishy man today. I think he works in my building. Tall, dark, and built. Hot enough to cause global warming, and proof that it exists. The most amazing dark blue eyes I've ever seen."

"News of hot men is always welcome. Gay or straight?"

I threw up my hands. "You're asking the wrong girl. You know my gaydar sucks."

"Come on. Give me your best guess."

"Fine. I vote for straight. Straight, hot, and single." I giggled.

"Introduce us. I'd be delighted to suss out which team he plays for. Either way, he's bound to find one of us attractive."

Duncan, the eternal optimist. No one would ever guess, but much of his life had been difficult. It wasn't something he talked about, but I knew his story. Raised in a small town, and the only child of fundamentalist Christians, Duncan was bullied for his sexuality at school and beaten for it at home. When he was fifteen, his parents died in a car crash, and Duncan was sent to Boston to live with his only living relative, his father's estranged older sister.

Living with Marjorie was the best thing that could have happened to Duncan. Marjorie was a modern businesswoman, and considered homophobia both ridiculous and ignorant. She introduced Duncan to a better, kinder world, where he was valued for his intelligence and talent, and his sexuality was simply an attribute, like height or ethnicity. In this new setting, Duncan's naturally sunny disposition reasserted itself, and he discovered an interest in photography.

We met during our first weeks of art school and became friends almost at once. Now, I looked into his blue-gray eyes, basked in the warmth of his happiness for me, and appreciated, once again, how lucky I was to have a true friend like Duncan—even if he was forever trying to set me up with attractive men. Many women would have appreciated such efforts, but I had my reasons for avoiding the dating scene.

"That guy was hot, but since I have zero time for romance, he'll have to just remain a fantasy. I need to get on my feet financially, and figure out whether I should stick with art, or pursue a commercial design career. Besides, you know my track record. When it comes to men, I'm cursed."

"That's what you always say," Duncan replied. His expression turned serious. "I understand that it's impossible to forget what happened with Matt. I can't imagine what it's like to be raped, and all of the emotional fallout that comes from such an act, so I really don't have any right to say this to you. But I'm going to say it anyway, because I love you. If you never trust a man again, Matt wins. And you're too strong to let one horrible experience hold you back from living."

"You're right," I said. "It's just hard, that's all. Someday, if I ever meet the right guy, I'll take that chance. But for now? Now, I need my beauty sleep. Tomorrow's going to be a long day."

4

My first day of work at Perfect Transcripts was a dreary, drizzly day, with the promise of winter in the chilly air. When I emerged from the subway, the gray sky sat heavily over the office towers of Kendall Square. I was ahead of schedule, so I decided to treat myself to a latte at Starbucks before work.

Unfortunately, by the time I'd finished my drink, the drizzle had turned into a downpour, and the wind had picked up. Although I didn't have far to walk, I could easily get soaked in this kind of weather. I picked up my briefcase and umbrella, and exited Starbucks, determined to stay as dry as possible.

I positioned my umbrella against the wind and began to walk toward Manning Tower. Rainwater pooled in potholes and eddied around street corners. I picked my way around the puddles and rivulets. Maybe if I was careful I could at least keep my ghetto shoes relatively dry.

For the first few blocks, I managed pretty well. Then, just two blocks from the shelter of Manning Tower, a gust of wind seized my umbrella and blew it inside out. I gripped the handle and struggled to save it, but the wind was so strong, it ripped the cloth away from several of the metal ribs. My lightweight coat offered little protection, and the cold rain drenched me to the bone in a matter of seconds.

I splashed toward the next curb, where I spotted a metal trashcan and hurled my traitorous umbrella into its depths. Through the rain in my eyes, I glimpsed the remains of two other umbrellas resting at the bottom of the trashcan. Despite my predicament, I had to laugh. At least I wasn't the only one who had suffered a near-drowning experience today.

I trudged the remaining block. Rainwater cascaded over my face, squelched inside my shoes and dripped off my body. When I reached Manning Tower, I pushed through the revolving door, and knew I needed to find a restroom before I arrived at Perfect Transcripts. Maybe I could lock myself in the restroom and wring out my clothes in the sink.

When I lurched into the atrium, I collided with another body. Thrown off balance, I staggered for a moment, but managed to stay upright.

"Sorry," I said. When I looked up, it was in horror—I'd just run into the sexy businessman I'd seen yesterday. Of all the people I could have run into, why did it have to be him? Even worse, the collision had left a large wet spot on the front of his impeccably fitted coat.

"I'm so sorry," I said. "I should learn to look where I'm going. Especially when I'm soaking wet."

"Not a problem," he said with a tinge of amusement. "You work in the building, don't you?"

"Yes. Today's my first day at Perfect Transcripts. I'm probably late by now. I'd better get going."

He looked me over from head to toe, and my cheeks reddened with embarrassment. I could only imagine how awful I looked.

"You can't go to work like this. You'll only catch cold. My office suite has rooms that I use when I need to work long hours, and there's a dryer. Come with me. Let's get you dried off."

Before I could object, he grasped my soggy arm and firmly led me to an open elevator. He pressed the button for the top floor, and the elevator began to ascend.

"We haven't been introduced," he said. "I'm Craig Manning. You are?"

"Juliana West."

I removed my wet coat and his eyes locked on mine. Under his intense gaze, I shivered, and realized just how cold I was. My nipples were rock hard—and no doubt fully visible—through my wet, clinging clothes. I felt naked and humiliated.

He took off his own coat, and placed it gently over my shoulders.

"You're shivering. Take my coat."

I pulled it around my body. Its warmth and concealment made me feel less exposed, and I managed a shaky smile.

"Thank you. I'm sorry to reward your chivalry by getting your coat nearly as wet as I am."

"It's just a coat. It'll dry."

He smiled at me, and my heart nearly stopped. Not only was he beautiful, but his smile was irresistible. At close range, he was even more gorgeous than I'd realized.

The elevator stopped and the doors opened.

"Follow me. My suite's this way." His deep voice was rich and silky, with an edge of darkness.

I trailed him past a large desk with two receptionists, each of whom looked up at me and stared. I couldn't blame them. I saw the company name on the wall of the reception area—Manning International.

"Thank you—but I really need to call work first," I said. "I'm new, and my boss will wonder where I am."

"Don't worry about your job," he said. "I know Berta Klein at Perfect Transcripts. In fact, I'm one of her best customers. I'll have one of my assistants call her and let her know that you'll be at work in an hour. That should give us enough time to get you warm and dry."

He led me down a hallway and opened a door at the end.

I followed him through the door, then through several rooms. As we moved through the space, I looked around. His decorator had excellent taste. The rooms and furniture mixed beiges and taupes with touches of dark, rich brown, and against the neutral palette, paintings provided splashes of lively color. He opened another door, which revealed a large, pristine bathroom, complete with twin sinks, a walk-in shower, and a spacious soaking tub.

"You can clean up in here," he said. He opened a closet and handed me a beige, waffle-weave robe and several large, fluffy towels. "There's a hair dryer somewhere in the cabinets. Just leave your wet clothes on the floor. I'll send someone to dry them for you. You can wait in here until they're ready. Take a hot shower. You must be freezing."

"Thank you. A hot shower sounds great."

He smiled. "Make yourself at home. Unfortunately, I need to get back to work. Otherwise, I'd stay." He turned and left the room.

After he left, I peeled off my clothes, and dropped them in a soggy mound on the bathroom floor. The walk-in shower was a revelation. Tiled in the same cream-colored travertine as the floor, it was equipped with a massage showerhead. I turned on the water, stepped under the hot, powerful spray and felt myself begin to thaw.

When I felt that I'd been restored to normal temperature, I turned off the shower, reached for a towel, and wrapped myself in it. A second towel served for my hair. When I opened the bathroom door, one of Manning's receptionists was waiting outside. She was an attractive blonde dressed in a chic, pale gray business suit.

"I'm Suzanne, one of Mr. Manning's assistants," she said. "Let me take your clothes and put them in the drier."

"I'm Juliana," I said. "And thank you."

She put my clothes into a hamper, and carried them out of the room. I looked around and realized that I was in Manning's bedroom. The room was decorated in warm grays and taupes, with a pale hardwood floor. A king-sized bed with an expansive white duvet occupied one end of the space, while the other end featured built-in bookshelves and a walk-in closet. Above the bed, a colorful painting of water lilies beckoned.

I couldn't resist a closer look. The vigorous, layered brush strokes and distinctive signature were unmistakable. Monet.

It wasn't as if I hadn't known that my handsome rescuer was wealthy. That much had been obvious. His name was Craig Manning. The building was called Manning Tower. The name of his company was Manning International. But the Monet in his bedroom made his wealth real to me. He could afford a painting that I knew was worth at least thirty million dollars.

I felt a twinge of disappointment. After today's little encounter, I definitely had a crush on Craig Manning, but now I knew for sure that he was out of my league.

I didn't want to get caught checking out Manning's bedroom while dressed in towels, so I returned to the bathroom. I found the blow dryer, and swapped my towels for the robe he'd given me. My long dark hair, thick and wavy, took some time to dry.

When I was finished, I noticed that my wet clothes had left a puddle on the floor of the bathroom, so I carefully cleaned up after myself. Then I returned to the bedroom and perched on a Corbusier chair. Suzanne had taken my briefcase as well, presumably to dry it, so I had nothing to do but sit, wait, and contemplate my humiliation.

I was late for my first day of work at my new job. To make matters worse, I'd slammed into the hottest man I'd ever seen—while soaking wet. Why hadn't I thought to wear a raincoat? It had been kind of Manning to help me, but that didn't change how dumb and pathetic I must have looked.

A knock sounded at the door.

"Come in," I said, rising from the chair as Suzanne entered. She carried a tray with a steaming cup of coffee and a plate of assorted cookies.

"Your clothes should be dry in twenty minutes or so," she said. "In the meantime, would you like a cup of coffee? If not, I can bring something else."

"Coffee would be wonderful," I responded. "Thanks so much."

She smiled. "You're very welcome. I'll be back soon with your clothes, and Mr. Manning had me call Ms. Klein. She's expecting you around six."

Just as I finished my coffee, Suzanne returned, carrying my briefcase and clothes. Dried and flawlessly pressed, my blouse and skirt looked better than they had when I'd put them on earlier in the day. Even my ghetto shoes appeared to have been polished.

"Here you are," she said. "When you're ready to leave, just go back to the living room. Then, take the door on the left side of the room, which opens into a hallway that leads into the reception area."

After she left, I dressed quickly, put up my hair, and applied makeup. I inspected myself in the mirror. I looked fine. Now I was ready to face Manning and his receptionists.

I took my briefcase, left the suite, and walked to the reception area. Suzanne was sitting behind the desk.

"Is Mr. Manning available?" I asked. "I'd like to thank him."

"I'll check." Suzanne picked up a phone and pressed a button. "Are you free? Ms. West would like to speak to you." She put down the receiver and motioned toward a door on the other side of the space. "Mr. Manning's office is just through that door."

I walked to the door, knocked lightly, and opened it. Craig Manning sat at a large, modern, glass-and-steel desk that was covered with paperwork. The wall of windows behind him revealed an expansive view of the river and the Boston skyline.

As I entered, he looked up from his work, and his eyebrows rose. "You look like a new woman."

"I feel like a new woman. Thank you again for everything, Mr. Manning."

His eyes took me in from head to toe, and his lips curved into a slow grin. "My name is Craig."

Is he flirting with me?

"Craig it is. I can't thank you enough."

"Sure you can. Have dinner with me tonight at Mistral."

Obviously, he *was* flirting with me.

"I'm scheduled to work until 10 p.m., and I have to get to work early tomorrow morning—at my other job. I'm sorry, but I can't."

"Tomorrow night, then?"

I was tempted. There was no denying my attraction to him, and he seemed genuinely nice. Still, the thought of dating such a wealthy man made me uncomfortable. We were from two different worlds.

But was it fair to make assumptions about Craig based on his wealth? I certainly didn't want to be judged based on my income. Perhaps we could have dinner on my terms—and on my turf. If he agreed, at least I'd know that he truly wanted to have dinner with me.

"I'd love to have dinner with you tomorrow, but only if you agree that it's on me. I'd like to do something to thank you. My budget doesn't extend to haute cuisine, but I can promise you the best burger in Boston."

He looked at me, and there was something in his expression that I couldn't quite define. Was it surprise that I saw in his eyes? I wasn't sure.

"Deal," he said. "Does 8 p.m. work for you? And where would you like to meet? I can pick you up in my car if that's easier."

"8 p.m. is fine. We can meet at 1100 Boylston Street. The Boston Burger Company. After today, I'm craving a Burger Bomb. Or maybe a Hot Mess."

That amused him. "Among other things, I do like my burgers hot."

His flirtatious humor surprised me—in a good way.

"Then I recommend the Jalapeno Burger. Or, if you're really feeling courageous, the Inferno Burger."

He laughed. "The Inferno Burger? What's an Inferno Burger?"

"A burger that's hotter than hell. Habanero salsa and spicy chili pepper mayo. If you decide to go there, make sure to have a cold beer on standby. You never know—it might be too hot for you."

He leaned back in his chair and appraised me. "I'm not sure if there's anything that's too hot."

"Then I'll look forward to seeing you tomorrow evening at Boston Burger." I pulled a pen and paper from my briefcase and scribbled down the address of the restaurant.

"Here's the address—and my phone number, just in case." I handed him the paper.

He took the paper and handed me his business card.

"My number's on here," he said.

I took the card and slipped it into my briefcase. "So, I'll see you tomorrow, then. I'd better get going now."

"Until tomorrow, Juliana." As I turned and left his office, I could feel his eyes on me, but not in a way that made me feel uncomfortable. As for me, I was walking on air. For the first time in years, I'd made a date—with an intriguing, exciting man. I could hardly wait to finish my shift, go home, and tell Duncan.

5

When I got home, Duncan was sprawled out on the couch, reading a book. When he saw me, he put the book down on the coffee table next to him and sat up.

"Give it to me," he said. "How was your first day?"

"Interesting," I said with a hint of mystery.

"How so?"

"First let's get to Perfect Transcripts, then we'll get to the really good stuff."

"But I want the really good stuff now."

"You'll need to wait. But I do have to say—it's epic."

"So not fair."

"Anyway, about work. Let's just say that doing transcription is a certain kind of hell because it's so boring, but at least the office manager, Moxie, has a sense of humor. And the owner, Berta, doesn't seem so bad either—she's just dog crazy. I mean, tonight her dog chewed up one of her plastic plants and then dropped a little turd in it. What does Berta do? She picks up the damned dog, pets him, and gives him a biscuit. Then she yells for Moxie to deal with the stinky, chewed up corpse. Moxie and I had to haul the plant out of the building. Naturally, it wouldn't fit in the trash chute."

"Gross," Duncan said. "But that aside, do you think this job's going to work out?"

"Oh, definitely. It's dull as hell, but they're nice people, and they'll give me as many hours as I want. So, I'm lucky to have it." And then I pointed my finger at him. "But enough about Perfect Transcripts. You're so not going to believe what I'm about to tell you."

"Finally, the good stuff."

He moved over on the couch and patted the cushion next to him.

I sat down. "I have a date tomorrow night."

"A date?"

"Mmm-hmm."

"With whom?"

"You can't handle it."

"The hell I can't. Spill it."

"I think I should get you an ice pack first."

"Oh, girl. Please."

"No, really. I think I should. And maybe even a drink."

"I'm losing patience…"

"I'm having dinner with the hot businessman I told you about yesterday."

Duncan looked at me with surprise. "You're what?"

"You heard me."

"Well, that was fast. How did you pull that off? I need a hot man." His voice became pleading. "Please. You know I'm your best friend. Share your secrets."

"I went to voodoo.com, paid my fee, and got my man."

"Be serious."

"It's all going to be wasted on you. You're far too poised to do what I did. Besides, I didn't exactly run into him on purpose."

"What do you mean you *ran* into him? Figuratively or literally?"

"Literally. After getting soaked in the rain. I must have looked like a drowned rat, or a dripping mop. Worse, I left a big wet print of myself on his coat."

"All right. So, how exactly did looking like a wet mop lead to a hot date? Details."

"After I ran into him, he took me to this suite of rooms next to his office. I took a shower and got dressed while one of his assistants dried my clothes. Afterward, I went to his office to thank him, we flirted a little, and then he asked me to have dinner with him. He asked me to go to Mistral, but I persuaded him to let me treat him to dinner at Boston Burger instead, as a thank-you gesture for helping me."

"What's his name?" Duncan asked.

"Craig Manning. He owns a company called Manning International, with offices in the building I work in. The building is called Manning Tower, and he has a Monet in his bedroom, so he's wealthy, which worries me a little. But he was kind to me, and he seems like a nice guy. The chemistry between us is pretty intense. When we were in the elevator together, after he put his coat around my shoulders, I nearly stopped breathing."

Duncan reached for his laptop, which was on the coffee table.

"Let's Google this guy." He shot me a mischievous look.

"Totally."

He entered Craig's name into the search engine, then let out a low whistle. "I knew we'd find something, but I didn't expect this. Look how many links."

We scanned the search results together. It looked like Craig Manning was some kind of celebrity. A search on Google Images produced hundreds of red carpet photos of him, usually with a gorgeous model or actress on his arm.

"Girlfriend!" Duncan exclaimed. "You told me he was hot, but what I'm looking at is beyond hot. He's gorgeous. Just look at those eyes. To die for."

"I know," I sighed. "But looking at all those models and actresses worries me. Maybe he's a playboy."

"He certainly gets around. Look at this bio. He produces movies, and he's into real estate—and biotech," Duncan said. "His bio mentions that he's involved in the development of a new cutting-edge anti-cancer drug."

I looked at the web page and remembered something. "I read an article about that drug in the *New York Times* a few months ago. It's supposed to be a huge breakthrough. If I remember correctly, the drug tells a cancer patient's own immune system to kill cancer cells."

Duncan clicked another link. "Look—he's a patron of the arts, too. Here he is at a VIP reception at the Institute of Contemporary Art."

In the photo, Craig stood next to the director of the Institute. Strikingly handsome in black tie, he looked like a movie star, not a movie producer.

"Don't show me photos like that, unless you want me to drool on your computer. You know my weakness for a man in a tux."

Duncan laughed. "This man doesn't need a tux to look good. He'd look amazing in just about anything—or for that matter, nothing."

"On the first date, no clothing will be removed."

"Just saying." He showed me a *Forbes* article. "This is interesting. Craig Manning didn't inherit his money—he made it on his own. He started his first business ten years ago from his college dorm room, and today he's a billionaire."

My initial excitement about tomorrow's date with Craig began to shift into fear.

"What could he possibly want from me? Based on what we've just seen, he can have any woman he wants. Why me?"

Duncan looked at me, and spoke quietly, "When I look at you, I see a smart, strong woman who deserves love, success, and all the best of what life has to offer. I know that this will be the first time you've gone on a date since the rape, and it's perfectly normal to be nervous. But you need to trust yourself. You're meeting Craig in a safe, public location. This is your chance to get to know him a little. Watch what he does. Listen to what he says. And keep an open mind."

6

The next afternoon, I rushed home from my teaching job to prepare for my date with Craig.

What the hell am I going to wear?

After trying on several options, I was beginning to get frantic. I wanted a balance between casual and elegant, and nothing I put on felt right.

Just then, I heard the sound of Duncan's key turning in the lock. I threw on a T-shirt and sweatpants, and ran to the living room to meet him.

He took in my T-shirt, sweatpants, and damp hair, and gave me a look of mock horror. "Sweatpants on a date? And the wet mop look may have worked for you once, but this time around, I recommend that you dry and style your hair."

I laughed. "You know perfectly well that I'd never leave the apartment looking like this. But. I. Have. Nothing! I've torn through my entire closet—zip! My room looks like a hurricane blew through it. It's the fashion equivalent of a dark night of the soul."

"I take it you're asking for my expert assistance."

"I'm begging you to save me from myself. Before I do something ruinous."

"You're going to a burger joint, so it won't do to overdress. Of course, underdressing is even worse."

I groaned. "Every outfit I've tried seems wrong."

"You need something casual but sexy."

"Such as?"

"Jeans. Your champagne silk blouse, with a button or two undone. Your black boots with the stiletto heels. Red lipstick. Wear your hair down, but flat iron the hell out of it."

"You're a genius, Dunc."

"Better move your ass. With that mop of yours, flat-ironing it into submission may require the help of Christian Grey."

I arrived at Boston Burger a few minutes early, and when I spotted Craig at the crowded bar, I caught my breath. He was dressed casually in jeans and a sweater. It was the first time I'd seen him wearing anything other than a business suit, and he looked hotter than ever. A shiver of anticipation threaded through my body, and I couldn't tear my eyes away from him.

Craig turned and our eyes met over the crowd. He got up and walked toward me.

"There you are." He smiled at me. "You look beautiful. Let's get a table."

"Maybe away from the bar, so we can hear each other," I suggested. "It can get a little noisy in here."

"How what that?"

"I said—oh, very clever."

"Just teasing." He beckoned a nearby hostess, who promptly seated us and handed us menus.

Close up, Craig Manning was less perfect than I remembered, but in some way, perhaps because of his sense of humor, he was more gorgeous than ever to me. I spotted the faint white line of an old scar on his right cheekbone, and a second, similar scar just above his left brow. The bridge of his nose was ever-so-slightly asymmetrical, as if it had been broken at some point. Given his athletic appearance, I decided that he'd probably played sports in school, and acquired a few scars along the way.

He put his menu on the table without opening it. His smile twisted into a pair of dimples, just to either side of well-sculpted lips.

"I'm going to try the hotter-than-hot burger that you recommended."

"The Inferno Burger? I warn you, it's really hot."

"I'm counting on that. What are you going to have?"

"The Green Monstah. Guacamole, pico de gallo, and cheddar jack cheese."

"Red Sox fan?" he asked.

I placed my hand on my chest. "If I give the wrong answer, will you still want to have dinner with me?"

He grinned. "Full disclosure. I'm a fourth-generation fan, but I try not to discriminate against supporters of other teams."

"That's a relief. My whole family is crazy about the Red Sox, so I'm technically a fan by birth. I don't really follow baseball, but I enjoy seeing a game once in a while at Fenway."

Our waitress arrived and took our order. I requested a Black and Tan with my burger, and Craig ordered a pint of Guinness with his.

"So, baseball isn't your passion. What is?"

"Painting and design."

"You're an artist?"

I nodded. "A painter. But recently, I've been thinking of going into commercial design. I minored in business, and I'm fascinated by design and marketing."

"I'd like to see your paintings sometime."

I pulled out my phone and brought up photos of my most recent work.

"Here." I handed him the phone, feeling more than a little nervous. As a patron of the arts, Craig probably knew a lot about painting, and I had no idea what he might think of my work.

The depth of his interest surprised me. Our beers arrived, but his attention remained focused on the paintings.

After several minutes, he put the phone down and looked at me.

"Your paintings are excellent," he said. "They're beautiful, and highly original as well. Do you show around here? Or in New York?"

"Not yet. Someday, I hope to—"

Just then, his phone rang.

He glanced at the screen and said, "I'm sorry, but I have to take this. It's not a personal call, just business. Please excuse me."

"No problem."

Craig got up from the table, walked across the restaurant, and stepped outside to escape the noise of the restaurant. Through the window, I watched him, sipped my beer and enjoyed the view.

As I watched him, I admired how his jeans hugged his ass and how his fitted, zippered sweater accentuated his muscled torso. In addition to striking good looks, Craig Manning had style.

He paced back and forth energetically. He gripped his phone to his right ear and spoke into it with obvious animation. Occasionally, he punctuated his conversation with vigorous gestures of his free left hand, or ran the hand through his thick black hair. I wondered what this impassioned conversation might be about. Was something wrong?

When he was finished, he reentered the restaurant.

"Sorry about that," he said.

"That's OK," I said. "That conversation looked pretty intense. Is everything all right?"

"Let's just say that everything is under control."

"Speaking of your business, I've read a little about your new anti-cancer drug. It sounded pretty exciting."

He cocked his head at me. "You follow business news?"

I knew from experience that artists were often stereotyped as eccentric, unworldly innocents. But that wasn't me.

"I read the *New York Times* top business stories. I minored in business because it interests me. And as an artist, I'm a one-person business of sorts."

For a moment, Craig seemed taken aback, but he recovered gracefully. "Forgive my surprise. I'm used to hearing artists talk about creativity and inspiration. But business? Rarely the case, but refreshingly the case when it comes to you."

"Tell me more about your new drug. Based on what I read in the *Times*, it sounds like a major breakthrough."

When he was finished telling me about it, the waitress arrived with our burgers. Craig looked at his Inferno Burger, gave me an amused look, picked it up, and took a bite. I crossed my fingers that he would like it, since I'd been responsible for choosing the restaurant.

Fortunately, he loved it.

"You weren't kidding," he said between bites. "It's red hot and rare on the inside, exactly how a burger should be."

"I love this place," I said. "I've been coming here with Duncan—my best friend and roommate—ever since it opened."

His phone rang again. He put down his half-eaten burger, wiped his fingers hurriedly on his napkin, and looked at his phone, which was next to him on the table.

"I'm really sorry, but I have to take this one too. I promise I'll be just a minute."

I nodded in acknowledgement, and watched him get up and go outside for the second time. I decided that since he'd said he would only be a minute, I would just pick at my fries until he returned.

But one minute soon turned into ten. I looked out the window, saw that he was still deep in conversation, and decided to just finish my meal. I was nearly done when the waitress returned to our table.

"How's your burger?"

"Heavenly," I said.

"Can I get you anything else? Another Black and Tan?"

My glass was nearly empty. "Sure. One more."

"And your friend?"

I looked at Craig's glass. It was empty, and his half-eaten dinner was getting cold. I looked out the window. He was still on the phone. He'd said he would only be a minute, and he'd been gone for quite some time. If I were honest with myself, I was getting annoyed.

"I don't know when he'll be finished with his call. At this point, I guess we should both pray that he has unlimited minutes. As for what he wants, I have no idea."

"OK. I'll get that Black and Tan for you right away, and come back later to see if your friend wants a second round."

"Thank you."

I finished my burger just as Craig returned.

"I apologize, Juliana," he said. "My company's involved in a lawsuit in connection with the new cancer drug."

I just looked at him. "Would you like your meal reheated?"

"No, it's fine, I'm not that hungry right now anyway. I would like another Guinness, though. This lawsuit is really getting to me."

For a second, I thought I'd glimpsed red-hot anger beneath his smooth facade, but then, our waitress returned with my Black and Tan, and Craig ordered a second Guinness.

I wondered if his behavior tonight was typical. Did he always take phone calls, even during dinner? I had no way of knowing, so I decided to keep an open mind, put my annoyance aside, and try to enjoy the rest of the evening.

After the waitress left, I looked at him. Any trace of frustration had vanished from his face.

"That call seemed pretty serious," I said. "Do you want to talk about it?"

He shook his head. "No. I don't want my lawsuit to ruin our evening any more than it already has." He looked into my eyes, reached across the table, and took my hand. "I'd much rather focus on getting to know the intriguing woman sitting across from me."

When he touched me, a tingle of excitement ran through my body. I looked him in the eye.

"What would you like to know?"

He leaned closer, and lowered his voice to a sexy whisper. "Everything." He leaned back in his seat. "But for now, let's start with the basics. What do you like to do in your free time?"

"I love movies—especially classic movies. I like to take long walks, and read books. I love visual art, and enjoy going to museums.

Contemporary art, ancient art—it all fascinates me. What about you?"

The waitress returned with Craig's Guinness. He released my hand, and took a long pull on his drink before he answered.

"I'm a big movie buff—always have been. When I was in college, sometimes I'd blow off my classes and see two or three movies in the same day. I have a house on the ocean—in Truro, on Cape Cod—where I spend weekends whenever I'm able to get away. My favorite long walk is on the beach there."

"I spent a few days in Truro with friends once. The beach there is stunning," I said.

"On another note, you said that you like museums and visual art. I just remembered that I have tickets to a black tie fundraiser at the Museum of Fine Arts. It's this Friday at 6 p.m. Would you go with me?"

I could hardly believe my ears. Maybe our paths were just destined to cross.

"I'm already going—with Duncan. But perhaps we could all meet at the museum? I'd love to introduce you and Duncan."

"Perfect," he said. "It's a date."

7

I put in a full day of transcription work, and then I headed home to dress for the fundraiser at the Museum of Fine Arts. Although fundraisers were good networking opportunities for artists, the ticket prices were usually too steep for my budget. But a friend had given Duncan tickets, so we were about to spend the evening rubbing shoulders with the movers and shakers of Boston's art world.

As if that weren't enough, Craig also would be there. I looked forward to introducing Craig to Duncan. I couldn't wait to get Duncan's impression of Craig. Duncan was an excellent judge of character, and I trusted his opinion more than my own.

For the event, I chose my favorite little black dress. A sleek, shimmering snippet of Armani, it had been a lucky find in one of Boston's many secondhand shops. I pulled my thick, wavy hair into a chignon, and added funky silver earrings. Finally, I completed my look with subtle lining and shading of my eyes—my best feature—and my favorite lipstick.

Duncan was handsome in his black tie, and he waited impatiently for me to finish getting ready.

"Done primping yet?" he called from the living room. "We're already fashionably late."

"Coming, daaahling," I responded in my best imitation Carol Burnett. "Perfection takes time—not that there's enough time for me to achieve that. But I'll do what I can."

I rounded off my preparations with a final mirror check, stepped into the living room, and struck a pose.

"You and that dress are a lethal combination," he said.

"I want to poison the world with it."

"I think you might. Is my tie straight?"

"You're good. We'd better head to the subway now."

"Subway? Dressed like this? Are you serious? Let's splurge on a taxi. My treat. It looks like it might rain again, and I refuse to let the weather destroy what's taken me thirty minutes to pull together, and you a full two hours."

"Two hours?"

"At least."

"Whatever. A taxi is a brilliant idea, but I'll pay for the one on the ride back, OK? Now that I'm making a decent living, no more sponging off my best friend."

"Don't be ridiculous. You're hardly a sponge. Do you remember when you won that painting award in school, and insisted on spending the money on a week in New York for both of us?"

"Of course I remember that week. We stayed in that dingy hostel near Union Square and walked for miles. All over Midtown and Chelsea. Gallery after gallery."

"Remember the night we tarted ourselves up and drank martinis at the Waldorf? We felt as if we'd stepped into a time machine that had flown us back to the nineteen-thirties."

I smiled at the memory. "We should go to New York again soon. Or Vegas. Maybe in the spring." I squeezed Duncan's shoulder with affection. "That is, of course, after I type my way out of my financial black hole. We deserve it."

"You're on, Jules. Let's make it happen."

As we sped toward the Museum of Fine Arts, I gazed out the taxi window, and watched the silhouetted trees and twinkling lights of the city flash by. In the pools cast by streetlights, bursts of colorful October leaves revealed themselves to us, as did clusters of people strolling the sidewalks and enjoying the warm fall evening. Soon, we arrived at the Museum.

When we entered the brightly lit atrium, the evening was in full swing.

The space was packed with the usual glittering mash-up of socialites, financiers, curators, and gallerists, and spiced with a handful of Boston's more prominent artists. Against the glass, marble, and steel of the modernist space, their collective chatter echoed and blurred into a single continuous noise.

"Let's get a drink, then we can look around for your new man," Duncan said.

"My new man? You're way ahead of me. I like Craig, but we've only had one date, and he spent half of it on the phone with his lawyer."

"Which would annoy anyone," Duncan said. "But you don't know the details of his lawsuit situation, which could be intense, so let's give him a break and not jump to conclusions."

We made our way through the crowd around the bar, and Duncan caught the bartender's eye. "Two Belvedere martinis. One with a twist, one dirty."

Tattooed and with multiple uncomfortable looking facial piercings, the bartender looked like an art student making a little extra cash. He knew his job though—our martinis arrived quickly, and they were chilled to perfection.

"Not bad," Duncan said, after taking a sip. We made our way out of the crush around the bar, and moved toward the less-crowded end of the atrium.

"Juliana!" A voice called out in the crowd. "Come here. There's someone I want you to meet."

I immediately recognized the warm, throaty voice of Elsa Nielsen. Elsa was one of a handful of prominent Boston art collectors who enjoyed discovering and purchasing the work of emerging artists.

She was also a relentless networker. Prepared to make small talk, which wasn't exactly my strong suit, I turned around and found myself facing not only Elsa, but Craig Manning.

For a moment, I couldn't breathe. He looked amazing. His flawlessly fitted tux hinted at the lean, muscled form beneath. As our eyes met, his gaze swept over me, and his lips curved into a slow, appreciative smile. Transfixed by his gaze, I felt exposed—and aroused.

Elsa made introductions in her usual flamboyant manner.

"Juliana West. Duncan McNeill. Craig Manning. Juliana's a painter—very interesting work. Duncan's a faaabulous photographer. Divoon, divoon, divoon. Both are in my collection, of course. Craig, darling, you need to pay attention to these two—mark my words, they'll both be art stars in a few years."

"I'm already paying attention to Juliana," he said. "We've met before, though I've not yet had the pleasure of seeing her paintings in person. Duncan, it's always a pleasure to meet another of Elsa's discoveries. As we all know, she has an amazing eye."

"Flattery," Elsa laughed. "At my age, it keeps me alive. You don't even know. Why are you looking at me like that? I'm serious. At this point in my life, whenever I receive a compliment? Here's my dirty secret. I skip my Lipitor."

Someone called out her name. "I'll catch up with you as soon as I talk with dear Bootie," she said. "You know how she is." She lowered her voice. "It could happen at any moment. We all know that it could. Don't look at me like that. It's the truth." Then she vanished into the crowd.

"I'm going for another round," Duncan said. "Jules, I know what you want. Craig, what are you drinking tonight?"

"Vodka martini with a twist, and thank you."

"Excellent," Duncan said, and then he disappeared into the mass of people around the bar.

Craig turned his attention to me. "You look beautiful," he said.

"You don't look half bad yourself," I said with a smile. "How was the rest of your week?"

"Busy. I had to make an unexpected trip to Los Angeles, in connection with a movie that I'm producing. What about you?"

"I've had a great week. Dinner with you two nights ago. Drinks after work last night, with a few of my co-workers. We went to Absinthe—that's where Duncan works as a bartender. And then there's tonight. Elsa's promised to introduce me to Genevieve DuBois."

"I know Genevieve well. You'll like her." He looked thoughtfully at me for a moment. "You know, Genevieve should see your paintings. She's a trendsetter. If she buys your work for her collection, others will follow. If Elsa doesn't come back soon, I'll introduce you to her."

I was moved by his support. "Thank you. That's very kind of you."

"Not really. I'll be doing Genevieve a favor. In a few years, when you're showing your paintings in New York, she'll be able to say that she was among the first to discover your work."

"You're as bad as Elsa," I laughed. "But I hope you're right. Like every artist I know, I dream of seeing my work in a New York gallery someday."

Just then, Duncan returned with our drinks.

"Thank you, Duncan," I said, taking my martini from him. He handed another to Craig, and then he raised his own glass to us.

"Cheers," he said.

We clinked glasses and drank.

"Juliana mentioned that you're a photographer," Craig said to Duncan. "What's your favorite camera?"

"The new Nikon top-of-the-line DSLR. As it happens, I just bought one a few months ago." Duncan's face lit up, and he began listing the capabilities of his beloved camera. Craig couldn't have hit on a subject closer to his heart. I sipped my drink and enjoyed the moment. My best friend and my new romantic interest had clearly hit it off.

∼

Half an hour later, when we'd moved on from camera geekery to movies, Craig's phone rang. He looked at the screen, and gave me and Duncan an apologetic look.

"Unfortunately, I need to take this," he said. "Please excuse me for a moment."

Of course you have to take it. Why wouldn't you take it? I thought.

He walked briskly away from the crowd, his phone at his ear.

I looked at Duncan. "You know, I'm beginning to suspect that he and his phone are surgically attached."

Duncan shrugged. "He runs a large business. He seems like a great guy, Jules."

"I guess I was just hoping that tonight would be different."

"Look on the bright side. Now that Craig's left, you can spend some time with Elsa. Wasn't she going to introduce you to a collector or two?" He looked around the space. "There's Elsa—over by the big Chuck Close painting."

"You're right. Craig's phone call is my opportunity. Let's go," I said.

I crossed the atrium to where Elsa stood. She was in conversation with two people whom I didn't recognize. As I approached, she saw me, came toward me, and took my arm.

"Juliana! Come with me. I've been looking for you everywhere. You simply must meet Genevieve."

She led me toward a tall, angular woman, who was draped in a flowing bronze and gold Donna Karan caftan dress. She wore her platinum hair in a flawless chin-length bob.

"Genevieve, meet Juliana West, one of my favorite young painters. Juliana, I'm delighted to introduce you to Genevieve DuBois. Genevieve's built one of the best art collections on the East Coast."

Genevieve had a polished, sixty going on fifty look, and I wasn't sure whether to credit good genes or an amazing plastic surgeon. Probably a bit of both. As Elsa fluttered away, likely to make other introductions, Genevieve smiled warmly at me.

"Wonderful to finally meet you," she said. "I've heard so much about your work from Elsa. And from others, as well."

"And I've heard so much about you. And your collection, of course," I said, trying to contain my excitement.

"My collection is my passion. It represents the best of Boston painting over the past hundred years. My late husband's father began it, and I've added a few works every year for nearly forty years now. When I'm gone, the museum will get most of it—aside from a few bequests to friends and family, of course."

"Elsa's told me how amazing your collection is. Many years from now, when the museum gets it, I'm sure it will be an important addition to their collection."

"Not so many years from now, I'm afraid." Genevieve said. "This old girl is older than she looks. Come on, guess my age."

"Sixty-two?"

"Not even close. I'm a tribute to my plastic surgeon. Not to mention the lovely man who does my Botox. Why, at this point, I'm nearly as much of a work of art as anything in my collection."

I found her irreverence charming. "Good for you. I hope I look half as good as you when I'm sixty-whatever."

"You have good bones. Classic features. You'll be fine, unless you insist on smoking or tanning yourself into a piece of jerky, of course. Like Anne Summers, poor thing." Genevieve lowered her voice, and gestured at a middle-aged woman standing near the bar. "Look at her," she said. "Look at that leathery hide. Years of roasting herself to obsession on a tanning bed. She clearly had tanning disorder. Remember, there's only so much Botox can do. And of course, don't get fat. Nothing ages a person like rolls of fat. Or a tanning bed." She shuddered.

"Tanning disorder," I said. "You've just described one of my college roommates. Eve fried herself year-round. Even during the winter, she looked as if she'd been smoked alive. I never understood her obsession with tanning, because she was a beautiful woman, talented and smart. We used to warn her that she'd have skin cancer at thirty, but she didn't want to hear it."

"They never do. When I told Anne one day over lunch that her face matched her handbag, she called me a bitch."

"I'm sure you meant well," I said.

"Actually, it was an intervention. Someone needed to tell her that she was going too far. But Anne's the sensitive type. Everyone in our circle expects everyone else to be nice. Whatever that means. Let's just say that she didn't take it well, and that she didn't take anyone's advice. God, people are weak."

Time flew by as we moved on to talking about my work, and before we parted, Genevieve asked for my card and promised to make a studio visit. I hoped it would be soon, because she was one of the most fascinating people I'd ever met. She had a scathing wit and a heart of gold.

Realizing that the evening was coming to an end, I looked around for Duncan and Craig. People were retrieving their coats, and the bar was closing down. I spotted Duncan near the entrance, but didn't see Craig anywhere. Had he left? I had no idea. I hadn't seen him since he left to take his phone call.

"There you are," Duncan said. "We should get going before they kick us out of this joint. Let's get a cab."

I agreed. "I've already told you—this is my treat. I'm not getting soaked again this week."

"That's fine."

"Do you see Craig anywhere? I'd like to say goodbye before we leave, but I don't know where he is."

Duncan looked around. "I don't see him. Do you have his cell number?"

I looked in my purse, and realized that I didn't. "Damn. I left his number in my other purse."

"Then let's wait a few minutes. If he doesn't turn up, you can call him from home."

We mingled for a few moments before Craig appeared. My mood lifted when I saw him emerge from the thinning crowd. God, I found him attractive.

"Can I give you a ride? My car's waiting just around the corner," he said.

"That would be great. Our apartment is in Davis Square. If it's too far out of your way, we can always take a cab."

"It isn't. Come on. Let's go outside. Here's the car."

His limo pulled up, and we piled in.

As we drove across the river toward Cambridge, Craig and Duncan resumed their discussion of favorite movies. I leaned back into the spacious leather seat, more than a little grateful to get off my feet after over two hours of standing in heels. Occasionally, I joined in the conversation, but for the most part, I relaxed and enjoyed listening to Duncan and Craig.

When we reached Davis Square, Duncan directed Craig's driver to our apartment. In the rain, streets and buildings glistened against the night sky.

The driver opened the door for us, and as I prepared to step out, Craig surprised me by taking my hand.

"When can I see you again?"

I was surprised by the warmth of his touch, and how it affected me. "Maybe some evening next week?" I said.

"How about early next week?" he asked. "Maybe a movie? I know you love movies. There's a Hitchcock series playing at the Brattle every Tuesday evening. This week they're showing *North by Northwest* at 6 p.m. We could see the movie and then have dinner together."

"Hitchcock? Are you serious? Tuesday night it is."

"I can pick you up here around a quarter past five—would that work for you?"

"Absolutely. I'll see you on Tuesday."

He released my hand, and I stepped out of the limo. Duncan followed. We said our goodnights to Craig, and then went inside.

8

When we stepped into the apartment, I removed my heels and flopped down onto the couch. Duncan sat next to me.

"Did I just hear you set another date? Craig is totally into you, Jules. I have a good feeling about him."

"I really like him, Duncan. It just worries me that his world is so different from mine. He's super wealthy. Worse, he's wrapped up in business 24/7. And I'm positive that beautiful women are throwing themselves at him on a daily basis. Maybe it's unrealistic to think that we could ever make a go of it. Am I taking the first step toward getting hurt? You know I had doubts about Matt early on, and look at what happened with him."

"Craig's not Matt. Matt was a cynical, manipulative bastard. He lied to you and abused your trust. But you're not a naïve girl anymore. You're a strong woman. You know what you want—and what you don't want."

I sighed. "I'll admit this to you, because you're the one person in my life who I can completely trust. I'm afraid of being hurt again. Now that I know what it means to risk my heart, risking it isn't easy. Of course I want to fall in love again. At least someday, and with the right man. Craig seems like a good person. I genuinely like him, and I'm attracted to him. I just doubt that it could ever work out."

"You're getting ahead of yourself," Duncan said. "Once you get to know Craig a little better, then you can decide if you want to take things further—or not. It's not as if you're in love with him. So, you know, give the man a chance."

"As usual, you're right. I'm probably overthinking this. It's just been so long that I've forgotten what it's like to date."

"I saw how he looked at you," Duncan said. "At one point, I thought he was going to set your dress on fire."

I laughed. "He is hot, isn't he? I have to restrain myself from drooling every time I look at him."

"He's a very handsome man. As a bonus, he has a charming personality. But let's get to what really matters. Is he hung like a porn star?"

"You're shameless!" I said.

"At least I'm honest about it."

"I'll tell you this much. He wore 501s to our dinner date, and what I saw looked substantial."

"So you checked out his package. Good for you. And not so good for you. You've got it bad, Jules. Fortunately, there's a cure. It's called sex. S-E-X."

"Let's just say it's a little too soon for that. I barely know him. My body might want to jump into bed with him, but my brain is in charge this time around. Craig is good looking and charming, but so was Matt—until I started to fall for him. Then it turned out to be all about conquest. What Matt wanted, Matt got. One way or another."

Duncan leaned toward me, and his expression turned serious. "Listen to me. As a bartender, I've seen it all, and my intuition tells me that Craig's a good guy. I understand that it's impossible to forget what happened with Matt. But as I've said before, this isn't only about trusting Craig. It's about trusting yourself."

Sometimes it seemed as if Duncan knew me better than I knew myself. The intensity of the pull I felt toward Craig made me feel uncomfortably vulnerable, especially because I didn't trust my own instincts. And how could I after what had happened with Matt?

I raised my hands in surrender. "You're right. I'm of two minds right now. The physical part of me wants to tear Craig's clothes off, and the emotional part wants to run before I get in too deep."

"Fine. But what else do you feel?" Duncan asked.

"That I need to get to know Craig better. Take my time. Have patience."

"Then that's what you should do," he said.

9

On Tuesday afternoon, I finished work and rushed home. I needed to decide what to wear for my movie date with Craig. I tried and rejected several outfits before I settled on slim beige pants, low heels, and an off-white silk blouse. I rooted through my limited jewelry collection and selected a chunky, eccentric necklace by an up-and-coming local jewelry designer, which I paired with silver ball stud earrings. The combination of cool silver with warm wood and amber added just the touch of color that I wanted.

As usual, I kept my hair and makeup simple—hair in a loose chignon, light foundation, smoky eyes, and pink lip gloss. I threw on a black, three-quarter length trench coat over the ensemble, inspected myself in the mirror, and decided that I looked good.

Not bad for an hour's work.

I heard a car pull up outside and looked out the window. It was Craig—in a silver Porsche 911 convertible.

Seriously? I thought.

I grabbed my purse and left the apartment. Craig stood beside his car, leaning against the passenger side door. He looked fantastic. He wore tan slacks that hung elegantly from his hips and a white button-down shirt, worn tails out with a couple buttons undone at the throat. His brown loafers and a navy blue blazer completed his casual, slightly preppy look. A touch of stubble lined his jaw.

"Hi Juliana," he said when I left my apartment. He opened the car door for me, closed it when I sank into the leather seat, and then he walked around the car and got into the driver's seat.

"Put on your seat belt," he said. "We've got plenty of time, so let's take the long way around. We can drive along the river, then park in the Charles Street garage and walk to the Brattle Theatre. Would you prefer the top up?"

I thought of my hair, then of the pleasure of feeling the air rush by. "Top down," I said. "The night is warm."

"Good choice." He put on his own seat belt, started the car, and pulled away from the curb. The Porsche's powerful engine thrummed beneath us as he drove, and then it broke into a full roar when we reached the river and the higher speed limit of Memorial Drive.

We reached Cambridge and Harvard Square far too soon. Craig parked the car, then put the top up, and we strolled the couple of blocks to the Brattle.

When we reached the box office, Craig purchased two tickets. "Where would you like to sit?" he asked.

"Six rows or so from the front, near the middle."

"Good. That's about the right distance from the screen here."

As we seated ourselves, the previews began to roll. Then *North by Northwest* began. I soon lost myself in the story and the characters, almost forgetting Craig's presence until the end credits.

"Want to get something to eat?" he asked, when the movie was over and we left the theatre. "We could go to Casablanca. Or maybe Dali. Do you like sangria?"

"Let's go to Casablanca," I said. "It's closer, and unfortunately, I need to make an early night of it. Tomorrow morning, I teach."

10

A fter dinner, we walked hand-in-hand in the direction of the garage. The night sky was an intense dark blue, against which the trees and tops of buildings were silhouetted. The autumn evening was warm, and the streets of Harvard Square teemed with life. College students mixed with locals, and with the occasional street musician or juggler. When we reached the car, Craig turned to me, and looked into my eyes.

"There's something I need to do before I drive you home," he said.

"What's that?"

"This." He leaned forward and kissed me gently on the lips. I responded instinctively, and my lips parted as he deepened the kiss. Surprised by the intensity of my response, part of me wanted to stop right now. To assert that we didn't know each other well enough to be even this intimate.

But my body had already surrendered. His hands roved downward, gripped my ass, then slipped upward again, and brushed lightly over my hard nipples. Before I could stop myself, my hands raked through his thick, dark hair. I tugged him closer, then brushed my fingertips along the roughness of his stubbled jawline. His scent intoxicated me with hints of wood and dark, resinous incense. As our bodies came into full contact, I felt the hardness of his erection pressing against me.

He pulled away slightly and smiled wickedly. "Just a taste of what I want to give you, Juliana."

My traitorous body throbbed in anticipation of what that meant. Still, determined to resist, I placed both hands on his chest and gently pushed him away. "It's too soon. We don't know each other well enough yet."

He raised my right hand to his lips, and kissed each finger in turn.

"I want you to trust me, and also to feel safe with me. That's not easy for you, is it?"

"No," I admitted. "Trust is hard for me."

"Someone hurt you. Someone you loved."

"Yes." It was as if he'd read my mind. He lifted my chin, and our eyes met.

"Tell me about it, Juliana. Trust me at least that much."

I wasn't ready to tell him the whole truth. Not until we knew each other better. The knowledge that I'd been raped might make Craig treat me as if I was damaged—or fragile, which was everything I'd worked so hard not to be. But I wouldn't lie to him, either.

I took a deep breath and composed myself.

"I fell for the wrong guy a few years ago. It ended badly, so much so that I haven't had a relationship since then. I promise to tell you the whole story someday, just not tonight. But it's only fair to tell you that I have major trust issues." I paused. "If you don't want to deal with that, I understand. You're an amazing, beautiful, intelligent man, and I'm sure you can find any number of women to date who don't come with so much emotional baggage."

Craig wrapped his arms low around my waist. "Perhaps I could. But none of them would be you. I want you to know that you can trust me, Juliana, and that it's OK with me if we take things slowly. I hope you believe me when I say this—I would never pressure you in any way."

I almost couldn't believe my ears. I'd confessed my trust issues, and Craig hadn't run for the hills. Maybe things could work out between us, after all.

"But a meal or a movie here or there isn't going to cut it. To build trust and get to know each other better, we need serious time together."

"What do you have in mind?"

"You'll see."

11

Over the next few weeks, Craig and I spent every free evening together. Sometimes, we saw a movie or went out for dinner. Other evenings, we hung out at his place or mine, and shared conversation over a bottle of wine. As I got to know Craig, I realized how right Duncan had been about him. Craig's business acumen and hard work had made him a billionaire, but he was unpretentious and down to earth.

I learned that Craig had grown up in Woods Hole, a little town best known for being the home of the ferry to Martha's Vineyard, as well as a number of marine science labs. He shared with me that his father had died in the first Gulf war when he was very young, and that he'd lost his mother to cancer when he was eighteen. After that, Craig went to college at M.I.T., where he started his first company out of his dorm room.

But neither one of us were inclined to talk much about the past. Mostly, we talked for hours about everything in our day-to-day lives. His business, my painting. Books and movies that we both loved.

I made him laugh with stories featuring the colorful, eccentric world of the arts, and he turned out to have a deadpan sense of humor, describing people and situations from the business world in comic relief, while somehow keeping a straight face, something that I'd never been able to pull off.

When we were together, time flew by.

Meanwhile, my physical attraction to him—strong from the outset—only grew. One Saturday night, after dinner and several glasses of wine, I started to unbutton his shirt and kiss my way down his neck, but he stopped me.

"We've both had a few drinks. The first time we make love, I want both of us to be sober. I want each of us to be fully present so that we remember everything."

The next day, we drove along the North Shore and stopped for lunch in a little restaurant by the ocean. Between the savory lobster risotto and the homemade apple pie, Craig made a suggestion.

"Would you like to spend next weekend together? We could go to my house on the Cape, and enjoy a couple of peaceful, uninterrupted days together. You could even bring your painting things. The house has an enclosed porch that overlooks the ocean, and has great natural light. You can paint there."

Uninterrupted sounded good to me. My one and only issue with Craig was that he never quite left work behind. When his phone rang, or beeped to announce the arrival of an email, he almost always answered.

"The Cape's beautiful," I said. "On the ocean, or in the dunes, you feel far from the city, even though you aren't. You must love going there in the summer."

"I don't get there as much as I'd like. Work tends to keep me in the city. But the Warrens look after the place for me. There's a caretaker's cottage where they live year-round. Bill Warren is retired military and can fix just about anything, and his wife Mary is an amazing cook."

It sounded wonderful, and I knew what this meant. We would finally be intimate, and I was ready to take that next step with Craig. "I'm in. When would we leave?"

"Saturday, maybe? We can take the company helicopter and be on the Cape in time for a late lunch. You can paint all afternoon. I'll pick you up at noon."

"That sounds perfect."

After we drove back to the city and Craig dropped me at my doorstep, I danced up the stairs to my apartment, full of the realization that for the first time in years, I truly wanted a man with my whole being. I wanted Craig so badly, I was willing to push my fears aside and go forward, so much so that I felt excited about the prospect of intimacy. Over the past several weeks, I had come to trust Craig, and spending the next weekend together felt right. I was ready to take our relationship to the next level.

12

When Saturday arrived, it was with a bright blue autumn sky that matched my optimism. A quarter of an hour before I expected Craig to pick me up, he called.

"I had to take care of some business this morning, and I'm running a little late," he said. "Reilly will pick you up first, then drive back to Kendall Square to get me."

"Great," I said. Reilly was Craig's usual driver. He'd driven us several times before. "See you in half an hour."

I hung up the phone. Hopefully, whatever Craig needed to finish wouldn't take long. He'd had to work long hours all week, and I missed him.

When the doorbell rang, I hurried down the stairs with my two bags, one filled with clothing, the other with brushes, paint, and several small canvases. I opened the door, saw Craig's sleek black limo waiting at the curbside, and locked the door behind me as Reilly took my bags.

"Hello, Ms. West," he said.

"Hi, Reilly."

He deposited my bags in the trunk, and then opened the door for me. I stepped inside and eased myself into the comfortable leather seat.

As we drove away from Davis Square, the reality of what I was about to do hit me. I felt excited, but also anxious. I hoped I wasn't about to make a huge mistake.

We reached Kendall Square, and Reilly pulled up in front of Manning Tower. A moment later, Craig appeared. He wore faded jeans, loafers without socks, and a thick cable-knit sweater. I thought that he looked sexier than ever. Even though he carried a briefcase under his arm—no doubt filled with work—even that couldn't dampen the thrill of seeing him.

Craig got in, and closed the door.

"Hi, beautiful," he said. As we embraced, the limo began to move.

"Hi, yourself," I murmured in his ear. "I've missed you. I've hardly seen you all week."

We enjoyed a lengthy kiss before he released me from his embrace.

"I know, and I regret that we haven't had more time together," he said. "I've been buried in work. But I promise to make it up to you this weekend."

"I can't wait."

∽

An hour later, we arrived at the airport. Craig had spent most of the drive reading and scribbling notes, while I enjoyed the passing scenery. Reilly stopped the car next to a white helicopter with an orange swirl on its side. Craig opened the door, and we got out.

"We should be all set to take off," he said. "Come with me. Reilly will get your bags." He helped me into the helicopter, which turned out to be every bit as luxurious as the limo. Two pairs of spacious leather seats faced each other.

Craig guided me to a seat, made sure I was buckled in, and handed me a headset that resembled heavy-duty headphones with an attached mike. "To cancel the noise," he explained. "You'll be able to hear me, as well as Jack—the pilot—and we'll be able to hear you."

He seated himself across from me, buckled in, and slipped on a headset. "Can you hear me?" His voice was slightly tinny, but clear.

"I can."

"Good. Let's go, Jack."

The helicopter's rotors built up speed and transitioned from a steady whump-whump to a dull roar that was fortunately reduced in volume by the headset. Unconsciously, I gripped the arms of my seat.

"Have you flown in a helicopter before?" Craig said.

"No, just airplanes."

"The takeoff and landing feel different from a plane. You might feel weightless for a moment here and there, a little like riding a roller coaster. The rest is about the same."

I concealed my relief. Roller coasters never made me queasy, though boats sometimes did. Takeoff was smoother than I'd anticipated, and during the short flight to the Cape, Craig pointed out landmarks. Boston Harbor. The Bourne Bridge. In the distance, the slender gray tower of the Provincetown Pilgrim Monument.

"The house is in Truro, between Provincetown and Wellfleet," Craig said. "We'll be on the ground in a few minutes."

The ocean wind buffeted the helicopter during the descent, and I was grateful when we reached the ground. The rotors thudded to a halt. Following Craig's example, I removed my headset and seat belt. He helped me out of the helicopter, and led me from the helipad to the house. Built in a contemporary style with classic New England materials—weathered gray shingles and white wood trim—the two-story structure blended attractively into the surrounding dunes.

A screened porch surrounded the entire first floor. The expansive main living area showcased a large fieldstone fireplace and cathedral ceiling. Large windows filled the space with sunlight.

"Let's go to the kitchen," Craig said. "Knowing Mary Warren, I'm sure she's left us something delicious for lunch."

13

I followed Craig into a large, modern kitchen, and watched him rummage through the refrigerator. "How about a lobster roll and a green salad? I make a great vinaigrette."

"Sounds good. Can I help?"

"You can set the table while I finish here. We'll eat on the front porch."

The front porch turned out to have an elegant wrought iron table-and-chair set, as well as a matching swing, which faced the ocean and was covered in striped gingham cushions. I spread the tablecloth Craig had given me, and then laid out plates, salad bowls, and silverware. When I returned to the kitchen, he handed me the salad.

"I'll follow with the lobster rolls in a minute."

I returned to the porch, put the salad on the table, and sat down. Craig appeared a moment later. He balanced a platter of lobster rolls in one hand, and a silver bucket containing ice, champagne, and two flutes in the other. He set the platter and ice bucket on the table. Then he picked up the champagne, popped the cork, and filled our glasses before he sat down across from me.

"To our first weekend together," he said, extending his glass toward me.

"To our weekend," I said.

We sipped our champagne, and I looked out at the sunlit ocean. Blue-green waves rolled onto the pale sand, one after another, and the rhythmic rush of the powerful surf filled my ears.

"I can't wait to paint this," I said, taking in the view. "I've never tried to paint the ocean before."

Craig smiled. "I'm glad you find this place inspiring. Try a lobster roll. No one makes a better lobster salad than Mary, and she's managed to teach me how to toast the buns just right."

I picked up a lobster roll and took a bite. It was perfect.

"My compliments to you—and Mary. I haven't had such a fantastic lobster roll since the last time I was in Maine."

"What was the name of your hometown again? Waterville?"

"Yes. On the Kennebec River. But I have family near Bar Harbor and spent a lot of time on the coast as a kid. That's where I learned to appreciate a real lobster roll. The city restaurants favor gourmet bread instead of a simple hot dog bun, and the effect is ruinous."

"Agreed. Here, have some salad." He handed me the bowl, and I helped myself to a generous mound of greens. I tasted the salad and said, "You weren't kidding about your vinaigrette—it's wonderful."

While we ate, I looked out at the ocean again, and wondered what it would be like to live in such a beautiful place. I loved the New England coast, but I'd never lived on the ocean.

"What was it like to grow up in a small coastal town?" I asked.

"Busy in the summer, and dead in the winter. But growing up in Woods Hole introduced me to science. The marine labs in Woods Hole do a lot of interesting research, and I enjoyed hanging around the marine scientists. In fact, for a while, I wanted to be a marine scientist. But after my mother was diagnosed with breast cancer, I became more interested in cancer research."

"One of my grandparents died from cancer. It's a horrible death."

Craig nodded. "Seeing my mother wither away—and not being able to do anything about it—was terrible. No one should die that way, or watch someone they love die that way." He took a breath. "On a more cheerful note, I'm optimistic about the advances in cancer treatments. There will be a cure in our lifetime."

"It must be wonderful to know that your work has the potential to help so many people. I love painting, but art doesn't really help people."

"I disagree," Craig said. "What art gives us may not be quantifiable, but just because it isn't quantifiable doesn't mean it isn't real. Science heals the body, but art heals the soul. When I buy a painting, it's because that painting speaks to me on a very deep level. Looking at a painting can be a spiritual experience."

I was surprised by his words. Craig had just voiced exactly how I felt in my best moments as a painter. He was speaking my language. I'd been so wrong to ever think that he couldn't possibly understand me, or me him.

For a long moment, I searched for the right words. Then I spoke from my heart.

"You're right. I'm ashamed to admit it, but sometimes I get lost in trying to make painting work as a career. Sometimes I forget why I do what I do."

"It's easy to forget. That's why I keep a photo of my mother—from before she got sick—on my desk. And another in my wallet. She's there to remind me why I've committed a huge part of my life and business to cancer research."

"I'm so sorry you lost her."

As the words left my lips, I couldn't help but feel how inadequate they were. I didn't get along with either of my parents, but I was grateful that they were alive and well.

"Do you still have family in Woods Hole?" I asked.

He shook his head. "Mom was all the family I had. She probably would have liked another child—she loved kids—but after my father died in the first Gulf War, she had all she could do to raise me. I do have a stepbrother—Mom remarried when I was twelve, and my stepfather had a son from his previous marriage—but we were never close." His expression shifted, and I glimpsed a flash of strong emotion, but it vanished almost immediately, and then he changed the subject.

"Enough about me. What was it like to grow up in Maine?"

"As you know, I'm an only child. But my parents both came from large families, so there were lots of aunts, uncles, and cousins around. When my cousins and I were young, we had a lot of great times together as a family. We would swim and sail all day, then cook enough lobster for an army on the beach. We hiked and camped in the woods. We roasted marshmallows on sticks. Later on, the family fell apart, but I'll always cherish those early memories."

"What changed? If you don't mind talking about it."

I shrugged. "My parents and their siblings stopped getting along after my grandparents died. It happened slowly, over the course of five or six years, and it wasn't any one incident that caused it. They just got together less and less often, and only a few at a time. There were several divorces, including my parents'. Then there were a couple marriages that turned so toxic that divorce might have been better. Not to mention the fights over my grandparents' almost nonexistent estates."

"How old were you when your parents split up?"

"They separated when I was sixteen. They hadn't been getting along well for several years. Then my mother caught my father in bed with a twenty-year-old waitress, which was the last straw."

"That must have been terrible," he said quietly.

"It was. But on some level I knew he'd been cheating on Mom for years. I don't know how I knew, but I did. The waitress wasn't the first time Dad cheated, so the divorce wasn't a complete shock. I thought they might do better apart, which in fact turned out to be the case. Neither has remarried, but they've both found relationships that work better for them."

He furrowed his brow. "Still, it can't have been easy."

"It wasn't. But it was a long time ago. Life happens, many people have it a lot worse than I do, and I'd rather focus on everything that's good in my life. Painting. My friendship with Duncan, who's like the brother I always wished I had. Days like today." I met his eyes, and let him see my appreciation.

He got up from his chair. "Speaking of today and good things, how about this unseasonably balmy weather? Let's take a walk on the beach. Soak up a little sun. Then we'll get to work. The second floor porch is set up as your painting studio." He held out his hand to me.

"Sounds good to me."

I was moved that he had set up a painting studio for me, and decided, once and for all, that I could love him. In fact, I was already beginning to love him. I took his hand, and we left the porch for the beach.

We moved past the dunes toward the ocean, and the strong, salty wind whipped my hair. As we walked hand-in-hand along the water's edge, I continued to process all that he'd told me about himself. Suddenly, he stopped, bent down, and picked up a rock that he handed to me."

"Check this out."

Shiny and wet, polished by the waves, the rock was dark gray and egg-shaped. A rougher circle of white stone was embedded in one side.

"That's really neat. I've never seen a rock like this before." I turned it in my hands, running my fingers along the white circle.

"I found one similar to it on the beach when I was a kid. Anyway, I still have mine, so this one is yours."

"Thank you," I said. "It's a wonderful keepsake."

"Are you cold?" Craig asked. "Because you look cold. Here, take my sweater." He pulled his cable knit sweater over his head, and gently slid it over mine. It was far too large, but I liked that it smelled faintly of him. He stepped back and appraised me.

"That sweater's never looked so good."

He put his arm around my waist, and I rested my hand on his hip as we continued to walk. Alone on the seemingly endless beach, we approached the waterline, and Craig pulled me against himself and kissed me. As our bodies merged and our tongues met, my desire for him heated and intensified with each caress. My hands explored the contours of his muscled torso, then reached upward to touch his face.

After all these weeks of being with each other, I was ready. My body ached for his touch. As if he'd read my mind, his hands moved to my breasts, and caressed their tips. I reached for his jeans and felt his thick erection surge beneath my hands.

Craig broke the kiss and looked deep into my eyes. "Are you sure?"

"Completely." I wanted this. I wanted him, with every fiber of my being.

"In that case, let's take this back to the house."

14

By the time we reached the rear deck, Craig had disposed of both his sweater and my blouse. Surrounded by dunes and a wooden slat fence, the deck was open to the ocean air yet completely private, with a spacious hot tub at one end.

As we continued to explore each others' bodies, I began to tease Craig's T-shirt upward. He raised his arms and allowed me to pull the shirt over his head, which revealed the hard muscle that I had so far only felt.

I ran my fingers lightly over the rippled muscle of his abdomen, and he reclaimed my lips with a kiss that I felt all the way to my toes. Then he released my bra, tossed it to one side, and knelt, drawing me gently to the deck, before lowering his head to my naked breasts. His tongue alternately flicked and circled my nipples, now rock hard, as his hands cupped and caressed. I moaned, wanting more.

"Not yet," he murmured. His tongue moved from one nipple to the other. "I've wanted to do this for a long time, and I won't be rushed."

With one hand, he guided my jeans downward, then my dark blue silk thong followed. He lowered his head and parted the soft folds of flesh that concealed my most sensitive parts. He stroked me delicately with the tip of his thumb, and then with his tongue. My breath caught when his finger lightly penetrated the inner wetness just beyond.

"You're so beautiful, Juliana."

He added a second finger. Then a third. Longer, deeper strokes quickly pushed me to the edge.

"Please, Craig. I need you inside me."

He shot me a mischievous glance. "Greedy, are we? You'll get what you want... soon enough."

I couldn't hold on any longer, and came in violent waves. My body shuddered its release around his hand. He pulled me into himself and wrapped a strong arm around my waist.

"Now you're ready for me," he said, and rose to his feet, holding my eyes with his gaze. Slowly, deliberately, he removed his jeans and boxers, which revealed an impressive erection that jutted from the dark curls between his beautifully muscled legs.

"Before we go any further, I need you to know that I'm clean," he said. "I have protection, too, if you'd prefer."

"No need," I said. "I trust you, and I've been on the pill since I was sixteen—it makes my periods easier. I don't have any health issues either."

"Great." He grinned. "Condoms are, at best, a necessary evil."

He reached for my hand, but the heat between us made me fearless, and I knew what I wanted. It was something I'd never done before, something I hadn't ever imagined wanting. I sank to my knees as the pounding of my heart merged with the distant sound of the surf.

I took him into my mouth. My tongue swirled lightly around the thick head of his cock, exploring him. He tasted like the ocean air, salty and invigorating. I threw caution to the wind and went with my intuition. Licking him from base to tip, I took him into my mouth again, only deeper this time. I gently grasped his balls with one hand, while I stroked him with the other.

He breathed heavily and released a groan. "Ahhhh... If you keep doing that, I'm going to lose control."

"Maybe I want you to."

I met his eyes, pulled him in deeper and deeper, and continued to suck and caress him. I felt that he was close, so instinctively, I picked up the pace, delicately tonguing him as I took him deeper.

When he came, he called out my name and spurted volcanically. I took it all. After he finished, he dropped to his knees and took me into his arms. As he held me against his body, I could feel his heart pound from the force of his orgasm.

"I had no idea you were so... experienced."

"Am I?" I smiled and savored the moment. "That was a first for me."

"I knew you were special from the moment we met, but my imagination didn't extend quite that far."

"And here I thought all those smoldering looks you've been giving me were all about sex."

"Oh, they were. I did take you for more of an innocent, though."

"You're not completely wrong," I admitted. "My sexual experience is pretty minimal. Adolescent fumbles, mostly. Just call me an almost-virgin."

"I'm a lucky man, then. You have no idea how much fun we're about to have together." He grinned in such a way that communicated the general direction of his thoughts. Not that I objected. Not at all.

"Let's move to the hot tub," he said. "What we just did was an appetizer. This calls for a five-course meal."

15

I sank into the hot, bubbling water, then leaned back into the seat. Craig climbed in after me, sat down, and then pulled me toward him for a long, passionate kiss that left me breathless. I wrapped my legs around his waist, and realized that he was already hard again.

"If I'm not mistaken, you're ready for the next course," I said.

"I am, but are you?" He gave me a playful look, and resumed caressing my breasts, which felt full and heavy with anticipation. My nipples were rock hard, and his every touch sent delightful ripples throughout my body.

"God, yes. I'm starving."

"I bet I could make you come just by doing this." He cocked his head to the side. "But right now, I have something else in mind. Give me a minute. I'll be right back."

Curious about what he was up to, I released him, and eased back into the seat. Warmed and relaxed by the hot water, I closed my eyes, and reveled in the light pressure of the bubbling jets against my skin.

I felt more alive than I had in years. The calls of seagulls and the rhythm of the surf surrounded me, and I absorbed the familiar sounds with pleasure.

When Craig returned, I opened my eyes halfway, and watched him squeeze something from a black bottle onto one hand and smooth it over his erection. Watching him stroke himself took my breath away. Anticipation and fear warred in my mind.

"Lube," he explained. "The water washes away your natural lubrication. This will help." He joined me in the water, and seated me on his lap with my legs around his waist.

"Rest your hands behind my head," he said, "or on my shoulders. And keep them there. No touching. This time, I'm doing all the touching."

"Are you a control freak?" I teased. "Do you want to dominate me?"

"I guess you'll find out what I want soon enough."

We shared a slow, lingering kiss. He lowered his mouth to my right nipple, and kneaded my other breast with one hand. Simultaneously, his other hand found my clit, and his thumb began to circle it leisurely. I gripped his shoulders harder as my excitement built, and my initial fear dissolved into raw desire.

He lifted me from the waist and gently guided me onto his hard length, bringing me down on him, then up, a little deeper with each stroke.

"You're so tight," he said.

As he penetrated me, I felt myself open and expand to receive him. My body cried out for more. As I approached climax, he slowed the pace, which made me feel every silky inch of him.

"Look at me, Juliana. Look into my eyes and come for me." I met his heated gaze with my own, waves of sensation coursed through my body, and the force of my orgasm shattered me.

I collapsed against his chest as, with a final, powerful stroke, he came inside of me. When we were spent, we lingered for a long moment before Craig roused himself.

"Time to get out," he said. "Too much time in the hot water and you'll fall asleep on me." He gave me a playful nudge. "I'm not ready for you to fall asleep just yet."

He lifted me off him, climbed out of the hot tub, and then offered me his hand. Once I was back on the deck, he reached for a beige, fluffy stack of robes and towels that I hadn't noticed before.

"Here." He gently placed a beige cotton robe around my shoulders. "And a towel for your hair." I tied the robe in place and toweled my hair as Craig donned a similar robe.

"How about a glass of wine by the fireplace?" he asked. "The sun is setting, and it's a little cold to be outside."

"That sounds perfect." I followed him into the kitchen, where he took an already opened bottle of Côtes du Rhone from the sideboard and handed it to me.

"I let it breathe while we were in the hot tub. It should be OK to drink by now, though it'll be even better in twenty minutes or so." He retrieved two wineglasses, and handed them to me.

I followed him to the main room, where a fire crackled in a large stone fireplace. In front of the fireplace was a fur throw flanked by a pair of comfortable-looking leather armchairs, between which sat a low table.

Craig poured us each a glass of wine.

"To us," he said, and clinked his glass against mine.

I drank. The wine was delicious.

"Relax," he said. "I'll be back in a minute with some cheese and crackers."

I laid down on the throw, propped myself up on one elbow, and luxuriated in the warmth that radiated from the fire. Outside the windows, the vivid colors of the setting sun streaked across the sky.

When Craig returned, he carried a cheeseboard, which he placed on the low table. He sat next to me

"The cheeses are Saint-Marcellin, Cantal, and Comté," he said, and cut a few slivers from each. "Here. Try the Saint-Marcellin first." He fed me a piece, then ate one himself.

It had a soft, buttery texture and a subtle mushroom-tinted flavor. I'd never tasted anything quite like it. Between sips of wine, Craig continued to feed me bits of cheese. The Cantal turned out to be cheddar-like but crumbly, while the Comté was mild and sweet.

The wine, in combination with the fire, warmed me to my toes, and each brush of Craig's fingertips against my lips fed my desire. The sense of complete intimacy, and the intense connection that I felt with him was unfamiliar. I'd never felt such hunger for a man before.

"I owe you an apology," he said, lying down next to me on the throw.

"Why?"

"I promised you painting time, and you didn't get it. I got carried away."

"We both got carried away. I'll paint tomorrow. Unless we get carried away again."

"You'll paint tomorrow morning. Promise?"

"OK," I said. "I promise."

16

When I awoke the next morning in his bedroom, it took a minute to process my unfamiliar surroundings. Images from the previous day flashed through my mind. Our conversation, and the intense connection I'd felt with him. The searing kiss on the beach, followed by an evening of mind-blowing sex. I closed my eyes, rubbed them with both fists, then opened them again.

I got up, looked around the room, and realized that Craig wasn't there. I spotted a note, pinned to the bedside table with a rough granite stone, and read the strong, spiky writing.

Gone for a run. Back by 10 a.m. Coffee in the kitchen, painting supplies in the second floor front room.

I threw on my robe and padded downstairs to the kitchen. Craig had thoughtfully put the coffee in a thermal carafe, so it was piping hot. I drank one cup quickly, then sipped a second. When the caffeine struck as only caffeine could strike, I began to feel like myself again. I finished my coffee and decided that a long, luxurious shower was next on the morning agenda. I headed for the bathroom.

When I was showered and clean, I dressed quickly in a black tank top and denim shorts—my preferred painting uniform. I realized that Craig would be back soon, and decided to check out the room where he'd said I could paint.

I followed the second floor hallway from the bedroom to the front of the house, and opened the French doors at the end of the hall. Once I'd entered the room, I looked around.

I couldn't believe what I saw.

Several easels held blank canvases of varying sizes. Additional canvases rested against the wall, next to a wicker couch and matching coffee table. A large assortment of brushes in all sizes and shapes were laid out neatly on a long, wood-topped counter next to the bag of supplies that I'd brought with me. I opened the drawers beneath the counter, and discovered an array of paint tubes and painting mediums. Craig had thought of everything that I could possibly need.

Then there was the room itself. It spanned the entire front of the house, with windows on three sides, which bathed the entire room in sunlight. Adjustable blinds permitted complete control of the light. It couldn't have been more perfect.

I stepped over to the windows, and looked out at the beach and the ocean beyond. Not for the first time, I struggled to reconcile my impressions of Craig. On the one hand, he was all alpha male. He pursued whatever he wanted single-mindedly and without hesitation. On the other, he could be incredibly thoughtful. At times he could come across as serious and intense, but he also had a quirky sense of humor that matched my own.

A moment later, I spotted him on the beach. He walked toward the house, and as he approached, I noticed that his cell phone was at his ear. At 10 a.m. on a Sunday morning? Did he ever take a break? This was supposed to be our weekend together. I sighed, then something occurred to me, and I smiled to myself. His phone had been conspicuously absent when we made love. Maybe I did have the power to tear him away from his work, after all.

Several minutes later, I heard his footsteps on the stairs. He entered the studio, looked around, and put his hands on his hips. In his running shirt and shorts, he looked athletic and ruggedly handsome. Several locks of unruly, windswept hair fell over his forehead, and his jawline had a sexy layer of dark stubble.

"This is refreshing to see," he said. "I hope you have everything you need to paint."

"You've stocked this place with everything I could possibly need, and then some. You really didn't have to do all this."

"I just wanted to make sure that you would have what you need. Is the studio OK?"

"The studio's more than OK. It's fabulous. It's perfect." I rose onto my toes and kissed him lightly on the lips.

"I warn you, Juliana. If you start something, I may be tempted to finish it." His eyes swept appreciatively over my body. "Where you're concerned, my margin of self-control is a little thin. And we need to talk. Things got a little out of hand last night."

What does that mean? "OK," I said.

He sat on the couch and patted the cushion next to him. "I've been thinking. If we're going to continue our relationship, we need to discuss a few ground rules. I'd like sexual exclusivity, on both sides."

"Isn't that assumed?"

"I don't live my life based on assumptions. And I don't want to sound judgmental, but not all men are like your father. I'm no angel, but I've never cheated on a woman. If we're going to continue seeing each other, I need to know that we're on the same page."

"Of course we are."

"We should also talk about visibility."

"What do you mean by visibility?"

His expression became serious. "I mean visibility as in media visibility. The media will pounce on you as soon as they discover that you're my girlfriend."

Girlfriend? The word sent a thrill of excitement through me.

"Are you saying that paparazzi will chase me on my way to work because of our relationship?" I couldn't help but laugh. "If so, they'll be disappointed. I like my life, but it's hardly fascinating enough to sell newspapers or magazines."

Craig sighed. "Believe me, I wish that were the case. But unfortunately, the media rarely let truth get in the way of a juicy story. Over the years, many exaggerations and lies have been written about me. The fact is that being with me will put you in the public eye. That eye can be unfair, even cruel. I don't want to frighten you away—very much the contrary—but we do need to talk about it."

The thought of that kind of attention was more than a little unsettling. "Can't we keep our relationship discreet?"

"We can try, but you may not like the simplest solution."

"What's that?"

"I can continue to go to business and philanthropic events with other women. You would have to trust that there's nothing going on beyond friendship."

"What about their feelings? What if they want more?"

"These are trusted friends. They're successful actresses and businesswomen. They're already in the public eye, and accustomed to the pressure. It's not romantic in any way. It's just a convenient arrangement that benefits both parties. Wealthy, single men like me are targets for every ambitious gold-digger, washed-up actress, and budding ingénue. The simplest way to avoid unwanted attention is to have a woman on my arm." He looked me in the eye. "What we have together is real, and I don't want to fuck it up by throwing you into the media spotlight—until you're ready."

"Let me give this some thought. You know I want to be with you. But it's unnerving to think of my face being plastered all over the Internet."

"Just think about what's best for you, OK? I promised you painting time, and I'm going to keep that promise." He rose from the couch. "We can talk more later, once you've had a chance to think about what I've said. Lunch around one?"

"Works for me."

When he left the studio, I turned to the windows and looked out at the ocean. I wanted to be with him, but I also wanted the time and space to pursue a normal relationship. Unfortunately, a normal relationship didn't seem to be an option, which, if I was being honest with myself, I already knew.

There was no way that I'd be anyone's dark little secret. If I was going to be with Craig—and I was—certainly I could adapt to life under a media microscope. Otherwise, not being with him could compromise our relationship.

I'll sit on it for a day, and then talk with Dunc about it.

I grabbed several tubes of paint and a couple brushes, chose a medium-sized horizontal canvas, placed it on an easel, and began painting.

Painting had always been a retreat, a respite from the demands of life. I began by applying broad washes of color for sea and sky. Then I reached for a fan-shaped brush and blended and stippled touches of white paint.

Time flew as I worked. My progress was accompanied by the sound of the waves crashing against the beach outside, and punctuated by the occasional cries of seagulls.

At one o'clock, Craig returned. He carried a tray with a large salad of mixed greens and two glasses of sparkling water, which he set on the table.

"Ready to eat? I'll be back in a minute with the rest of our lunch."

He left the room and I heard him jog down the stairs. I put my brushes in water and went to wash my paint-smeared hands. By the time I came back to the studio, Craig had brought plates, cutlery, and sandwiches. We settled on the couch to begin eating.

"I like what you've done," he said between bites while gazing at my morning's work. "It verges on abstraction, but with a strong sense of place. Is it finished?"

"It's just a sketch. I usually work through a few versions before a painting is done. Still, I haven't had much time to paint during the past few months, and it feels fantastic to put paint on canvas again, regardless of the result."

"I'm glad to hear that."

"What did you do this morning, while I was painting?" I asked.

"Work. I spent most of Friday in meetings, so I used the morning to read and answer email. I'm not completely caught up yet, but I'm getting there."

Once again, I was reminded of the heavy weight of responsibility that Craig carried as the CEO of a large business. Reading and answering my own email rarely took more than a few minutes, let alone an entire morning, and I felt more appreciative than ever that he'd made time to spend this weekend with me, and even set up a painting studio for me.

When we finished our sandwiches, Craig got up and began stacking dishes on the tray. We carried everything back to the kitchen together, and put the leftovers away. When we were done, he turned to me.

"How would you like to spend the afternoon?" he asked. "You can continue painting, of course, or we could take a walk. It's a beautiful day."

"A walk sounds great," I replied. "Give me a minute to put on a sweater, and find my sandals."

We left the house together, and emerged into the crisp air and clear light of the lovely autumn day. As we walked toward the ocean, I reached for his hand. His fingers tightened around mine.

"I do trust you, Craig," I said. "And I want to be with you. Just give me a day or so to think through how I'm going to cope with dating a business celebrity."

"You'd have plenty of support. My public relations team handles everything from press releases and answering routine questions on my behalf, to wardrobe, hair, and makeup. Then there's the security team, of course."

"So someone else chooses your clothes for you?"

"In a way, yes. Samantha Day, my wardrobe consultant, knows what I like. She shops for me, and suggests combinations that work, like which ties go well with which shirts. Not that Sam manages to get me into a tie very often." He grinned. "Perk of being the boss, you know."

Wardrobe consultant. Security team. It all made my head spin. Every time I thought that I'd grasped Craig's world, something like this reminded me that I hadn't.

Trusting him had been an enormous step for me, and while I had no regrets about that, being with Craig was obviously going to change my life in ways that I couldn't predict, let alone control.

17

That evening, we flew back to Bedford where Craig's driver picked us up and drove us to Davis Square. When we reached my apartment, I took his hand and leaned in for a kiss.

"Thanks for a beautiful weekend. When will I see you again?"

He squeezed my hand. "Tomorrow night? Maybe we can go out for a drink after you finish work?"

"I'd love that. I'll text you when I finish work."

I walked up the stairs to the apartment, and unlocked and opened the door. Inside, Duncan was sprawled on the living room couch with his iPad. He sat up and patted the cushion beside him.

"You're glowing," he said. "Spill it. Tell me all about your weekend."

"Let me put down my bags and make us both a cup of tea. Then I promise to tell you everything."

"I'll make the tea, while you put your things away."

"You're the best."

While Duncan made tea, I put my bags in my room and started to unpack. As I removed clothing and toiletries from my bag, my hand brushed against the lucky rock that Craig had given me on the beach.

I pulled it out of my bag, turned it in my hands, and caressed its surface.

Smooth, dark gray, and interrupted by a circle of rougher white stone, the rock's unusual contrast felt symbolic. Craig was the white circle. Beautiful, unexpected, wonderful—but a radical interruption in my life. Being with him meant that my life would change, and I needed to prepare myself as much as possible. I placed the rock on my bedside table, and returned to the living room.

Duncan and I settled onto the couch.

"Tell me what happened."

I did.

"What a perfect romantic weekend," Duncan said. "I can't tell you how thrilled I am for you."

"I'm in love with him. I've never wanted anything as much as I want to be with him, but I'm not sure if I can be part of his life without losing my own."

"What exactly do you mean?"

"Look, Duncan. I knew that Craig was a business celebrity before we began dating, but now I'm faced with the reality of it, and what it means for me. To be honest, I'm a little freaked out. Eventually, our relationship will become public. We'll attend events together, and photos of us will be all over the Internet. Again, I went into this relationship with my eyes wide open, but I didn't think it would become reality. But now that it's here, I'm really not sure I'm ready to step that far out of my comfort zone. You know me—I'm shy." I shrugged. "I guess I'm at an impasse."

Duncan nodded thoughtfully. "I get where you're coming from. I really do. It won't be easy, at least not at first. But if you love Craig, and you want to be with him, then you need to share his life—all of it."

I shook my head. "Thank you. I needed to hear that."

"Anytime. I'm really happy for you, Jules. I like Craig, and I'm glad to hear that he's so upfront and honest with you."

"So when Craig and I take our relationship public, what should I expect? I have my ideas of what could happen, but I'd like to hear what you think."

"I'm no expert, but you should expect to lose some degree of privacy. Photos of you with Craig will be posted online, maybe articles about you as well. Much of the media coverage will be neutral and more or less accurate, but some will be inaccurate or unkind—that's the risk, and you need to decide if Craig is worth it. I think you already have. You may have to deal with some gossip at work, but do you really give a damn about that? You don't have to worry about it hurting your painting career though—the art world is nothing if not rabid for the slightest whiff of celebrity. Kind of like how blood in the water attracts sharks."

"Sharks? Blood? What am I getting myself into?" I rolled my eyes.

"You'll need to invest in a pair of big, dark sunglasses. Like Jackie O. Maybe something by Chanel. Or Dior. I'll help you find the perfect pair. In the right sunglasses, you'll look fabulously chic and glamorous. Of course, in the wrong ones, you'll just look like a demented insect."

"I haven't made any decisions yet, and already you're shopping for designer sunglasses."

"Someone has to think ahead," Duncan said, and then his expression sobered. "I know you, Jules. You hesitate. You second-guess yourself. But in the end, you go after what you want. And it's obvious that you want Craig."

"Thank you so much, especially for your honesty. I know I can always count on you for that."

"I'll always be there for you. Just like you are for me."

Once again, I felt lucky to have Duncan as my best friend. His own less-than-idyllic life had given him the perspective I sometimes lacked, and talking things through with him always provided new insights.

As I prepared to go to bed, a thought occurred to me—I could get a better sense of the media presence around Craig by doing a Google News search on him. Google would tell me much, if not all, of what I needed to know. I sat at the desk in my bedroom and opened my laptop.

Two hours later, I checked the time. It was just after midnight. Googling Craig had produced a dizzying array of search results. Interviews with Craig the business genius offering advice to young entrepreneurs. Images of Craig the philanthropist and Craig the movie producer, photographed at red carpet events, and always with a beautiful woman on his arm.

Or two.

One woman appeared more frequently than the others. Her name was Alessandra d'Acosta. Tall, dark, and classically beautiful with a lush, hourglass figure, she reminded me of the famous Italian actress, Anna Magnani. Alessandra's name was often romantically linked with Craig's. A search on her name revealed that she was an actress whose career was on the rise.

I was curious about Alessandra's history with Craig. Based on what I'd seen, I was almost certain that they'd been romantically involved at some point, and the most recent photos of them together were from an event that had taken place only a few weeks ago, not long after Craig and I had started dating. She was exactly the sort of person everyone would expect Craig Manning to date.

But Craig had told me that he often attended events with women who were just friends, and I trusted him. I wasn't about to cross-examine him about his past. I closed my laptop, and told myself to forget about Alessandra. So what if she was gorgeous, and an up-and-coming movie star to boot? Craig wanted to be with me, and I wanted to be with him. I just needed to learn how to deal with his world.

18

Monday morning arrived all too soon. I turned off the buzzer on my alarm clock, got up, and made myself coffee. Duncan's bedroom door was closed, and I envied him for getting to sleep in.

After I showered, dressed, and drank a second cup of coffee, I was off to Tremont to teach a morning class. I felt tired and more than a little distracted. I should have gone to bed earlier—or downed a third cup of coffee. But what I needed more than anything was to talk to Craig.

After the class ended at noon, I texted him.

Do you have time to talk? I'm free now, working at Perfect at 4.

I sent the text, and then stared at my phone. Nothing. Maybe he was in a meeting, or busy with something. If so, I'd just have to wait until tonight.

Happily, his text popped onto the screen a minute later.

In meetings until three. How about 3:15, my office?

Relieved, I quickly tapped an answer.

See you then.

I decided to take the train to Park Street, and walk to Kendall

Square from there. The unseasonably warm weather had held, but I knew there wouldn't be many more days like this before the New England winter arrived in full force. And walking, like painting, always helped to clear my head. I strolled down Beacon Hill, toward the Charles River and the gray stone towers of the Longfellow Bridge.

When I approached Manning Tower, I checked my watch, confirming that I was on time. I entered the building and took the elevator to the top floor. The attractive blonde I remembered from my previous visit was seated behind the reception desk.

"Good afternoon, Ms. West. Mr. Manning is expecting you in his office."

"Thank you."

The door to Craig's office was open. He stood in front of the wall of windows behind his desk, and looked out at the Boston skyline. Dressed in a tailored dark business suit and a slightly mussed white shirt with open collar, he appeared deep in thought.

I knocked lightly on the open door. He turned, crossed the office, and closed the door behind us.

"I've instructed Suzanne that we're not to be interrupted." He gestured toward the two Corbusier sling chairs in front of his desk. "Let's talk. Unless you'd like some lunch?"

"I'm not hungry, but thanks." I perched on the edge of one of the chairs.

Craig seated himself in the other, leaned back and smiled at me.

"It's great to see you," he said. "I was afraid I'd scared you off. Anyway, you have my undivided attention."

"Thank you for making time for us to talk. Last night and this morning, I thought about our conversation on the Cape and I've come to a decision." I hesitated, searching for the right words. "I need to find out if I can handle the pressure of being your girlfriend, in public. Hiding won't let me do that. I need to experience the intensity of your world."

As he listened, Craig's expression shifted from nervousness to relief.

"What parts would you like to experience, and how?"

"I want to understand you better. See a little more of your day-to-day life."

"So you're ready to go public? If so, that makes my day. Possibly my weekend, too." He looked thoughtful. "How about if we start in New York? This Thursday? At the Guggenheim gala?"

"As in the Guggenheim Museum?"

"Yes. The gala is an annual event benefitting the Guggenheim Foundation. Cocktails followed by dinner. Manning Biotech is one of the event sponsors. Some of the work for the upcoming benefit auction will be on view. Oh, and one of the event chairs, Caroline Holt-Fleming, is hosting an unofficial after-party at her Park Avenue brownstone for a handful of major donors and art world celebs."

"Let me think. I have to teach Thursday afternoon, and I'm scheduled to work at Perfect on Friday."

"When do you finish teaching? I can send a car to pick you up at Tremont, and we can fly from Bedford to LaGuardia."

"I'm done at four on Thursday. I guess I could just pack a bag with what I need, so long as I'll have time to take a shower and get dressed after we arrive."

"Don't worry about packing a bag. Samantha will take care of everything. Any chance you could get Friday off? We could do a long weekend in the city."

"I don't know about getting Friday off, but I'll ask. And I'll text you the location of the building where I teach on Thursdays."

He got to his feet as I rose from my chair. He took my hand, and pulled me into a lingering kiss that set my body on fire. His hands roved lightly over my ass, then moved around and up to my nipples, which were already at full attention. I could feel him getting hard against my leg, as well as the aching heat of my own desire. Mentally cursing the clock, I forced myself to pull away.

"Do you really have to go now?" he asked.

"Unfortunately, yes. I can't show up late for work. Rain check after I finish? Maybe we can go out for a martini, then spend the night together?"

"Text me fifteen minutes before you're ready to leave, and I'll have the car waiting." His eyes were full of mischief. "And after that martini, don't expect much sleep."

19

The clock moved all too slowly as I struggled to keep my mind on my work. No matter how hard I tried to focus, thoughts of Craig crept in. Finally, 9:45 arrived, and I texted him.

Leaving in fifteen minutes. See you downstairs a few minutes after ten?

I watched the screen expectantly for several minutes. No response. I made myself keep working until 9:55, then checked again. Still no response. I decided to go downstairs to see if he was already waiting for me.

I put on my coat, slung my bag over my shoulder, and left the office, phone in hand. After reaching the lobby, I looked around. No Craig in sight, just the usual security guards.

I checked the phone again. 10:03. No new messages. This wasn't like him, and I hoped that everything was OK. I waited until 10:15, and then called his cell. Direct to voicemail. I left a message saying that I was waiting downstairs. Then I called his office number. After several rings, he picked up.

"Juliana, I apologize. Something's come up. I can't leave just yet. Can you come up here and hang out for half an hour? It shouldn't take longer than that." He sounded stressed.

"OK. See you in a minute." As I took the elevator to the top floor, I wondered what had kept Craig at his desk so late.

As the elevator doors opened, I heard the sound of Craig's voice coming from his office, and realized he was on the phone—with his lawyer. Based on Craig's side of the conversation, it sounded like a fairly heated disagreement. I could hear frustration in his voice, and his hair was mussed, as if he'd been running his fingers through it.

Finally, he ended the call. "Just make it fucking happen, Jared. Tomorrow morning. First thing."

He hung up the phone and turned to me. "Sorry to keep you waiting. This lawsuit is driving me crazy. Would you mind if we didn't go out tonight? We can still have a martini here."

"Of course I don't mind."

We left his office, and walked across the reception area and down the hallway that led to his private suite, familiar from previous visits. As we entered the spacious living room, he gestured toward an alcove, which contained built-in bar cabinets.

"Belvedere, dirty, olives?" he asked.

"Your memory is spot-on." I raised my eyebrows in mock surprise.

"Oh, you're nothing if not memorable—in every way."

Watching his strong hands measure, shake, and pour, I couldn't help but recall the exquisite sensation of those hands on my body, and I remembered the king-size bed just a few doors away.

When he was finished, he gestured toward a large, dark brown leather couch, positioned to take advantage of the suite's spectacular view of the Boston skyline.

"Let's sit there. As you can see, the view's pretty good in clear weather."

We sat on the couch, and Craig raised his glass. "Cheers," he said, and then tossed back half his drink.

"Cheers," I said, and took a sip of my martini. It was perfect. Ice-cold and smooth as silk.

For a minute or two, we sat in a comfortable silence. I enjoyed the view and savored my drink. In the distance, Boston sparkled and shimmered. The steady motion of headlights on Storrow Drive traced the energetic, living flow of the city. At night, the vision of the whole dominated the individual parts, and became an immense living organism that pulsated with life.

I broke the silence. "The sky is so clear tonight. I feel as if I could reach out the window and touch the big CITGO sign."

Craig smiled, but his expression was distant. I wondered if he was still thinking about work, and if I should ask. I decided to give it a shot.

"It seems as if you've had a stressful day," I said. "Do you feel like talking about it?"

He sighed. "It's a long story. Sure you want to hear it?"

"Of course I do."

"I'll try to keep it short. Years ago, one of my companies—Manning Biotech—patented an anti-cancer drug. Since then, we've been working our way through the clinical trials required for FDA approval."

"Does the drug have a name?" I asked.

"We haven't made a final decision about the name yet," Craig said.

"So what are you thinking of naming it?"

"So far we've spent over a million dollars with a marketing agency that specializes in branding. They're working with us to create a name, design a logo and brand strategy, et cetera. Of the names they've proposed to date, Protix is the best. And I like the logo they've developed. But something about the name doesn't feel right to me. Not strong enough."

I thought for a moment. I liked *pro*. *Pro* implied progress, moving forward. What to put with it? Maybe *vita*? Latin for life? That would make Provita, but that sounded too much like a vitamin. Maybe Provitane?

I pulled out my phone and did a quick Google search to see if there was an existing drug or product with that name. After confirming that there wasn't, I asked, "What about Provitane? I just checked. There isn't another product with that name."

Craig looked stunned. "Provitane," he said slowly. "You know, I like it. I really like it." He shook his head. "So great. I spend a million bucks for a team to sit around conference rooms inventing drug names, and my genius girlfriend come up with a better one in under a minute." He kissed me on the cheek. "Thank you."

"Hey, I was just riffing. I'm glad you like it." I paused. "So, tell me more about this anti-cancer drug you've been working on."

"OK. The drug showed strong results, and we were able to fast track the approval process. It should be approved and on the market early next year."

He paused to sip his martini. "Six months ago, a company called Syngenomics filed for patent of a near-identical drug, what the industry calls a 'me-too' drug. If they had produced their drug independently, as they claim they did, that would be legal. The two drugs would compete against each other for market share. However, for reasons I won't bore you with now, I had good reason to believe that Syngenomics stole our research. So, we sued them for theft of confidential research information. If we win the lawsuit, then Manning Biotech will be poised to dominate the market for this drug. If Syngenomics wins, the profits from our new drug will be much less than projected, and Manning Biotech's stock price will take a beating. And knowing Walter Reimann—the CEO of Syngenomics—if the stock price drops low enough, he'll attempt a takeover. He's wanted Manning Biotech for years."

When I heard the name Walter Reimann, I froze. I knew that name. Walter Reimann was the father of Matt Reimann. As in Matt, my ex-boyfriend, the jerk who had raped me. I was speechless.

Craig's eyes darkened. "I know Reimann stole our research, and I know who helped him steal it. I just need more time to gather additional evidence."

I hadn't wanted to tell Craig about the rape. At least not yet. He knew that I'd been hurt in a prior relationship, but I hadn't told him how. I'd promised that I would tell him someday, when I was ready.

My silence had never been about hiding my past from him. I just didn't want Craig—or anyone—to see me as damaged goods. I wanted him to know me for longer before I told him about that rotten chapter in my life.

But what he'd just revealed changed everything. I had to tell him, and I had to tell him tonight. It wouldn't be right to conceal my history with the son of his business enemy.

"Well, this is unexpected," I said.

"What's unexpected?"

"There's something I need to tell you. I know the Reimann family."

His face showed surprise. "Really? How?"

"I dated Walter Reimann's son in college."

Craig's face shifted from surprise to an expression I had never seen before. Not angry, exactly. Primal.

"You dated Matt Reimann?"

"That's right."

"I hope you're not about to tell me that you're still friendly with him, because believe me, Matt Reimann is a fucking jerk."

"I know that—now."

"Why do I feel that there's more to this?"

"Because there is."

"Tell me."

To get through this, I knew I needed to stay calm, and relate the facts with as little emotion as possible. I took a deep breath and began.

"I met Matt in college, at a party. A mutual acquaintance introduced us. He was good-looking and charming. Popular with everyone, though there was always gossip about his womanizing. The first few times he asked me out, I refused because of his reputation. But he continued to pursue me aggressively. He showered me with romantic gestures and expensive gifts. He claimed that he'd fallen in love with me." I took a deep breath. "Eventually, I caved and decided to give him a chance after he said that he was fine with taking things slowly. We dated for a few months, and we became closer. I started to fall for him—at least the part of him that I knew."

Craig took my hand in his own, and looked at me. "He's the guy who hurt you, isn't he?" His eyes revealed the depth of his concern.

"He's the one," I said.

"Tell me what he did to you."

I steeled myself to go on. "He invited me to spend the weekend at his parent's house in Newport. His parents were hosting this big party, a political fundraiser of some sort. Everyone was drinking. I didn't get drunk, but I was definitely tipsy. Matt, on the other hand, *was* drunk—he'd been swilling whiskey all evening. After we went to bed—in separate bedrooms—he came to my room and demanded sex. I asked him to leave, but he said it was time to get what he'd paid for. He pulled out his Swiss Army knife, and said he'd use it on me if I resisted. Then, he ripped up a sheet and used it to tie me to the bed."

Craig gently turned my face toward his. Although his gesture was tender, the emotion I saw in his eyes was anything but.

"I think I can guess what happened next," he said quietly. "You have nothing to be ashamed of, Juliana. Did you file a police report? Or report him to the college?" His voice was tense with contained rage.

I forced back tears at the memory of it all. "No. I didn't tell anyone until a couple years later when I told Duncan. You and he are the only ones who know, aside from the therapist I went to for a while afterward. What would have been the point? No one who mattered would have believed me. Everyone knew that Walter Reimann paid for most of the new recreational center at our college—his name was on the building in big gold letters. And I'd just seen him host a political fundraiser, slapping backs and clinking glasses with half of the most powerful politicians in the state. Sons of powerful men don't get convicted for raping random college sophomores. The irony is that I'd more or less decided to have sex with Matt soon, just not that weekend, and certainly not when we'd been drinking." I shrugged. "What can I say? I was attracted to him. I thought we were in love. But I wanted my first time to be special—and romantic."

Craig pulled me into his arms. With my head resting against his shoulder, I couldn't see his face, but I felt his anger reverberating through his body.

When he finally spoke, his voice was controlled. "You were a virgin? How badly did he hurt you?"

"I was sore and bleeding—you know, inside. I was bruised just about everywhere, and my wrists and ankles were a bloody mess by the time I managed to free myself from the torn-up sheets he had used to tie me. By then it was dawn. Matt was passed out, dead to the world. I dressed, left the house as quietly as I could, ran several miles to the Newport bus station, and caught the first bus back to Boston." I paused. "You know what? I could really use another martini."

"Since killing Matt Reimann isn't an option at the moment, I guess I'll also have to settle for another drink."

Craig released me from his embrace and got up from the couch. As he stalked to the bar and began to mix our drinks, his every motion radiated contained fury.

While he made the drinks, what I'd just done hit me—I'd told Craig everything. Part of me felt relieved that I had—now he knew my deepest, darkest secret, and he hadn't rejected me. Instead, he'd taken me in his arms, and listened to me with compassion. My heart swelled with love for him.

Craig returned and handed me my drink. Although still visibly tense, he seemed calmer than before. He sat down, and raised his glass to me.

"To you, Juliana. You kept your head throughout a horrible, traumatic experience. You removed yourself from a dangerous situation as soon as you could. And you survived."

"Thank you for saying that. I did the best I could. My initial gut instinct about Matt was correct, but I didn't listen to it. That's one of my greatest regrets."

Craig shook his head. "Don't blame yourself. No is no, and any man who can't respect that should be shot." He looked at me. "Can I ask you one more question?"

"Of course."

"Has Matt Reimann ever bothered you again? In any way?"

"No. Initially, I took steps to avoid him, but as far as I know he never tried to contact me. I haven't had any contact with him since that night."

"What steps did you take to avoid him?"

"The fall semester was over except for exams, and I took the spring semester off. He was a senior, so I knew that by the time I returned to campus the next fall, he would be gone. I had two thousand dollars saved for spring-semester expenses, so I could afford to rent a cheap room. It was simple enough to get a job—I waited tables at a Greek restaurant in Watertown. I knew I'd never run into Matt in a place like that."

"Didn't anyone help you financially? Your parents, maybe?"

"Them? I didn't even bother to explain why I was taking a semester off to them. There wasn't any point. They've never forgiven me for choosing art instead of something more practical, like business or law. I did minor in business, but that wasn't enough. Besides, it's not as if they would have been able to help much—they don't have any money. But that's another story. For another day, if that's OK. I'm exhausted." I drained the remnants of my martini, and stood up. "I should get some rest."

Craig put down his empty glass and got up. "It's nearly 1 a.m. Want to stay here or drive to your apartment?"

"Your bed is closer than mine. I'm too tired to do anything but sleep, though." After raising the ghost of Matt, sex was the last thing I wanted.

"Fine by me. I'm exhausted, too." He put his arm around my waist, and we headed for the bedroom.

Craig led me to his generously sized walk-in closet. He pulled out a couple of drawers, removed a dark blue silk pajama shirt, and handed it to me. "For you." He retrieved a similar shirt and pants in charcoal gray for himself, then we began to undress. I quickly slipped out of my clothes, and put on the pajama shirt he'd given me. It was too large, of course, but with the sleeves rolled up, it was fine.

By the time I finished, Craig was already in bed. I joined him, and he gathered me into his strong arms. Soothed by his warm, comforting bulk, I fell asleep almost instantly. My last conscious thought was that he couldn't be real. He was too good to be true.

20

When I awoke the next morning, it took a moment to figure out where I was—in Craig's bed. The owner of the bed was sprawled next to me, with one long arm draped over my left thigh. His handsome features, peaceful in repose, contrasted with his tousled dark hair. His breathing was quiet, deep, and steady.

A bedside alarm clock indicated that it was 6:52 a.m. Not wanting to wake him, I lifted his arm from my body, and gently placed it by his side. I got up and decided to make coffee.

I padded barefoot into the kitchen, and spotted an Aeropress on the counter. Now I just needed to find the coffee. I began to rummage through the cupboards as quietly as possible.

"Juliana?" Craig called.

"In the kitchen."

After a moment, he appeared in the doorway, looking slightly bleary-eyed. "How long have you been up?"

"Just a few minutes. Did I wake you?"

"No, my internal clock is fixed on 7 a.m. I wake up at about the same time every morning—unless I'm in a different time zone. Then all bets are off. Put the water on, and I'll make the coffee."

Several minutes later, when we were enjoying our coffee, my mind flashed back to the previous evening, when I'd told Craig my most closely held secret, that I'd lost my virginity to rape. Even worse, that it was by the son of Craig's business enemy.

Craig had been nothing but understanding and supportive, but I couldn't help but feel exposed and raw.

Meanwhile, the object of my thoughts had drained his first cup of coffee and gotten up to pour himself a second. "Would you like another cup?" he asked.

"Not yet. Your throat must be lined with Teflon. I've never seen anyone down coffee so fast."

"The first cup is all about getting the minimum effective dose of caffeine into my blood. The second cup is for taste."

Demonstrating his point, he seated himself next to me, crossed his legs, and took a sip. "Usually I surf a few news sites on the Internet with my morning coffee, but looking at you definitely beats that." He winked at me.

"You're crazy," I said. "I know all too well what I look like in the morning. Hair totally out of control. Circles under the eyes. Sort of like a sleepy shrub in desperate need of pruning."

"In lieu of pruning, how about a hot shower? I give a great shampoo."

"A hot shower and a shampoo?" I said, getting up from my chair. "Lead the way, stud."

When we reached the bathroom, Craig shed his pajamas, turned the shower on, and adjusted the heat before getting in. I followed suit, and joined him under the steamy, soothing spray. He pulled me against his muscular body, turned me so that my back was against his chest, and reached for the shampoo.

As the hot water flowed over our bodies, he massaged the shampoo into my hair. Working from the crown of my head backward and down, his strong, hands massaged every inch of my scalp and neck. Blissfully relaxed, I was delighted—and more than a little relieved—to feel his erection rise against my back, banishing my lingering concern that telling him about Matt would affect our intimacy.

"My turn now," I said.

I grabbed the shampoo and turned to him. With his dark hair soaked and slicked back from his face—and with the hot water coursing over his beautifully muscled body—he was sex incarnate. I reached up, drew his face toward mine, and began to massage shampoo through his thick hair.

Our lips met in a searing kiss that didn't want to end. He pulled me against him, and cupped my ass gently. My hands slid down his body and caressed him.

"Are you sure that's what you want?" he asked.

"That's exactly what I want." I met his gaze, and let him see how much I wanted him. "I want you inside me. Right here, right now."

He raised me gently against the wall, then eased himself into me with exquisite care, moving in a slow rhythm that sent ribbons of sensation throughout me.

"Look at me, Juliana. Stay with me. Look into my eyes until we come together."

In his heavy-lidded gaze, I saw his intensity. As he continued his slow, unrelenting assault on my senses, the warm, spreading glow inside me burst into flame. And as he spurted his orgasm deep inside of me, I came hard. My body erupted like a firework, and dissolved in an explosion of embers.

Shuddering, we held each other for a long moment as the hot water continued to pulse against our bodies. Then he spoke.

"The way we are together amazes me, Juliana. You amaze me."

He released me, got out of the shower, and turned off the water. I followed, took the large, fluffy towel that he handed to me and wrapped it around myself. He secured his own towel, which hung deliciously low on his hips.

"One more cup of coffee?" I asked.

"Sure, but I need to keep an eye on the time. I have a 9 a.m. meeting and need a little time beforehand to prep. When do you have to work today?"

"I teach at 1 o'clock," I replied. "Then Perfect Transcripts from 5 to 10."

We returned to the kitchen, and Craig checked the time on his phone. "8:15 already. I have to get moving. You can relax, though. Stay as long as you like." He deftly set up a second brew of coffee, then made a beeline for the bedroom to get dressed.

By the time I poured myself a cup of fresh coffee, he reemerged, handsome in a dark red shirt that complemented his olive skin. He'd paired it with slim charcoal gray trousers and a matching jacket. I turned my face up as he bent down for a quick kiss.

"Off to work," he said. "If you're still here at 10:30 or so, maybe we can have a late breakfast together."

"Sure," I replied. "It's not as if I have to dress for work. My studio clothes are in a locker at the university anyway."

"The TV remote is on the coffee table in case you get bored."

"Perfect. So, I'll see you after your meeting."

He kissed me again, and then headed, a little reluctantly, for the door. When it closed behind him, I stretched, and reveled in how alive I felt. Love had finally found me in the form of Craig Manning, who surpassed every romantic fantasy I'd ever entertained. Gorgeous and intelligent. Strong and tender. Successful, but not egocentric.

I finished my coffee and dressed, not bothering to blow dry my hair. It was nearly dry anyway. I then went into the living room, picked up the TV remote and pressed the power button.

Nothing happened. I looked at the remote in my hand, and realized that it was a universal remote. There was probably some weird sequence of buttons I needed to press. I decided to look for the TV remote instead.

I went over to the television and began to open the cabinets next to it. The first cabinet I opened was empty. The second held shelves of DVDs.

I scanned the titles. Craig was definitely a big fan of classic American movies. There were some action and suspense titles as well. The lowest shelf appeared to hold DVDs that he had burned himself.

Curious, I pulled out a handful of them. As I flipped through the titles, I was impressed. He had a Joris Ivens film that had never been released on DVD. I had to wonder how he'd gotten his hands on that. I pulled out a second handful, and a name jumped out at me. Alessandra.

Alessandra d'Acosta?

With an ominous feeling in the pit of my stomach, I turned the television and the DVD player on manually, and then I put in the Alessandra DVD. I stared at the universal remote for a few seconds, and figured out how to set the TV input to the DVD player. Then I pressed the play button.

On the large, flatscreen TV, the video image was grainy and low quality. I turned up the volume, but there didn't seem to be any sound. The shot was of a poorly lit room, captured from above, as if by a surveillance camera.

At the center of the room was a large, empty bed with carved posts. A figure entered the room. A woman with long, dark hair wearing a flowing white garment. She turned her face toward the camera. Definitely Alessandra D'Acosta. She knelt beside the bed.

I didn't understand what she was doing. Was she praying? Was she waiting for something? A minute or two passed, and then she got up and removed the garment. Underneath, she was naked. In the center of the bed, she lay down spread eagle on her stomach, and remained unmoving. After a moment, a dark-haired man came into view, and my heart sank. It was Craig.

Naked to the waist, he wore fitted leather pants. He walked to the foot of the bed, and then I realized what was going on. He was tying her to the bed. Mesmerized, I watched in disbelief as he tied each limb in turn to the four posts of the bed.

My mind flashed back to the night Matt Reimann raped me. I remembered the sense of utter helplessness as he tied me to the bedposts with strips torn from the bedsheet. And then there was the pain—physical and emotional—as he forced himself into me.

I returned my attention to the video. Craig walked offscreen, then returned with something in his right hand that looked like some sort of whip. It was short, with numerous tails, and it appeared to be made of leather or rubber.

As I watched in shock, Craig began to whip Alessandra with measured strokes. With each stroke, the many tails of the whip spread across her smooth, white buttocks and thighs. I couldn't believe my eyes. Craig was into BDSM? He had made a video of himself whipping a woman?

After several minutes of stunned immobility, I snapped out of my initial disbelief, not sure why I was still watching. If this was what Craig was into, our relationship would never work out. After my traumatic experience with Matt, I couldn't imagine allowing anyone to tie me up, let alone enjoying it. It would only bring me back to one of the worst days of my life.

I was about to turn off the television when the scene changed. Now, the room was different, darker, with an X-shaped cross attached to a wall. Wall-mounted candelabras provided the only light. Bound, naked, and with her back to the cross, Alessandra's hands and feet were cuffed to the four terminals of the X. Her mouth was filled with a ball gag.

A string of saliva hung from one corner of her mouth. Her heavy breasts rose and fell with rapid breaths. Her eyes stared into the camera through black holes of smeared mascara. I couldn't tell if she was OK or not. As in the first video, the camera was positioned above the scene, focused on Alessandra's body.

Four men came into view, identically attired—nude to the waist, ripped, oiled muscles gleaming in the candlelight, black leather pants. All wore ornate half-masks that concealed the upper portion of their faces behind exaggerated, grotesque noses.

One of them, distinguished from the others by his highly decorated, gold-colored mask, appeared to be in charge. The sinister lines and hooked, rapacious beak of his golden mask caught the flickering candlelight, and seemed to change expression, shifting between cruelty and mockery. The gold-masked man turned his back to the camera, pulled his pants partway down and began to fuck Alessandra hard, while the three others watched and stroked themselves.

Another man approached Alessandra and began to strike her extended limbs with a riding crop, while he continued to stimulate himself with his other hand. A third man moved behind the gold-beaked leader, gripped his hips, and positioned his substantial erection so he could slam it into the leader's muscled ass.

In the dim light, the pulsing forms moved and merged together like a nest of snakes. Then a fourth man began to piss on the others. Rivulets of urine traced their way down the writhing, intertwined bodies.

Sick to my stomach, I realized that the leader—the man in the golden mask—was Craig. Despite the disguise, his build, his slightly long dark hair, and his strong jawline were unmistakable.

I'd seen enough. I turned the television off and removed the DVD, which I returned to its plastic case. Nauseous and light-headed, incapable of motion or decision, I sank to the floor, realizing that once again, I had let the wrong man into my life—and into my heart.

I had thought I was ready for intimacy, but I hadn't known what I was getting into. I definitely wasn't prepared for anything like this.

As the shock began to ebb, my confused thoughts resolved into two clear impulses. I needed to get out of here. I didn't want to see Craig now, and I didn't know if I'd ever want to see him again.

I got to my feet. I placed the DVD in the center of the coffee table, where Craig couldn't possibly miss it. I picked up my purse, then paused for a moment, struck by an overwhelming sense of loss. And fear. *What if he had done that to me? What if that was next for me?*

I pulled myself together, then took a Kleenex from my purse and dabbed my eyes. Next, I armored myself with my dark, generously sized sunglasses. Finally, I took a deep breath and straightened my posture.

I opened the door to the hallway that led to the reception area, closed the door behind me, and strode decisively toward the elevator.

"Ms. West?" the receptionist called.

"Yes?" I said.

"Mr. Manning is in a meeting in the conference room. It's

expected to finish in fifteen minutes or so. He said you were planning to have breakfast—"

I cut her off. "Something's come up. Please let Craig know that I had to leave earlier than expected."

"I'll do that, Ms. West. Have a nice day."

I needed to leave. My impulse was to run. I punched the down button on the elevator harder than necessary, and the door popped open with an insultingly cheerful "ding."

As the elevator began its descent to the ground floor, I slumped against the wall. The Craig I thought I knew wasn't real. The man I loved didn't exist. The real Craig was someone else. Someone I didn't know and wasn't sure I wanted to know.

From what I'd just seen, I now knew that he was capable of things that would forever remind me of being raped by Matt. And if I stayed with him, God only knew when that would happen to me.

21

Somehow, I made it through the rest of the day, likely on some kind of autopilot I didn't know I possessed. I more or less sleepwalked through my afternoon class. At the end of class, I saw that I had three voicemails from Craig, but I couldn't bring myself to listen to them. At this point, what could he possibly say to me?

I called in sick to Perfect Transcripts, then took the subway to Davis Square and walked home. As I climbed the stairs to the apartment, I crossed my fingers that Duncan was at home. I really needed my best friend.

No such luck. The apartment was empty. I changed into sweatpants and a T-shirt, and flopped onto the couch.

I needed to clear my mind with something, anything. I flipped through a few channels of bad TV. I thought about ordering takeout. Maybe Chinese. Maybe a pizza. Definitely something delivered to the door. I knew I should eat something—I hadn't eaten all day—but when I thought of food, it made me nauseous, so I did nothing about it. I thought about watching a movie or reading a book, if only because I needed to put Craig out of my mind. Somehow, I needed to forget about his existence, as if that were possible. But no movie or book was that powerful, and I knew it.

Around eight o'clock, I heard the sound of a key turning in the lock, and it gave me a start until I realized it was Duncan. Thank. Fucking. God.

"Jules! Spent the night with Craig, did you? I'm envious. It's been months since—"

I held up my hand. "It's over. Craig and I are done."

"What are you talking about?"

"It's over."

"I don't understand. Everything—"

"Everything is bullshit, Dunc."

"Why? What's happened?" He sat down next to me on the couch.

My voice was shaky but clear. "He's into BDSM. And group sex. And video taping it all."

Duncan's eyebrows shot up. "He told you this?"

"Oh, no. Not at all. I found a DVD in his suite. It was of him and his ex, Alessandra d'Acosta. Much of what I saw reminded me of what Matt did to me."

Duncan put his arm around my shoulders. "Have you talked to him since then?"

"No. I just left the DVD on his coffee table, where he couldn't miss it."

Duncan sighed. "The DVD might not be recent. It could have been made when they were together. Lots of people experiment in a healthy relationship. Bondage. Multiple partners. Toys. Whatever. It could have been a one-time thing. I don't mean to take his side, Jules. I'm just playing devil's advocate because my impression of Craig is that he's a really nice guy. Are you sure you're not overreacting? Maybe you should just talk to him about it."

"Look, I get what you're saying. I admit that I don't know anything about BDSM. Whatever consenting adults do together is no one else's business, and I don't mean to judge Craig, or anyone else. But the thought of being tied up obviously scares the hell out of me, for reasons you and I both know."

"No wonder you're upset, especially after what you've been through."

"On the DVD, Alessandra was bound and gagged. She was drooling, and struggling to breathe. She looked like she had been crying. I'm not saying it was nonconsensual. I couldn't tell for sure. But either way, I can't be with a man who gets off on hurting women."

Duncan looked stunned. "That's about the last thing I would have expected from Craig."

"Tell me about it."

"At some point, maybe you'll talk to him about what you saw," Duncan said.

I shook my head. "Not anytime soon. I need time and space to even begin to wrap my head around this. If I was with him now, I wouldn't feel safe. Confronting him could anger him. Then what? Another rape? What I'm feeling right now is related to being a rape survivor, but it's going to take time for me to sort things out in my mind. I thought I'd put the rape behind me, at least enough to have a normal relationship. But it all came back when I saw that video. Emotionally, I was back in that room, tied to that fucking bed, hurt, bleeding, and terrified for my life. Obviously, I've still got issues, and I don't know if it's even possible to work them out. Right now, I need to figure things out on my own. If I can't, it's back to therapy."

Duncan put his hand on my knee, and we just sat in silence for a moment while we waited for me to calm down.

Later, when the doorbell rang, Duncan ran to the window to see who it was.

"Craig's outside. Do you want me to tell him to go away?"

"Please tell him to go away. There is no way in hell that I'm seeing him now."

Duncan went downstairs, and closed the door behind him. A couple of minutes later, I heard raised voices. Then I heard Craig's car drive away, followed by Duncan's footsteps coming up the stairs.

"What did you tell him?" I asked.

Duncan sat next to me on the couch.

"I told him that you stumbled on the DVD of him and Alessandra having sex, and that, because of the content and because of what you've been through in your past, that you needed space. He was obviously distressed, but he did leave when I asked. He wants you to contact him when you're ready."

"I'm not sure that I'll ever be ready."

"I don't know," Duncan said thoughtfully. "Could Craig deceive both of us so easily? It still doesn't make sense to me."

"Since when does life make sense?" I said bitterly, getting up from the couch.

As I stood, my left hand grazed the rock Craig had given me on the day we first made love. It rested on the coffee table on top of my phone bill. The circle of rough white stone embedded in its smooth gray surface had come to symbolize his presence in my life—the beautiful, unexpected force of nature that he had been in my life.

I picked it up and turned it over in my hands. I ran my fingers across its smooth gray and rough white surface, and I thought of that day on the Cape when we found it on the beach. Then I thought of all the days that followed.

And then I thought of that video.

I walked into my bedroom, opened a bureau drawer, and shoved the rock so far to the back that it disappeared.

Just as I hoped Craig Manning would.

ON THE BRINK, VOL. 2

1

Boston
Six months later

I hurried down Boylston Street, on my way to work. The sparkling April sunlight, gentle breeze, and bright, shimmering greens of new spring foliage made a delightful contrast to the long, cold winter that had held Boston in its icy grip until just a few weeks ago.

I entered the Prudential Tower and walked briskly to the elevators. Barlow Interactive, my employer, occupied the 40th floor. A midsized agency specializing in interactive design, Barlow was energetic, youthful, and growing fast.

Life was good and getting better. I had a wonderful new job with fabulous career potential, and even my painting career seemed to be getting off the ground.

The only ingredient missing was romance.

Since my breakup with Craig, I hadn't felt a single flicker of interest in any man. Maybe what I'd felt for Craig had been a once-in-a-lifetime thing; maybe I'd never experience anything like it again. Sometimes I felt that part of me had died with our relationship. Or maybe he'd brought a part of me to life for the first time, a part of me that I hadn't known existed.

I wasn't sure. Not that it mattered. I'd sent him away, for both our sakes. Given my history as a rape survivor and Craig's attraction to bondage and domination, it could never have worked out.

Last fall, after I'd stumbled onto a DVD of Craig and his ex-girlfriend Alessandra d'Acosta participating in an orgy, I'd cycled through a range of emotions—anxiety, anger, fear, betrayal, disappointment—but once I calmed down and talked things through with Duncan, I realized that my feelings were hopelessly tangled up with my history.

Craig hadn't done anything wrong. He hadn't lied to me, or betrayed me. He hadn't pushed me to do anything I didn't want to do. But now I faced the reality that I would never be able to satisfy him, never be able to give him what he really wanted.

So I stayed away. It was for the best. For both of us. But as the months wore on and Craig continued to occupy my thoughts, I began to worry. Maybe I'd never be able to stop thinking about him. Maybe I'd never feel anything for another man. Was I destined to spend the rest of my life alone?

I reminded myself to focus on the positive. After all, my life had turned around over the past few months, and I was grateful for my good fortune.

My good fortune began a few weeks before Christmas when Connor Barlow, the handsome co-owner of Barlow Leighton Gallery, spotted one of Duncan's photos in an arts benefit auction and requested a studio visit to see more of his work.

When Connor came to see Duncan's work at the small but cozy Somerville apartment we shared, it turned out to be nothing less than a double act of fate: love at first sight for Connor and Duncan, and a two-person show at Barlow Leighton for Duncan's work and mine. Now, Duncan was naturally spending much of his free time with his new boyfriend, and while I missed him, I genuinely liked Connor, and was happy that my best friend had finally found love. No one deserved it more.

As if that weren't enough luck for one month, a few weeks after Duncan and Connor got together, while at a Barlow Leighton event, Connor made the introduction that led to my new job.

"Lara Barlow, Juliana West. Juliana, my twin sister Lara. You two need to talk. If I'm right—and I usually am—you two may just hold the answer to each other's most annoying problems." He winked conspiratorially at his sister, then turned away to continue greeting the stream of arriving guests.

Lara was a tall, slender blonde with full lips and stunning bright blue eyes that revealed humor and intelligence. The navy silk sheath dress she wore could easily have been paired with pearls for a classic look, but she'd opted for an edgier approach and contrasted the simplicity of her dress with a wide, felted-fiber necklace that merged ancient Egyptian form, traditional hand felting technique, and bright, contemporary colors.

"I love your necklace," I said with a smile. "And I'm delighted to meet you at last. I've heard so much about you from Connor and Duncan. But I hope you know what Connor's talking about, because I don't."

Lara laughed. "I've heard a lot about you, too. And fortunately for both of us, I know exactly what my brother is plotting. I need to hire a digital media designer. I've heard that you're an excellent one, and I've heard that you're looking for a job…"

Now, thinking about all these months of working with Lara at Barlow Interactive, I smiled to myself. Lara was creative and lively, and had an irrepressible sense of humor. After we began working together, our friendship quickly solidified. Most days, we had lunch or coffee together, or enjoyed an after-work martini. We talked for hours about life, relationships, work, and everything in between. I felt truly fortunate to have found such a fabulous best girlfriend.

When I reached my office, I tossed my briefcase onto a chair and sat down at my desk. I opened my email and read the most recent, from Lara.

Coffee in my office at 9:30?

I replied immediately.

9:30 it is. I'll bring the coffee.

I scrolled through my email inbox, and answered a half dozen emails. Soon, it was time to meet Lara. I stopped by the lunchroom and made two cups of coffee, and then proceeded to Lara's office.

When I entered with two steaming cups of coffee in my hands, Lara's face brightened.

"Have a seat. We need to talk about this weekend. Are you up for hanging out in Maine at the Barlow compound in Harpswell? Please say yes. Otherwise, I'll be the only girl for miles around. Connor will be there, with Duncan, of course. We'll probably all drive together, in Connor's SUV. We could take off at noon on Friday, and come back to Boston sometime on Sunday."

"I'd love to go. A change of scenery sounds perfect."

"Great! I'm so glad. It'll be a blast—I promise. Long walks, fresh air, and good food. Can't wait for you to meet the rest of the clan. You haven't met our brothers, Jake or Nick yet." Lara's eyes narrowed thoughtfully. "I don't know why I didn't think of this before! Nick's too young, but Jake's about right—two years older than Connor and me —and single. You'd be perfect together, and then we'd be sisters for real. Nick was supposed to be my sister, but that didn't exactly pan out. Poor Nick. When Mom first found out she was expecting, she asked Jake, Connor, and me whether we wanted a little brother or a little sister. Jake and I requested a sister. Connor asked for a pony."

"A pony?" I said.

"He wanted to call it Rainbow Brite."

"That's hilarious."

"Now, about you and Jake..."

"You are *not* setting me up with your brother. Talk about inviting disaster. Seriously, Lara, at this point, if I'm going to date anyone—and that's a *big* if—it's not going to be the brother of my best girlfriend and my brand new gallerist, who incidentally happens to be my other best friend's boyfriend. Romance may pass, but friendship is forever, right?"

"I'm not sure I agree with that," Lara replied. "My parents have been married for over thirty years, and they're still a couple of romantic fools when the mood strikes them. You know, holding hands, exchanging meaningful looks—that kind of thing. It used to embarrass me when I was a teenager, but now I know just how lucky they are. One day, I hope to find the sort of love that they have. Anyway, don't you want to at least check out a photo of Jake? I mean, before you completely reject the idea."

"Fine. But I won't change my mind."

With a hint of mischief in her eyes, Lara picked up a framed photo from her desk, and handed it to me. "Jake's the one in the middle, between Connor and Nick."

I looked at the photo and had to admit that Jake was easy on the eyes. Like his brother Connor, he had a swimmer's build—tall and muscular. His arms were draped casually over his brothers' shoulders, he wore a faded dark green tank top and loose khakis that had been cut off at the knee. I noted wavy, sun-streaked brown hair, sea-green eyes, tanned skin, and a wide, generous smile that reminded me of Lara's.

"I took this picture of my brothers in Harpswell last summer," Lara said. "We'd just returned from sailing in the bay. A handsome lot, aren't they? All the way through high school and college, I had to deal with girls sucking up to me to get to Jake. They tried with Connor, too, but my twin is and has always been gay. Though it was fun watching the girls bat their eyelashes at him. Nick's five years younger than Connor and me, so he wasn't a target then, but of course that's changed. At this point, at least half my girlfriends have revealed themselves to be shameless, cradle-snatching cougars."

I sighed. "Lara. I'd love to spend the weekend with you in Harpswell, but if you want me to come, you have to promise to refrain from any attempts to set me up with your brother. You and I are like sisters already. It's not as though I have to marry one of your brothers to make it official. Believe me, I plan to enjoy our friendship for the rest of my life. Besides, I'm just not fully over Craig. I've accepted that it could never have worked out, but I still think about him more than I probably should. I wish I didn't, but the truth is that I do."

Lara knew all about Craig—and Matt. At this point, there wasn't much about me that she didn't know.

She relented. "Fine. I promise. No set-ups."

"Thank you." I hoped that she'd given up the idea.

"On another topic, want to go shopping?"

"Shopping?" I asked. "Now? It's barely 10 a.m. And we're buried in work."

"This shopping is work related. The office needs a new color laser printer. I don't want to delegate such an expensive purchase. And I need the exercise. Desperately. This morning, my scale reported an unspeakable number. Two pounds above my target zone. I'm officially fat."

"You? Fat?" I shook my head. "You spend so much time in the gym, they should give you an award. Princess Cardio-Kickboxing-Fierce-Fit of the Year. Or something like that."

"This is serious, Juliana. I'm cursed with fat genes. I was chubby in eighth grade. The kids used to call me 'Larda.' Choke on that one for a minute. If I don't watch my weight, terrible things happen. Just imagine Jabba the Hutt in a blonde wig—and then imagine that beauty on a fat scooter."

After I managed to stop giggling at this improbable image, I wiped my eyes and said, "Lara. Listen to me. As your friend, I would never lie to you. If you needed to lose weight, I would be the first to support you. But you're *not* fat."

"Maybe you don't see it, but trust me. I can feel those two pounds. Just like I feel the public shame for having gained them. I blame the Italian food we ate last night."

"I'm bloated too. But it's just water weight. Never go near a scale the day after Italian food—it's too traumatic."

Lara rolled her eyes. "When I got on the scale this morning and saw that number, I felt light-headed, which makes no sense since, with my extra chunk, my feet were planted on the ground more firmly than ever. Then I began the epic struggle of shoving my fat ass into Spanx. Thank goodness only the cat witnessed my complete humiliation."

"Spanx *defines* humiliation. Mine look like they're designed to fit an eight-year-old. A skinny, stunted, little runt of an eight-year-old."

Lara giggled. "Sad but true. Whenever I contort myself into Spanx, it's like a game of Twister. What's worse? Obviously, trying to extract myself from its powerful Spandex clutches."

We laughed.

"So. Shall we go?" Lara asked. "We can power walk to Staples in twenty minutes or so. After we choose a printer and arrange a delivery time, let's have lunch. Something fat-free, of course."

"How about Sweetgreen? We can pile on the roughage, do aggressive shots of purifying juice, and then spend the rest of the day in the bathroom losing all of last night's gluttony."

"That sounds oddly appealing—in a gross sort of way."

"A girl has to do what a girl has to do."

"I'll warn you now—I refuse to chew raw kale. Or choke down wheatgrass juice."

I lowered my voice to a whisper and leaned toward her. "Want to know an ancient Incan secret for flushing away the weight?"

"What secret? Tell me now. Is torture involved?"

"I'll tell you everything—but only if you promise not to set me up with your brother."

Lara rolled her eyes and pushed back her chair. "All right. Let's do this shit."

"You have such a way with words."

"That's not what I meant."

"Consider it Freudian."

"Just give me ten minutes to check my voicemail. Then you can tell me your Incan secrets."

As I left to check my own voicemail, I felt a wave of affection for Lara. Of all the wonderful things that had come my way over the past few months, my friendship with Lara was the dearest to my heart. I was looking forward to a weekend of conversation, fun, and laughter in Harpswell.

2

On the drive from Boston to Harpswell, I talked and laughed with my friends, and time passed quickly. We drove through Brunswick, then left Route 1 for a quiet country road. Half an hour later, Connor turned the SUV onto a gravel drive, and we drove through the trees for a minute or so before reaching a sprawling, gray-shingled house.

Connor stopped the car and turned off the engine.

"Welcome to Chez Barlow. Nick and Jake should already be here."

We got out, retrieved our bags, and headed for the front door. Before we reached it, the door burst open, and a golden retriever bounded out, tail wagging. The retriever ran to Connor, who dropped his bag so he could grasp the dog's collar.

"Take it easy." he said to the dog.

"He's gorgeous. What's his name?" I asked.

"Barkley. As a puppy, he was super cute, but he barked at literally everything," Connor replied. He petted Barkley with his free hand, then released him.

Somewhat calmed by Connor's voice and touch, Barkley loped around Lara's legs, then ventured over to me. I put down my weekend bag and extended a hand for him to sniff.

A deep male voice spoke. "Don't worry. He's really friendly. Although he still jumps when he gets excited—I have to work on training him out of that. You must be Juliana."

I looked up and recognized Jake Barlow from the photo on Lara's desk at work. "And you must be Jake."

"That's me," he said, and gave me a friendly grin.

In person, he was even more handsome than he was in the photo Lara had shown me. I knew from Lara that he worked in their father's investment firm, but he didn't look like he spent his days sitting in an office. His sun-streaked hair, muscular build, and lightly tanned skin hinted at a love of the outdoors. Close up, his green eyes revealed flecks of gold, and there was a faint echo of Connor in the way he moved and held himself.

"Let's bring your things inside, and introduce you to the rest of the gang."

Jake picked up my weekend bag effortlessly, and gestured for me to precede him into the house.

We passed through a slate-tiled entryway, lined with sandals, boots, and an assortment of coats, into a large open space with a vaulted, open-beam ceiling. The far side of the space was mostly glass, with double doors opening onto a spacious deck that overlooked the water.

Jake put my bag down, and we joined the others on the deck. As I stepped onto the deck, I felt the crisp, salty air wash over me. I took a deep breath and drank in the light sea breeze and the stunning ocean views.

At the end of the lawn, grass met dark, jagged rocks that stretched to the waterline below. Waves crashed against the rocks, and cast salt spray into the air. In the distance, I saw several pine-forested islands edged with seaweed-draped rocks and slightly obscured by a touch of haze. The ocean stretched away from us into an infinity of blue sea and sky, its surface dotted with a scattering of tiny, faraway boats.

Lara took charge of the introductions.

"Juliana, meet Nick. And his girlfriend Ariel."

At first glance, Nick Barlow didn't resemble his siblings. Dark-haired, with a solid, stocky build, Nick was slightly taller than Lara, and a couple inches shorter than his older brothers. But when he smiled, I could see the family resemblance. His girlfriend Ariel, a pale young woman with long auburn ringlets, seemed shy but nice.

Later, over food and wine, I enjoyed watching the Barlow siblings alternate between light-hearted sparring and humorous stories from their shared childhood. Their affection and respect for one another was so different from my own family. I hoped that someday, when I had children, that they would grow up within a loving and supportive family like the Barlows.

Not that having a family was on the horizon. At the moment, it didn't seem even remotely possible. I'd had two relationships—Matt and Craig—and both had failed spectacularly. Dating Matt had been the biggest mistake of my life. And while dating Craig hadn't been a complete mistake—unlike Matt, Craig was a good person—it still had ended disastrously.

Watching my friends talk and laugh, I pushed away thoughts of romance. Maybe someday, I'd be lucky enough to find the right man. Focusing on my career and my friendships—that's where I was now, and that's exactly where I wanted to be.

3

When I awoke the next morning, it took a moment to register where I was. Maine. Harpswell. The Barlows' house. A sunlit second-floor room with a sloped ceiling, just down the hall from Lara's room. I got up, threw on my robe, went down the hall, and glanced through Lara's half-open door. She was still asleep, the top of her blonde head peeking out from beneath a mound of colorful quilts. After a quick shower, I opened the window in my room to check the temperature. Although the sun was warm, the sea breeze was on the chilly side. I threw on khaki capris, a T-shirt, a lightweight fleece pullover, and sandals, and then went downstairs in search of coffee.

A half-empty French press sat on the kitchen counter. I poured myself a cup and took a sip. The coffee was still hot and fresh. I walked to the glass doors and stepped onto the deck, where I found Jake sitting in a deck chair, a cup of coffee in his hand and Barkley wagging his tail at his side. Over a T-shirt, he wore a dark green V-neck sweater that brought out the striking green color of his eyes. Well-worn jeans and salt-stained boat shoes completed his casual look.

"Good morning," I said, taking a nearby chair. "Mind if I join you?"

"Not at all," Jake replied with an easy smile. "Barkley and I would enjoy some company, wouldn't we?" He scratched the dog's ears affectionately. "Is Lara up yet?"

"No, she's still asleep. She and I stayed up pretty late last night, talking about more or less everything."

"Sounds like fun. I'm glad to see Lara making new friends. She's had a rough time over the past few years in that regard."

"She's mentioned that some of her college friends were uncomfortable with her success at Barlow Interactive."

"Lara's not a complainer," Jake said. "But I know what she's been going through, because I experienced something similar a few years back. It's never easy when people you thought of as friends turn out not to be."

"Losing friends is painful," I agreed. "You have to tell yourself that they were never real friends, and that you're better off without them in your life. Still, it hurts."

"It does. But that particular cloud does have a silver lining. Losing false friends opens up space in your life for new friends." He smiled at me. "Real friends, like you."

I returned his smile. "I love Lara, and cherish our friendship. I don't make friends easily, but Lara and I connected immediately—on so many levels."

I sipped my coffee, a little surprised that I was having a meaningful conversation with a guy I'd just met the night before. For the most part, I was reserved, and careful about what I said to people I didn't know well.

But talking to Jake was easy. As an investment banker, he carried the responsibility of making multi-million dollar decisions on a daily basis, but he clearly wasn't a stress case. He came across as self-assured yet relaxed.

Suddenly, Barkley jumped to his feet, leapt off the deck, and took off like a shot, barking as he disappeared into the woods.

"Probably a deer," Jake said. He got to his feet and picked up a dog leash. "Still, I'd better go after him. Last year, he got into a scrap with a porcupine, and ended up with a face full of quills that required a trip to the vet."

"I'll come with you." I got up and followed Jake onto the lawn. We jogged together towards the edge of the woods.

"Barkley," Jake called. "BARKLEY!" He turned to me. "He must have gone farther in. Let's take this path—it goes through the woods toward the beach—and keep calling him."

"OK," I agreed.

As we jogged down the rough path, we continued to call the dog. But the need to step over tree roots and push aside low-hanging branches slowed our progress.

I tripped on a tree root and landed on my hands and knees. Jake heard me fall and turned around.

"Are you OK?" he asked with concern. He held out a hand and helped me to my feet. When our hands touched, a thrill raced through my body, but I brushed it aside. He was, after all, devastatingly handsome. No red-blooded woman could be completely immune.

I brushed dirt from my knees. "I'm fine. Just a bit dusty; that's all."

Jake looked me over closely, then bent down. "You've hurt your knee. I'll take you back to the house."

I glanced at my knees. The right one was scraped and bleeding, but not badly. I appreciated his thoughtfulness—and the concern in his lovely green eyes—but it was nothing more than an ugly scrape. The only real damage was to my capris, which were torn, but that wasn't a big deal.

"It's just a scratch. I'll clean it up after we find Barkley."

"Are you sure?"

"Thank you for asking, but I'm fine. Really."

"We're almost to the beach now, and the house isn't far from there. Maybe Barkley's beat us home. I wouldn't be surprised if he's waiting for us on the deck."

We continued down the path, and soon emerged from the woods onto the rocky shoreline.

"Barkley," Jake called again. "Oh, there he is." He pointed down the beach.

The dog sprinted toward us.

"Watch out," Jake said. He stepped in front of me. "He's soaking wet. Must have taken a swim." As he reached Jake, Barkley jumped. Jake caught him by his front paws. "Oh no you don't. Down, Barkley. DOWN!"

The excited retriever obeyed, but then shook himself, spraying us both with ice-cold seawater.

I wiped my face and laughed. "Now I'm *really* awake."

Jake laughed with me. "Thank you for being a good sport. Around water, he's just a big puppy. Lots of fun, but terrible manners." He leaned down. "Come here, boy. Time to go home."

Barkley loped around us, wagging his tail.

"Looks like he wants to play," I said. I reached down, picked up a stick of driftwood, and handed it to Jake. "You can probably throw this farther than I can."

Jake hurled the stick into the water, and the dog charged after it. "You've just made his day."

We strolled down the beach until Barkley emerged from the water, the stick clenched between his jaws. He ran to us, dropped the stick, and gave Jake an expectant look.

"Alright. One more." Jake picked up the stick and was about to throw it, when Barkley jumped for the stick in Jake's hand, missed, and landed with his front paws against my chest. The dog's weight threw me off balance and I stumbled, but Jake caught me from behind. For a moment, I felt the strength of his arms around me, and the hard muscle of his torso and thighs against my body. He released me and inspected the damage.

"I apologize, Juliana. You're soaked. And covered in sand. We'd better get you inside before you catch cold. The water's arctic at this time of year."

I laughed. "I'm fine. Seriously. Nothing that a hot shower won't fix."

"Take off your fleece, and put this on." He pulled his sweater over his head. As he did so, his T-shirt rode up and gave me a tantalizing glimpse of tanned, muscular abs. I groaned inwardly. This wasn't good. I'd forbidden Lara from setting me up with Jake for a host of good reasons. And now, here I was lusting after his body.

"Won't you be cold?" I asked.

"I'm relatively dry, and we're not far from the house."

Realizing that he wouldn't take no for an answer, I slipped out of my wet fleece, before realizing—too late—that thanks to the chilly sea breeze and the sight of Jake's perfect abs, that my nipples were rock-hard beneath my damp T-shirt. I hoped he wouldn't notice.

No such luck. His eyes paused on my chest and widened briefly, before returning politely to my face. He handed me his sweater, which I quickly put on. The sweater carried his scent—temptingly masculine with a hint of citrus.

Jake bent down and hooked the leash to Barkley's collar.

"Let's get you inside," he said to me. "The sooner you get warm, the better."

As we walked toward the house, I couldn't resist sneaking an occasional glance at Jake. The ocean breeze blew his hair back from his face and threw his handsome features into relief. Was I crushing on him? Maybe a little. But I sure as hell wasn't going to do anything about it.

4

When we returned to the house, I left Jake and Barkley on the deck and went upstairs, where I took a quick shower and put on clean, dry clothes. As I put a Band-Aid on my knee, I reminded myself that nothing could come of my little crush on Jake Barlow. He'd given no sign of a similar attraction to me. On the contrary, he'd been a complete gentleman. And no matter how hot he was, Jake was Lara's brother, and therefore off limits.

On the other hand, there was no reason why we couldn't be friends. Jake was much more than a handsome face and a ripped body. I'd genuinely enjoyed talking and dog-chasing with him, and there was certainly no harm in appreciating his company.

When I came downstairs, Lara was finishing a bowl of cereal and Connor was making a fresh pot of coffee.

"Jake and Duncan are out on the deck," Lara said. "Let's join them."

I followed Lara outside, where Jake was telling Duncan a story about Connor's first attempt at starting his own gallery business.

"So Connor moved all his stuff into one tiny room in the back, and he turned the rest of the apartment into a sort of gallery—"

"Do I hear my name being taken in vain?" Connor asked, as he stepped onto the deck, coffee in hand.

"Just bragging about you." Jake grinned. "I was telling Duncan about your first gallery."

"Thank goodness I had just finished college and couldn't afford to buy anything," Connor said. "I couldn't possibly cram everything into an eight-by-ten foot room anymore. At this point, I need half that space just for shoes."

"Queen," Lara said. "He has more shoes than I do. And it's a well known fact that I suffer from a serious shoe fetish."

"Princess. Please. Of course I have more shoes than you. I treat my shoes with the respect they deserve. You destroy yours by walking to work every day. On frost-heaved brick sidewalks, no less. Death to heels. Your closet is filled with the corpses of murdered shoes."

"It's the aerobic part of my exercise regime," Lara replied, flipping her hair back and staring her twin brother down. "Twenty minutes each way, forty minutes total. Doing it in heels works every single leg muscle." She turned to me. "Connor doesn't believe in aerobic exercise. Thanks to the fat-annihilating power of testosterone, he gets away with his ignorance. At least for now."

"Twins," Jake said. "They've been sniping at each other and finishing each others' sentences since birth. On another topic, does anyone want to go kayaking? I was thinking of going to one of the islands, maybe bringing a picnic lunch."

"Duncan and I are going for a drive," Connor said. "I want to show him some of my favorite places around here. Then we'll pick up lobsters and mussels for dinner tonight."

"I think Nick and Ariel plan to go into Brunswick for the day," Jake said. "That leaves you, Lara. And Juliana."

"I'd love to, but I can't today. Maybe tomorrow," Lara said. "I have to finish writing a proposal. But you should go, Juliana. If you enjoy kayaking, that is."

"I do like kayaking, but I haven't done it in years. Are you sure I wouldn't slow you down?" I asked Jake.

He shook his head. "Not at all. We could paddle out to one of the nearby islands, explore all around, and find a spot for a picnic."

"That sounds like fun," I said. "I'd love to go. But Lara, are you sure I can't help you finish the proposal? Then we could all go."

Lara shook her head. "It's easier to just push through the first draft. I should be finished by the time you and Jake get back. Then you can look it over and give me some feedback." She got up and motioned for me to follow her. "Come on. Let's set you up with some kayaking gear."

5

After Lara outfitted me with wetsuit, beach shoes, fleece and windbreaker, I headed downstairs to help Jake prepare our picnic lunch. I found him in the kitchen, making sandwiches. His black wetsuit fit like a glove. It was all too easy to imagine how he'd look without it, and I caught myself doing just that.

It was a harmless moment of fantasy, and I succumbed to it for a moment. I imagined unzipping his wetsuit slowly, revealing well-formed pecs and washboard abs. He was relatively fair, so he'd probably have only a dusting of chest hair, which was just how I liked it. A light trail of hair would lead downward, toward—

I squelched this line of thought. I was *not* going to imagine my best girlfriend's brother naked. Things between Jake and me needed to stay uncomplicated—and platonic.

"Ham or turkey? Mustard or mayo?" he asked.

"Turkey with mustard," I replied. "Can I do something?"

"Sure. Find the mustard for me. It's probably buried in the back of the fridge."

I located a jar of Dijon mustard and handed it to him. He finished the sandwiches and placed them in his backpack.

"Ready to go?" he asked, swinging the backpack onto one shoulder. The motion tossed several locks of sun-streaked hair into his face. He pushed them back with one hand and smiled at me, his green, gold-flecked eyes contrasting against his tanned skin.

"Let's do it," I replied, returning his smile. Was he flirting with me? Or was it my imagination? Maybe I shouldn't have agreed to go kayaking alone with him, but I'd already said yes. The moment to decline gracefully had passed.

He led me to the boathouse.

"Here," he said, handing me two life vests and picking up paddles for both of us. "I brought the kayak down to the beach earlier."

We walked across the lawn and down to the beach, where Jake rested the paddles against the kayak. In his skin-tight wetsuit, with the ocean at his back, he made an all too attractive portrait. Sleek and streamlined, but bulging in all the right places, including—

Too late, I realized just where my thoughts were going. I turned away and hoped that my face looked less flushed than it felt. So Jake was hot. In form-fitting black neoprene? Dangerously hot. If I kept staring at him like this, the contents of my head would be obvious to everyone, including him. It didn't require mind reading.

"It's a perfect day for this," Jake said, reaching for one of the life vests. "See that island?" He pointed. "That's where we're going. There's a place that you can't see from here where we can beach the kayak."

He slipped into his life vest, and zipped it. I followed suit.

With ease, Jake lifted the kayak onto his left shoulder and carried it to the edge of the water, where he set it down. Then he secured the backpack containing our picnic supplies to the kayak with a bungee cord. "You're much lighter than me, so you should sit in front," he said as he held out a hand to help me in.

"OK." I took his proffered hand and stepped into the kayak, doing my best to ignore the thrill of attraction that shot through my body when my hand touched his. I seated myself and Jake handed me a paddle. Then he got into the kayak and seated himself behind me.

"Have you been in a tandem kayak before?" he asked.

"No, just solos," I responded.

"Here's how it works. You set the pace, I follow. It's easier to steer the boat from the stern, so I'm responsible for direction. Let's warm up with a couple loops near the dock."

He pushed us off, and we began paddling. It felt wonderful to be on the water, breathing in the fresh ocean air and sensing the motion of the waves against the hull.

"You're doing great," Jake said. "I thought you hadn't kayaked in years."

"Thank you," I replied. "I wasn't sure I'd remember, but when I touched the water with the paddle, it all came back."

"Now that we've got our rhythm, let's head for the island," Jake suggested.

"OK," I agreed.

Jake turned the kayak, and we paddled into the light breeze. The wind caught my hair, and I felt a sense of exhilaration and freedom. Since moving to Boston for college, I hadn't done any of the outdoor activities I'd grown up doing—swimming, kayaking, cross-country skiing. It felt fabulous to be out in the elements, to taste the salty ocean air, to hear the sound of the waves and the cries of gulls as they swooped and dived for fish. And I had to admit, it wasn't so bad to enjoy all this with a terribly handsome man.

Time flew by as we crossed the water. As we approached the island, I spotted the beach that Jake had mentioned. As we reached it, Jake got out of our kayak, then held it steady while I climbed out. He detached his backpack from the kayak, slung it over his shoulders, and then turned to me.

"Let's bring our things up there," he said, pointing to a sheltered spot just above the high tide line. "You can take the paddles, and I'll bring the kayak."

We made our way up the beach to the area Jake had indicated, set our things down, and removed our life vests. I watched his dexterous movements, and my wetsuit fantasy resurfaced in full force. Embarrassed, I turned away, and bent down to examine a seashell in an effort to conceal my face, which was probably flaming.

"Hungry yet?" Jake asked.

Hungry for what? I thought.

"There's a good picnic spot not far from here," he added.

I just blinked at him. "I'm ravenous," I said. *If you only knew how ravenous.* "I'd forgotten what a great workout kayaking is."

Jake led us up a narrow, rocky path that snaked its way toward the tree line and ended in a sun-drenched, grassy slope. "Here we are," he said, slipping his backpack off and opening it. He'd chosen the location well.

With trees and rocks on three sides, our picnic spot was protected from the wind, but offered a stunning view of the open ocean. A few small fishing boats were visible in the distance. Around the boats, birds circled, screamed, and dove for discarded bait. In the distance, dark blue sea faded into lighter blue sky.

He removed the container with our sandwiches, followed by a bottle of wine, two tumblers, and a large beach blanket, which he handed to me. I spread the blanket on the grass and Jake weighted the corners with rocks. We both sat down on the blanket.

"Thank you for bringing me here," I said, meaning it. "The view is breathtaking, and it was amazing to be in a kayak again."

"Glad you like it," he said. "The sun here is pretty hot, though. Mind if I take off the top half of this wetsuit?"

"Of course not," I said. What else could I say? I had the feeling that I was about to be reduced to a quivering puddle of lust. I would just have to limit my exposure by staring at the view instead of at him.

He unzipped the top, removed it, and tossed it aside. His upper body was everything that I'd imagined it would be—and then some. His well-defined arms and chest were in perfect proportion to his narrow hips and strong thighs. The warm sunlight gleamed off his tanned, muscled form, and highlighted every contour.

I would just have to tough this one out. I wanted Jake Barlow, and I couldn't have him. Now that I'd admitted that to myself, maybe we could just get on with lunch. Conversation. Admiring the view.

Jake smiled at me, and in his smile I saw a hint of something I couldn't quite define. "Thank you for coming with me. It's a rare pleasure to share my favorite picnic spot with someone who appreciates it. Let me open the wine—once I find the corkscrew, that is." He rummaged in his bag. "Here it is." He opened the bottle, filled the glasses, and handed me one.

"To your first kayaking adventure since—when was it, anyway?"

"Summer camp, I think. The summer after eighth grade." I clinked my glass against his. "To kayaking. And to you, for bringing me to this beautiful spot."

6

After we finished lunch, Jake suggested we take a walk. "Feel like stretching your legs? From the west side of the island, there's a great view of Casco Bay."

"I'd love to take a walk," I said. I genuinely wanted to be friends with Jake. When we'd talked over coffee earlier in the morning and ran after Barkley, we'd really connected.

Admittedly, there was this little problem that part of me kept thinking about tearing his clothes off. But as long as I didn't act on my attraction to Jake, there was no reason why we couldn't be friends.

Since I was connected to his family through friendship and work, we would probably run into each other now and then. Openings at Connor's gallery. Office parties at Barlow Interactive. Weekends like this one.

We packed the remnants of our picnic into Jake's backpack, then set off, following a path along the top of the rocks and bushes that ringed the island.

"You seem to know this place well," I said. "Did you come here often as a kid?"

"Our parents used to bring us to this island at least once every summer when we were kids. Later on, I'd sometimes come here with one or both of the twins. We always spent summers in Harpswell, except for Dad, of course. He usually had to go back to the city during the week." He paused. "You mentioned summer camp. Was that something you did every summer?"

"For seven weeks every summer, from age nine to fourteen. The camp was on a lake in western Maine. I loved everything about it: kayaking, riding horses, swimming, and of course, having other kids around—there were about three hundred campers. I always looked forward to it. Especially because I got to be around other kids. Being an only child can get pretty dull during the summer."

"I guess I was lucky. I always had my brothers and sister around. On the other hand, having three younger siblings could get pretty crazy at times. Not that I was an angel myself. My mother's the angel. Four kids in seven years? She's a saint for putting up with us."

"I imagine it would be wonderful to be part of a large family, but I can't imagine keeping up with four small children all at once."

"You haven't met our mother," Jake said. "Half saint, half drill sergeant. She's the kindest person I know, but make no mistake, she knew how to keep us in line."

Jake stopped. The path we had been following had ended abruptly in a mass of thorny rugosa bushes.

"We can go a bit farther if you don't mind climbing down the rocks. Would you like to see a tidal pool? There's a good-sized one not far from here."

"I'd love to," I said, looking down. While the shoreline was rocky, it wasn't steep, the rocks looked dry enough, and my shoes had rubber soles.

Jake stepped onto a large rock, then held out his hand to me. "Let me give you a hand up."

We worked our way down the rocks, stepping over the spaces between them. Whenever we needed to make a longer leap between rocks, Jake went first, then took my hand, pulled me across, and steadied me as I landed. On one particularly long jump, I lost my balance and crashed into him. He absorbed the shock expertly, pulling me against him.

Held against the hard muscle of Jake's torso, I felt his strength and breathed in his clean, masculine scent that was mixed with the salty sea breeze. The unexpected sensation of his body against mine made me dizzy. I reflexively clutched him for a moment while I regained my balance. I felt his chest expand as he took a long, slow breath. Then he released me and stepped to the next rock.

"Almost there," he said.

We walked across the surface of a large outcropping of rock, reaching the edge of a hollow in the rock that contained the tidal pool, which was maybe a dozen feet across. Jake dropped to his knees.

"Here it is. Isn't it amazing?"

It was. Colorful patches of algae, clumps of seaweed, and bright yellow sponges clung to the rocks. Small crabs scuttled around, appearing and disappearing beneath strands of seaweed. I spotted several sea stars, in colors ranging from pink to purple with touches of orange. One sea star slid slowly along the sand at the bottom of the pool. Anemones waved their fronds gently in the crystal clear water. It was a small, self-contained world, a tiny, jewel-like microcosm of the ocean's wealth of life.

"It's magical," I replied.

We watched in silence for several minutes. Jake pointed out a hermit crab, several types of snails, and a sea urchin half-hidden in a small crevice. Then he got to his feet.

"The tide is rising, so we'd better head back," he said. "The trip back should be faster." He held out his hand and helped me to my feet. I felt an unexpected rush when he did so.

"Thank you," I said, trying to remain collected. "It's inspiring to see such beauty. I could watch it for hours."

Jake smiled. "We'll have to come back soon, then."

He held out his hand, I took it, and we began to make our way back toward the beach where we'd left the kayak. Soon, we were back on the water, pointed toward the Barlow dock.

As Jake had predicted, the return trip was faster. With the wind at our back, we arrived at the beach more quickly than I'd expected.

Jake stepped out of the kayak, then helped me get out. I stood on the beach, looked back at the island, and inhaled a deep breath. It had been a marvelous day.

After we put away the kayak and our gear, Jake surprised me by turning to me and taking my hand.

"Thank you for spending the day with me," he said. "I had a wonderful time."

"So did I," I replied, meaning it.

He gave me a long look, as if searching for something. Then he surprised me again, with a gentle kiss on my lips. I responded, parting my lips as the kiss intensified. He pulled me into his arms, and molded my body against his own. For a long moment, we stood, arms around each other, kissing, with the dull roar of the surf behind us.

I snapped back to reality, ended the kiss, and pulled away from his embrace. "I really like you, Jake, but I'm not sure this is a good idea."

"Why not? I was drawn to you from the moment we met. We're both single, and we're obviously attracted to each other."

"I just don't want to rush into anything," I said. "Please don't take this the wrong way, Jake. It isn't about you. It's about me. About my past."

He looked deep into my eyes. "I won't rush you. I just want to see you again, after this weekend, when we're both back in Boston. Promise you'll think about it?"

I relented. "I promise."

7

Around midnight that evening, Lara and I were sitting next to the outdoor fireplace on the deck and enjoying a glass of wine. The others had drifted off to bed, one or two at a time, and the fire had burnt down to a mound of glowing embers. I'd been dying to tell Lara about the kiss all evening, and was glad to finally have the chance to talk to her alone.

"I have to tell you something."

"Spill it."

"After we went kayaking, Jake and I kissed."

Lara grinned at me and shot one fist into the air. "I knew it! I had a feeling about you and Jake. I know my brother, and I'm not blind. I've seen how he looks at you."

"I really like Jake. But I'm not sure that dating your brother is a good idea. I don't want to do anything that might risk my friendship with you."

Lara's expression turned serious. "I understand where you're coming from. But dating Jake won't affect our friendship unless you suddenly turn into some random liar or cheater, and I already know that you won't. You're a good person, Juliana. So is Jake. And we're all adults. If you and my brother start seeing each other, you have my blessing. Although, come to think of it, in matters of the heart, my curse might be more beneficial." She sighed. "It's been almost two years since anyone asked me out. My height eliminates eighty-five percent of the male population. My personality drives away the rest."

"There are plenty of tall men out there," I said. "And you have a great personality. I don't disagree that some men might find your strength and intelligence intimidating, but I think you're looking at it from the wrong angle."

"What do you mean?"

"Instead of focusing on why men don't ask you out, think about the kind of man you need. You need a man who's not easily intimidated. A man who can stand up to you. A man who'll call you out when you go overboard, instead of going passive aggressive and sulky, which always is a sign of weakness. In other words, you need a man who appreciates your strength, not one who sees it as a challenge to his own."

"I couldn't agree more," Lara said. She raised an eyebrow. "So. How does one find this prized specimen of masculinity? What's his native habitat?"

"Business," I replied. "Conferences and meet-ups for young entrepreneurs. I heard Craig speak to one such group last fall, at M.I.T. The question-and-answer session afterward really impressed me. The people in the group were intelligent, thoughtful, and creative—like you, Lara. You'd fit right in. They meet once a month, usually at one of the bars on Boylston or Newbury Street so members can network over cocktails. Maybe we can go to the next meeting together."

"I like that idea," Lara said.

"I'll be your girl Friday. I'll stick to your side like glue while the frogs come and go, and conveniently disappear the moment Prince Charming arrives at your side."

"At this point in my non-existent love life, anything's worth a try. What have I got to lose?"

"That's the attitude."

She took a deep breath. "It's been so long, Juliana."

"I hear you."

"I want someone in my life. I can barely remember what it's like to have a man at my side, let alone have sex."

"You'll find him."

"Will I?"

Naturally, I couldn't be sure, but I couldn't imagine that she wouldn't. I loved my friend, and she was a catch. At some point, given the right circumstances, it had to happen. "I believe that you will."

"Maybe. Anyway, back to you and Jake. Are you going to give it a chance?"

"I'd like to—I really would. I just need to make sure that I'm over Craig first. Once I am, I'll feel ready to allow someone else into my life. I don't want to hurt anyone, especially Jake. I need to make sure I'm over Craig so I don't bruise someone else's heart."

Lara groaned. "Not Craig again. He's ancient history. It's been six months since you ended it with him. How do you expect to stop obsessing about that man if you refuse to date anyone else? Don't you think it's time to move on?"

She had a point. Six months had passed. I still thought about Craig every day, but I'd accepted that we weren't meant to be together. And I'd enjoyed Jake's company since I'd been here. Especially today. Today had been wonderful with him. How could I deny what I'd felt each time I'd looked at him, and each time he'd reached for my hand? I couldn't. The attraction between us was intense and mutual. What was I waiting for anyway?

Lara was right. There wasn't any real reason to hold back from living my life. I smiled at her. "Thank you for talking me through this. You're so right. I'm going to take my chances with Jake."

"Thank God for that," she said.

8

After the weekend in Harpswell, Jake and I continued seeing each other. Sometimes we went out for dinner or a movie, but more often we hung out at his condo or at my apartment. We cooked dinner together and talked about our lives and experiences, and often, we just sat together with a martini, me resting my head against his chest, and saying nothing at all. We shared our stories, our experiences, and our dreams and ambitions for the future. We even discussed previous relationships, and I told him about Craig—and Matt.

Telling Craig about Matt had been hard for me, but telling Jake was somehow less difficult. Although Jake and I hadn't known each other long, I felt at ease with him in ways that I had never felt at ease with Craig. The sense of comfort and security I felt with Jake was new to me, and I relished the effortlessness of our conversations. There was no judgment when we spoke. We just talked—and we listened—each knowing that neither was perfect. Or expected to be perfect.

As our intimacy grew, my attraction to Jake only increased, but he didn't push for sex. I sensed that what he knew about my history was causing him to wait for me to make the decisive move. And one

Saturday afternoon, two weeks after we met, I decided that it was time.

We were in the living area of Jake's second-floor condo on Marlborough Street. The day was warm. A soft breeze entered through the open windows, rippling the floor-length, translucent white curtains. Shimmering bands of sunlight reflected across the hardwood floor. Barkley sprawled on the floor, basking in the sun's warmth and chewing on an old tennis ball. We began to watch an action movie, but it was soon dismissed in favor of making out on the couch.

As we kissed, one of Jake's hands roved under my blouse, caressing a nipple. His other hand wandered between my ass and my crotch, stroking me lightly through my clothing. I slid my hands under his T-shirt, explored the corded, muscled contours of his torso, and then decided to go for it. I moved a hand downward, and traced the generous bulge in his jeans.

"Shall we take this into the bedroom?" I asked, smiling at him as I felt his erection thicken against my hand.

He returned my smile. "I was hoping for that."

As we got up from the couch, Jake pulled me into a searing kiss, holding me with one strong arm and unbuttoning my blouse with the other. I slipped my fingers under the waistband of his jeans, and pulled him closer.

By the time we reached the bedroom, we were both shirtless, and Jake had removed my bra. He dropped to his knees, trailing kisses past my navel, and then slowly unzipped my jeans and slid them off before guiding me down onto the bed and removing the rest of my clothing.

"You're so beautiful," he said. He looked into my eyes as he traced the contours of my naked body with his hands. I ran my fingers through his thick, wavy hair, and drew his lips to mine. We kissed deeply, and then he moved down my body. He lingered over my breasts, and caressed their hardened nipples before gently parting my legs. His tongue explored my clit and stroked it leisurely. I felt my desire build as my core warmed in response to his touch.

I gripped his solid biceps and tugged him upward—I wanted him inside of me. With a twinkle in his eye, he let me roll him onto his back and unbutton his fly. And as I released the final buttons and tugged down his jeans, his erection sprang free, tenting his boxers impressively. I removed the boxers, and said, "Oh my."

My breath caught as I saw Jake naked for the first time. He was a magnificent sight. A light trail of hair ran from his navel to the light brown curls between his muscled thighs—it matched the dusting of hair on his chest. In the bedroom's dim lighting, his tanned skin and sun-streaked hair took on tones of bronze and gold. From between his legs, his erect, beautifully formed cock greeted me. He was even larger than I'd imagined.

I ran my fingers lightly over him and appreciated his girth. He reached into the bedside table, and I heard the sound of a foil packet tearing. He rolled the condom on, reclined on his back, and then reached for me.

"Straddle my hips, and use your hands to guide me," he said.

I realized that he intended for me to be on top, and positioned myself as he'd suggested. I took him in one hand, and lowered myself onto him gradually, enjoying the slow, delicate sensation of opening and expanding myself to take him in. He gripped my hips firmly. He used the strength of his arms to slide me up and down on him. Already slick with arousal, I felt myself becoming increasingly wet as our motions synchronized in a mutual rhythm that built inexorably toward climax. As our momentum increased, Jake slid his hands upward, cupped my breasts, and tweaked their engorged tips. He moved a hand downward and began circling my clit with his thumb. My excitement intensified as he stroked my most sensitive parts, and within moments, I came. A few seconds later, Jake followed. He buried his mouth into my neck, and said my name.

Afterward, he took me into his arms and held me close. I drank in his clean, masculine musk, mixed with a sharper note of citrus. He turned his face toward me and touched my nose with his own. Several locks of brown-gold hair fell over his brow, and his green-gold eyes looked deeply into mine.

"I've fantasized about this moment since the day we met in Harpswell," he said.

I kissed him lightly on the lips. "Me too." It was the truth. Since meeting Jake, I'd thought of little else.

"Let's rest for a few minutes. Then we can pick up where we left off."

I nodded in agreement. His eyes closed, and his breathing took on the slow, regular rhythm of sleep.

Cradled in Jake's embrace, I struggled to reconcile my conflicting thoughts and feelings. I was strongly attracted to him, and I loved spending time with him. And as I'd anticipated, he was a tender, thoughtful lover, and sex with him had been good. Very good, as a matter of fact. Yet I couldn't help but feel that something wasn't quite right. I just couldn't put my finger on it.

A wave of guilt washed over me. What was wrong with me?

In every way that I could think of, Jake was the Prince Charming of my wildest fantasies. He was a dream come true. It was easy to imagine spending the rest of my life with him. I could envision the picture-perfect wedding, with Lara standing by my side as maid of honor, and Duncan, Connor, and Nick forming a handsome trio of groomsmen. I could see him and me sitting together on the deck in Harpswell, watching our children play.

My confused feelings finally coalesced into something resembling a conclusion. The problem wasn't Jake. It was me.

Jake's lovemaking wasn't just sensitive and passionate. His every look and gesture had been loving. Tonight, he'd made me feel loved and safe.

The person I didn't trust was myself. I'd only known Jake for a month, and we'd just been intimate for the first time. I wanted to stop holding back and to trust my feelings, but I couldn't. Not yet. I'd been terribly wrong before, and I might be wrong again.

I reassured myself that Jake was different from any other man I'd known and that my trust issues would subside with time. Then I drifted into sleep, wrapped in the comfort of his strong arms.

9

Over the next month, Jake and I spent every free moment together, and our intimacy continued to grow. We agreed to be exclusive, and got tested to confirm that we were safe to make love without protection—I was already on the pill, so pregnancy wasn't a concern. Jake turned out to be a playful and adventurous lover, and the sex just kept getting hotter. He also turned out to be an unabashed romantic who showered me with small, thoughtful gifts and gestures.

One evening in late May, he surprised me with dinner. It had been a long and strenuous day, punctuated by intermittent downpours of rain. Lara and I had taken the Amtrak to New York early that morning, pitched a proposal to a prospective client, and returned to Boston on a late afternoon train.

Exhausted from twelve hours of trains, taxis, and presentations, I reached Jake's condo at around 8:00 p.m., grateful that the rain had finally stopped. I trudged up the stairs to the second floor and let myself in.

"Jake," I called. "It's me." As I hung my raincoat and put away my umbrella in the entry closet, my nose registered a delightful, savory aroma, with just a hint of sharpness.

"In the kitchen," he called.

I sniffed the air blissfully. My ever-thoughtful man. He'd known when I would arrive because I'd phoned him from the train, and he must have ordered takeout. Aside from an uninspiring, plastic-encased salad in the Amtrak restaurant car, I hadn't eaten all day. The scent of hot, delicious food made me salivate with anticipation.

I slid my heels off my aching feet, and padded into the living area. The table was set with white linens. Glasses and cutlery glimmered in the warm, soft light of a pair of candles. A bottle of champagne rested in an ice bucket. Through the windows behind the table, the setting sun illuminated the rain-cleansed sky with vivid streaks of blue, orange, and gold.

Jake stood in the kitchen, stirring something on the stove. It wasn't takeout. He'd made dinner for us. On a weeknight, no less. How had he managed to find time to shop and cook? He'd been so busy at work recently, that he rarely left his office before 7 p.m. Deeply moved and completely surprised, I went into the kitchen, stood beside him, and wrapped an arm around his hips.

"You didn't have to do this, but thank you," I said. "What have you made? It smells incredible."

He leaned down for a lingering kiss as he continued to stir with one hand. After he released my lips, he said, "Sherried tomato soup. Chicken with forty cloves of garlic. Mashed potatoes. There's dessert, too, but that's meant to be a surprise."

"Dinner, champagne, candles—it's all a marvelous surprise, Jake. Can I do anything?"

"Not tonight. You've had a long day, and dinner is fully under control. Sit down and relax while I open the champagne."

I acquiesced and sat at the table, grateful to get off my feet. Jake opened and poured the champagne, sat down himself, and then touched his glass to mine.

"To your successful presentation in New York. Lara texted me that you two kicked ass."

I took a sip of champagne, then smiled at him. "Thank you, but you're the one who kicks ass, Jake Barlow. How did you find the time to do all this? You've been slammed with work for the past few weeks."

"I told the team they'd have to live without me for the afternoon and left the office early today. I made a quick stop at Whole Foods, then came home and started cooking."

After we finished our champagne, Jake brought out the soup. As he sat across from me, he said, "My buddy Christopher swears by this recipe. I hope you'll like it as much as I do."

I brought a spoonful of the thick, creamy soup to my lips and took a sip. Aromatic and steaming hot, it was the ideal soup for a rainy day. Its rich, sherry-tinged warmth was so comforting that I felt my body start to relax and release the tension I hadn't realized I was carrying.

"It's amazing, Jake. Heavenly. Don't be surprised if I beg you to make this soup again. Especially when it's rainy and damp."

"I know what you mean," Jake replied. "Rainy days demand comfort food."

After we finished the soup, he got up and said, "Stay here. I've got this." He disappeared into the kitchen. A few moments later, he emerged with two plates of chicken, gravy, and mashed potatoes.

"You'll definitely love this," he said as he placed the steaming plates on the table, and then sat down. "It's not as pretty as the soup—but wait until you taste it."

I took a bite and agreed. It was fabulous. In the moments when our eyes met across the table, I felt the heat of his gaze. The flickering candlelight caught the gold in his hair and in his eyes, and as we ate, I wondered again how I ever had been so lucky to meet a man like Jake, and to be able to call him my boyfriend.

Later, on one of the sofas in the living room, I curled into Jake's arms, and together, we sipped champagne and fell into a comfortable silence. While I lay there listening to his heartbeat, my mind flashed back to last night's lovemaking.

Jake had kissed and licked his way down my body with a kind of slow, devastating sensuality. He made love to my lips, my neck, my breasts, and all the way down my body, briskly setting it on fire. By the time his talented tongue penetrated my inner wetness, I was so completely turned on that I'd orgasmed almost at once, which delighted him.

His response to that was to deliver a leisurely, full-tongued lick that made my entire body shudder. We then changed position and he slid slowly inside of me, filling me and sending ripples of heat through my sensitized body.

Thanks to these tantalizing images, I felt myself getting wet now. A tempting thought crept into my imagination. Jake had surprised me, delightfully so. Perhaps I could manage to surprise him.

"I think I've had enough champagne," I said, giving him a suggestive look. "How about you?"

"But I want something in my hands," he said.

"So do I."

I ran my hand downward and massaged him lightly through his trousers. He was already rock hard, just how I wanted him.

I sat up and pushed him playfully back so that he was lying way down on the couch. I quickly disposed of his trousers and underwear, knelt between his muscled thighs, and took his substantial erection in my hands.

"See?" I said. "Look how full my hands are."

"Juliana—"

"You know, if I had a third hand, I bet I could also fill that. But why bother when I have my mouth?"

I tossed my hair back and bent down. I trailed soft, wet kisses down his length, then licked him from root to tip. He let out a soft groan. I took the head of his cock into my mouth and began swirling and flicking my tongue.

His eyes, heavy-lidded with desire, looked at me, and his full lips parted slightly as I continued to suck him, only now with one hand caressing his balls. His rigid member throbbed inside of my mouth. Every nuance of his response turned me on.

"You're so beautiful," he murmured, his voice low and intense. "You're so fucking sexy."

Relishing his masculine scent and salty flavor, I took him deeper and tongued the sensitive area beneath the head of his cock. As his arousal mounted, I picked up the pace, alternating between fucking him with my mouth and teasing him with licks and kisses. I felt him shudder, and moments later, he came explosively.

When he was spent, Jake pulled me into his arms and kissed me deeply. "You're amazing."

I smiled at him. "Thank you, but I'm really not responsible. It's you, Jake Barlow. You make me think dirty thoughts."

"Maybe it's contagious." He grinned wickedly at me. "I've had nothing but dirty thoughts since the moment I first laid eyes on you."

"Such as?" I asked.

I could feel him starting to grow hard against my thigh. So, he had been having dirty thoughts. Good—I wanted to know what they were.

"So, why don't you tell me," I said. "I want to know your fantasies." I ran my fingers through his thick locks. "If you tell me yours, I'll tell you mine."

"Deal." He rolled his eyes upward, miming deep contemplation.

"Is it that difficult?" I teased.

"I do have more than one fantasy, you know? Which one should I tell you about first?"

"Surprise me."

"OK. Sometimes I think about how hot it would be to do it in a public place, an exposed place, like one of those glass elevators that are in hotel lobbies."

"What do you imagine?" I asked, curious.

"We're taking the elevator to our hotel room. We kiss and touch each other. And we're so turned on, it doesn't occur to us to wait until we get back to the room. I hit the button. The elevator stops. We're stopped in mid-air, between floors, in this glass elevator. We're alone, but exposed. We see people walking around in the lobby below, and other elevators move past us, filled with people. All of them are looking at us."

He was fully hard now. I gripped his erection and slowly started to stroke him. "What happens after you stop the elevator?" I asked.

He was breathing heavier now, and God, was this man a turn-on. "We're still kissing," he said. "I press your ass against the elevator wall. Then I slip my hands beneath your skirt. You're naked underneath. My hands squeeze your lovely ass, then touch the wetness between your legs. I undo my pants, lift you onto my cock, and thrust into you. You're hot and wet around me, and as we begin to move, I'm aware of other elevators zipping past us. Everyone is watching but I couldn't care less if they're watching, because it gets me off. I like being watched. So, I focus on you, take you hard and fast against the wall, and I watch your tits bounce each time I thrust into you, and our bodies merge until we come together, in a mind-blowing climax."

I had to be honest—I was turned on. Not so long ago, my response to Jake's fantasy would have shocked, perhaps even horrified, me. But the past month with Jake had been eye-opening, to say the least. I'd become more confident in myself as a woman, more comfortable with my own sensuality. Jake had brought out a side of me that I hadn't known existed. A more adventurous side that was playful and open to experimenting. Maybe even a bit kinky?

For the second time that evening, I acted on my arousal. "This building doesn't have an elevator, but we could try the sex-against-the-wall thing. If you're up for it—and if your cock could talk right now, it would say you're obviously up for it—then why don't you choose a wall and fuck me against it?"

His eyes lit up. He swept me into his arms and tore off my clothes. And then he did just that.

10

The next week, Jake surprised me again. Maybe I should have seen it coming, but I didn't.

It all began innocently on Thursday, with the unfortunate death of a shoe. One of my Nine West black heels—my lucky heels that had seen me through so much—totally bit the dust when the heel snapped off. I'd bought them on sale at DSW a couple years before when I was still in school. I'd worn them to cocktail parties, art openings, graduation, job interviews. They'd carried me down the streets of Boston and New York, and saying goodbye to them was a little like losing an old friend.

"Goodbye, shoes," I said, tossing them into a trashcan. "May you walk tall in shoe heaven."

Thankfully, the shoes could be replaced with another pair. Perhaps even identical, or as close to identical as possible. Maybe on Saturday I'd go to DSW, and if they failed me, there was always Macy's just a couple blocks away. I'd probably have to pay full price at Macy's, but at least now I could afford it. For the first time in my life, I didn't have to count every penny, and I felt grateful for my good fortune.

Saturday morning, I woke at Jake's condo to a beautiful, warm spring day, and soon decided to go shopping. I slipped into one of Jake's button-down shirts, went into the kitchen, and made coffee. Jake put on a pair of jeans and joined me. After the coffee finished brewing, we sat at the table, absorbing our morning caffeine and basking in the warm sunshine that streamed through the windows.

"What does your day look like?" Jake asked.

"For starters, I have to brave the crowds at Downtown Crossing. I broke a heel a couple days ago, and need to find a new pair before Monday."

Jake looked at me thoughtfully. "I've got to go in to the office today—I need to catch up on some paperwork. Why don't I drop you off at Downtown Crossing? Once you've finished shopping, you can give me a call. Maybe I can pick you up as well. I shouldn't need more than a couple of hours in the office."

"You're a doll," I said, and leaned over to kiss him appreciatively. "But are you sure you don't mind? Traffic's terrible in that area on Saturdays. I don't mind taking a cab."

Jake shook his head. "Not a problem. I'll avoid the worst of the traffic by dropping you a block or so away, on one of the side streets."

An hour and a half later, showered and dressed, we left the condo and got into Jake's dark green BMW sedan. He drove to Downtown Crossing, then stopped the car on a side street, just a block away from the shopping district. I unbuckled my seat belt and leaned over to give him a kiss.

He unbuckled his own seat belt, and surprised me by sliding his hands over my breasts, tweaking my nipples lightly. Then he slipped a hand under my skirt.

"Jake!" I exclaimed. "You're going to get us arrested for indecency!"

He grinned. "Not if you do as I say." Mischief was written all over his face. "Come on, Juliana. I dare you to have car sex with me."

I looked out the car windows. The narrow side street that we were parked on was deserted, shadowed by surrounding buildings. A block away, throngs of shoppers milled along Washington Street.

"Afraid?" Jake teased.

I looked him in the eye. "Not at all. I just don't want to get caught." My hesitation wasn't only about the risk of someone catching us. In truth, my own excitement left me feeling unnerved. I could feel myself warming and opening. My core throbbed, wet with anticipation. What was happening to me? Risk was hardly my middle name.

He met my gaze without flinching. "We won't get caught so long as you do what I tell you."

I stared him down. "Dare accepted. What do I do first?"

"Recline your seat all the way back."

I did.

"Perfect. Stand up, just enough to let me slide underneath you."

It was a little awkward, but we managed. Jake was lying on his back, and I ended up perched on his right knee, facing the windshield.

"Straddle my legs." He slipped my thong down. "Don't turn around. Stay facing away from me."

Straddling him spread me wide open. He gripped my left hip with one hand, undid his jeans with the other, and then guided me onto his erect cock.

As he entered me, I began to realize where this was going. Fully reclined, Jake was invisible to anyone more than a couple feet away from the car. He couldn't see much past my back and the car interior. On the other hand, I was completely visible, the car windows giving me a full view of our surroundings.

I looked at him over my shoulder. "Aren't you getting the short end of the stick, Jake? You can't see anything."

"That's easily fixed. Open the moonroof. That way, if anyone looks down onto the streets from a building, they'll see me underneath you, driving my cock into you. Of course, with the roof open, they'll also hear if you scream with pleasure—like you did last night." He smiled broadly, but I saw the implicit challenge in his eyes.

He'd taken it to a new level. Could I remain silent while he did his utmost to make me scream my lungs out in ecstasy?

I reached over and pressed the button to open the moonroof. *Game on.*

Jake began lifting and moving me in rhythm with his thrusts. For a moment, my body took over, overwhelmed by pure sensation. Then reality clicked back into place.

My focus sharpened and honed in on the hordes of passing shoppers a mere block away. I heard the hubbub from the street, the dull roar of traffic—punctuated by the horns of annoyed drivers—and the din of many voices merging into a single sound. Images and sounds washed over me and filled my eyes and ears as Jake penetrated me to my core. People strolled past, unaware of our existence, let alone what we were doing—all while Jake pushed me relentlessly toward climax.

The sheer contrast heightened my response. I felt electrified and alive in ways that I'd never experienced before. Every inch of my skin hummed with vitality, and I felt my life force surging through my body. We continued our rhythm, now faster as our mutual arousal built, and we ground against each other with intensified passion. The sensations that assaulted me blurred into the inexorable drive toward orgasm, and I bit my lower lip to avoid screaming my pleasure to half of downtown Boston.

When we were finished, I looked over my shoulder at Jake, who had a huge smile on his face. He was clearly delighted with himself. But then, why shouldn't he be? We extricated ourselves, and Jake slid back into the driver's seat.

Just then, a Boston City Police car cruised past us, and I couldn't help bursting into a fit of giggles. Jake joined me and laughed uproariously.

"We'd better stop laughing," I said, wiping my eyes. "If a second police car comes by, they'll think we're on drugs."

Jake grinned. "Until they see your underwear on the floor of the car. That alone would tell them everything they don't need to know."

I looked down. My thong was indeed much the worse for wear. Jake or I—maybe both of us—must have stepped on it. I picked it up gingerly, then dropped it again. "Guess the first thing I'm shopping for is underwear."

"Why bother?" Jake asked. "It's futile, you know. I'm just going to tear them off in a couple hours."

I punched his bicep lightly. "You're a sex maniac. And apparently an exhibitionist. I can't believe you want me to run around Downtown Crossing naked under my skirt, just waiting for the next gust of wind to expose everything."

He raised a hand. "Guilty as charged. Fortunately, you don't seem to mind."

11

After Jake and I went our separate ways—me to Washington Street to shop, Jake to his office to work—I walked toward Macy's, intending to replace my destroyed underwear. Fine, I might have a touch of exhibitionism in me, but it didn't extend to accidentally flashing the entire population of Washington Street. I suppressed a giggle. Part of me couldn't believe I'd gone along with Jake's sex-in-public fantasy, let alone enjoyed it as much as I had.

My stomach rumbled loudly. I looked at my watch, saw that it was nearly noon, and realized that I hadn't eaten anything all day. No wonder my stomach was staging a minor revolt. I decided on a quick bite at Starbucks. A muffin would tide me over for a couple of hours. I walked into Starbucks, and nearly did a double take.

I couldn't believe my eyes. In eight months, I hadn't run into Craig Manning once. Of course, today would be the day. I'd just had hot car sex with Jake and was wearing no underwear. I vowed to carry a spare thong in my purse for the rest of my life.

Craig stood at the counter, as strikingly handsome as ever. Nothing about him had changed. His dark, polished elegance. The aura of utter confidence that radiated from him like a magnetic field. He was buying a cup of coffee. I stood just inside the door, frozen in place, unsure of what to do. Before I could react, he turned and spotted me. His face lit up. I was floored. Was he actually happy to see me?

"Juliana!" He smiled disarmingly. "Now this is a nice surprise."

"Hello, Craig." I didn't know what more to say. It had been months since I'd pushed him out of my life, and while I knew I'd made the right decision, I'd also come to terms with the undeniable truth that, at least on some level, a part of me would always love Craig.

He'd been my first real lover. We'd shared many beautiful, unforgettable moments together, and he'd been nothing but good to me when we were together. Unfortunately, the conflict between his sexual proclivities and my own issues meant that we were completely wrong for each other. The gulf between us was beyond insurmountable.

"Please. Sit down for a minute. We need to talk."

I did feel bad that I'd never cleared the air with Craig. What with my history, finding the DVD of him participating in an orgy had set off every possible alarm bell in my head. It had taken time to even begin to wrap my head around it.

Still, what was the point of talking? So much time had passed that it constituted a barrier in itself. And what would have been the point of talking sooner? It wasn't as if there was any hope for us working things out. Our differences were irreconcilable. And I was falling in love with Jake.

But maybe this was the closure I needed, so I agreed.

"OK. Perhaps you could find a table? I'll join you as soon as I get my coffee."

I bought a small coffee and a blueberry muffin, then sat down across from Craig. For a long moment, we sipped our coffee in silence. I felt awkward and tongue-tied. Maybe this wasn't such a good idea. But here I was. I had to make my best effort to tell him how I felt.

"I've really wanted—" he said.

"I've been thinking about—" I said.

We'd both started to speak at the same time.

"You go first," I said, giving him what I hoped was an encouraging smile.

"Ladies before gentlemen," he replied.

"I owe you an apology, Craig. I feel terrible that I didn't talk to you again. I know we were wrong for each other, but I wish I'd behaved—well, honestly—with more maturity."

He sighed. "There's no need to apologize, Juliana. Once I realized what you'd seen, your reaction made sense to me—especially given your personal history."

"Maybe. But I should have talked with you."

"I wish you had. But I'd rather not focus on that at the moment. We're talking now, and there are a couple things I need to say to you."

"I'm listening."

He looked at me with that intense, dark blue gaze that always made me feel exposed, as if he were reading my mind, seeing my every thought.

"I want you to know that I still love you. I want to be with you."

My lips parted in shock, and at first no words emerged. A shiver ran down my spine. "Craig—"

"Let me finish, Juliana. I've waited months to say these words. Give me another chance. Give us another chance."

I was speechless.

"Say something, Juliana. Please. Tell me how you feel."

I gripped the sides of my seat to steady myself, unable to believe what I had just heard. He still loves me? He wants another chance eight months after our breakup nearly destroyed me? I had to stay calm. I couldn't let this—let him—rattle me or knock me off course. I'd worked too hard to get where I was today.

I took a breath and began. "Craig—you were my first real love, and getting over you was the most difficult thing I've ever done. I'll always care for you, but let's face it. Our relationship was doomed from the start. You belong with a woman from your own world. Someone beautiful and adventurous. Someone who fits into your life in ways that I never could. I wish you nothing but the best, but I can't agree that we were ever right for each other."

He didn't reply.

"Also, I've met someone," I said.

Craig gave me a penetrating look. "Do you love him?"

"We've only known each other for two months. It's a little soon to call it love, but I am falling for him and I am happy. Very happy." I paused. "What I have with Jake isn't complicated. In fact, it's easy. We have fun together, and we get along incredibly well."

There. I'd said it. I was falling for Jake. He made me happy. I was finally in a relationship with better odds of survival than a snowball in hell. Sitting across from Craig, feeling the indefinable, nearly irresistible pull that his physical presence had on me, something clicked in my head. While Jake did push my comfort zone sometimes, it was never in a way that made me feel off-balance. With Craig, I'd struggled to find my balance, perhaps due to the complexity of his life, and the demands of his work on his time and attention.

Craig looked thoughtful. "I know that being with me was never simple."

"Please don't get me wrong," I said. "Being with you was wonderful. Life-changing, even. I'm just—I don't know how to say this. I guess I just want a simple life. No drama." I shook my head ruefully. "I wish you the best, and I hope that we can be friends."

He raised his eyebrows at me. "Friends? I want much more than friendship from you, Juliana. That said, I hope you agree that there's no reason whatsoever for us to avoid each other. Boston can be a small town, as you know, and our paths will cross again, I'm sure."

He glanced at his watch, then got up from his chair. "I'd better get going—I have a meeting scheduled in twenty minutes. Good luck with your life—and your new boyfriend." Then he strode out the door.

12

Over the next few days, I spent far too much time thinking about Craig, and his declaration that he still loved me. As I sat at my desk Friday afternoon, my thoughts turned once more to our brief encounter. Aside from mentioning to Jake that I'd run into Craig and had a cup of coffee with him, I'd kept it to myself.

Telling Jake was one thing. On the rare occasions that I'd talked about my previous relationships, Jake had listened. He'd been attentive and supportive, and he never pushed me to go beyond what I felt comfortable revealing. And besides—it wasn't as if I had anything to conceal.

But Duncan and Lara were another matter entirely. They'd listened to me obsess about Craig for months after our breakup. If I told Lara or Duncan that I'd spoken to Craig, let alone seen him face-to-face, neither of them would let it go until they'd dragged every last detail out of me. And the last thing I wanted was an interrogation.

Despite the fact that nothing had changed between Craig and me, knowing that he wanted me back attracted my thoughts like a moth to a flame. Thoughts and images of him hovered around the edges of my consciousness, and frustrated me to no end. It had taken months to get him out of my head the first time, and now it felt as if the clock had been turned back.

Then I stopped myself and thought of Jake. The mere thought of him warmed my heart. Our lives blended so seamlessly together, without any of the complications that had troubled my relationship with Craig.

I knew that what I had with Jake was different from the life-changing, mind-bending passion I'd experienced with Craig, but that didn't make it less meaningful. Craig had arrived in my life like a bolt of lightning, cleaving the sky and scorching the earth. Our passion for each other had been incendiary from the moment we met.

Jake and I had been more of a slow burn. The intensity of our lovemaking and the depth of our connection to each other had developed over time. Every time we made love, the flame between us burned a little hotter. With ease, I could imagine spending the rest of my life with Jake. Getting married. Choosing our first house. Having children together—I envisioned adorable, tow-headed twins, romping with Barkley on the lawn in Harpswell, while Jake and I sat nearby, watching the children and enjoying a glass of wine.

Just then, a light knock against the open door of my office startled me and interrupted my thoughts. I looked up, and saw Lara standing in the doorway.

"Lara! What's up?"

"You've forgotten, haven't you?"

"You mean about tonight's opening? Of course I haven't forgotten. Is it four o'clock already?" We'd planned to leave work an hour early to dress for tonight's VIP reception at the Institute for Contemporary Art. Most of the people invited to the reception were major donors—Lara and I only had tickets because her parents had given us theirs—so I doubted that I'd see many people I knew, but I might meet some collectors. Elsa Nielsen would definitely be there. Maybe Genevieve DuBois as well.

Lara groaned. "You artistic types. No grasp of time. Fortunately for you, I'm used to it. Connor's the same way. Anyway, come on. Let's get out of here. We need to tart ourselves up for tonight."

13

Two hours later, we were ready for action.

Lara was stunning, as usual. Tonight, she'd chosen a strapless, ankle-length sheath by Dior. Although the silhouette was classic and minimal, Lara's dress incorporated a funky combination of patterns and textures, in whites, pale grays, and subtle pinks. She'd completed the look by putting her hair up and adding pearls—simple earrings paired with a four-strand choker—and a dangerously delicate-looking pair of Jimmy Choo heels.

I'd stuck with my usual black, but thanks to a real paycheck, I'd splurged on a halter back-cutout cocktail dress several weeks earlier. An exposed back zipper gave it just a hint of edginess, and I loved the subdued glitter of its beaded neck and hem. With my new black heels and a pair of Swarovski stud earrings, I was psyched for a night out with my friends.

We left Lara's Beacon Street condo building and got into our waiting taxicab.

Once we were en route to the Institute for Contemporary Art, Lara turned to me. "Connor and Duncan are still planning on showing up, right?"

"Duncan said they might be a little late," I replied. "Jake wanted to meet us too, but he's stuck wining and dining prospective investors. He'll text me if he manages to escape early. Otherwise, he might be able to meet us afterward for a drink."

"Great! Let's make a night of it. Remind me what we're supposed to be looking at between martinis. Please tell me it's not all video art. Or performance. You know how I feel about art that demands more than thirty seconds of my time."

I laughed. Lara's impatience was legendary, but she often made fun of herself.

"It's a mix. A video artist—Andrej Zakrajsek—I think he's from the Czech Republic. I'm not familiar with his work. Then there's a group show of contemporary paintings, which should be interesting. Julie Mehretu's in it—I love her work."

Our taxi reached our destination and pulled up near the entrance. I paid the driver, dismissing Lara's protests.

"My turn—I do have a fabulous job with an excellent salary, remember?"

"Fine. But when we leave, I'm paying. No arguments."

We walked into the soaring lobby of the building, which was directly on the waterfront. Towering glass walls on two sides offered dramatic views of the Boston skyline and the inner harbor. The descending sun scattered its warm rays across the harbor, and edged the massed skyscrapers of the city with gold.

The VIP reception was in full swing. Clusters of the well-heeled and perfectly coiffed shook hands, exchanged air kisses, sipped cocktails, and made conversation. Waiters circulated, bearing trays of hors-d'oeuvres and champagne. Hard, polished surfaces dominated the atmosphere—sparkling glass, polished steel, and glittering diamonds were captured and illuminated in frozen moments as cameras flashed relentlessly, documenting the event for the society pages.

Lara nudged me. "Isn't that your ex across the room? Talking to Elsa Nielsen?"

I looked. "Yes, it's him. I guess it's no surprise to see Craig here. He's a big supporter of the arts."

"Looks like he's heading our way," Lara said, mischief in her voice. "You have to introduce us. That is, if the two of you are on speaking terms and if you feel comfortable doing so. I'm dying to meet him."

My upbeat mood evaporated as I suppressed the impulse to turn around and walk out the door. Talking to Craig was the last thing I wanted right now. Still, as he'd said when we'd run into each other the previous Saturday, this sort of encounter was inevitable. For my own good, I needed to get used to it.

"Good evening, Juliana." I recognized his public face. The deliberate, flawless smile that wasn't quite real.

"Good evening, Craig. Allow me to introduce my friend and colleague, Lara Barlow," I said with careful politeness. "Lara, this is Craig Manning."

Craig shook Lara's extended hand. "Lara Barlow of Barlow Interactive?"

"That's me," Lara said, visibly surprised that he knew who she was.

"I remember seeing a *Boston Magazine* article about you last fall —" Craig stopped in mid-sentence as one of the waiters approached with glasses of champagne on a round, glimmering silver tray. "Champagne, anyone?"

We each took a glass. I sipped mine delicately, repressing the urge to down the entire glass. I disliked small talk, and it felt incredibly weird to make polite conversation with this man, with whom I'd once been so intimate and in love.

"Have you met Andrej? The video artist?" Craig asked. He waved at a stocky, dark-haired man, who promptly made his way over to us.

"Juliana. Lara. I'd like to introduce Andrej Zakrajsek. His work is on exhibition upstairs."

Andrej took my outstretched hand, bowed slightly, and kissed the back of it with old-world European flair. After kissing Lara's hand as well, he smiled broadly and with enthusiasm. Despite teeth that had never crossed paths with an orthodontist, he was an attractive man.

"So good to meet you," he said with a strong Slavic accent. "I apologize in advance for my English—it is not so good."

Craig laughed. "Your English is much better than my Czech, Andrej. It's great to see you again." He turned to us and said, "Andrej and I met in Prague two years ago when he had a big show at the Futura Centre for Contemporary Art."

Suddenly, the good humor left Craig's face. Moving toward us was a woman, radiant in emerald green with long, raven-black hair that framed a face of classic beauty and cascaded over her shoulders. She was nearly as tall as Lara, and she exuded charm. She was the embodiment of glamor and poise, and many people watched her as she approached.

"Andrej!" she exclaimed, in a low, lightly accented alto. "And Craig! How marvelous to see you here!" She kissed Andrej quickly, then Craig, whose arm she grasped familiarly. Something about her jogged my memory. I knew I'd seen her before, but I couldn't recall where. She released Craig and turned back toward the rest of us.

"We must toast the great success of my friend Andrej. We have known each other many years, since we were young students in Prague."

I began to put two and two together. Given Craig's visible discomfort, the woman in green had to be one of his ex-girlfriends. Probably an actress, or a model. Probably one of the many women I'd seen on the Internet, standing by Craig's side at one red carpet event or another. It was obvious that he was trying to drag her away before any introductions or conversation could take place.

She shrugged away Craig's arm with an air of aggrieved petulance.

"I *will* have champagne now. Waiter!"

She hailed the closest waiter, who promptly equipped her with a glass of champagne. About to propose a toast, she raised her champagne flute, but then paused, turning to Lara and me. Her previous annoyance had evaporated, and she once again radiated serene control.

"I am so sorry. Please excuse my terrible manners. I should introduce myself first." She smiled graciously. "I am Alessandra d'Acosta. And you are—"

I froze. *Alessandra d'Acosta?* The ex-girlfriend from the sex video I'd found in Craig's apartment? I knew they'd remained friends after they broke up. Had she and Craig gotten back together?

Looking exasperated, Craig completed the introductions. "Alessandra, meet Juliana West. And Lara Barlow."

Something indefinable flickered across Alessandra's perfect features. Did she know who I was? Or was it my imagination? Then she smiled exuberantly and raised her glass. "To old friends —and new."

After we drank, Alessandra asked, "So, Juliana West, what do you do? Your name is not familiar to me." Her voice dripped with faux sweetness as her eyes evaluated me from head to toe, disdain apparent in her expression.

Bitch. Why was she going after me? Craig must have talked with her—about me. Why else would she act jealous? Why else would she feel the need to sharpen her claws? Fine. Two could play at that game.

"I paint. And design websites. What about you—what do you do?" I knew perfectly well that Alessandra was an up-and-coming movie star, but why give her that?

Her eyes narrowed with suspicion. "I am an actress," she said loftily. "In movies, of course. I am in many movies, both in the States and in Europe."

I smiled disingenuously. "Now that I think of it, I believe that I have seen one of your movies. Unfortunately, I can't seem to recall which one, but I do remember that it was rather edgy and dark." I glanced at Craig, and sensed his discomfort. *Too bad.*

"Maybe *Winter in Prague*? It has received many awards in Europe."

I shook my head slowly. "No, that's not it. Prague is a beautiful city. This film wasn't particularly beautiful. In fact, it was almost disturbing."

She laughed, but with an edge of mockery. "Perhaps you have seen my most recent film, *La Vie en d'Or*. In English, *Golden Life*. Even Americans have seen this film."

"No, it wasn't that either."

"You don't see many movies, do you?"

"I see plenty of movies." I snapped my fingers and looked straight at her. "And look—the title just came back to me. The movie I saw you in was called *Golden Showers*. Or something like that."

I thought I heard a muffled giggle from Lara. Craig looked horrified. Only Andrej seemed blissfully unaware of what was going down. Alessandra's face revealed her surprise, but she recovered quickly.

"One of my finest performances," she purred. "Wouldn't you agree, Craig?"

Craig looked at her with a grim expression. "You're nothing if not a born performer, Alessandra."

"Your performance was unforgettable," I agreed. "But the script was hackneyed, the action uninspiring, and the lighting—well, frankly, the lighting was terrible. But as a professional, I'm sure you're aware of that."

She glared at me.

"Not to mention the issues with your makeup," I continued cheerfully. "Tell me, has waterproof mascara—an American invention—made it to the Czech Republic yet? If so, you really should consider making the switch. Trust me, you won't regret it."

If looks could kill, I would have been dead on the spot. Beside me, Lara shook silently with repressed laughter. Even Craig looked amused.

"Come on, Alessandra," he said. "I just saw the Staunton-Millers arrive." He took her by the arm. "If I'm not mistaken, you know Tootie and Addy from New York. Let's go over and say hello to them."

"But of course, Craig," she said, resurrecting her dazzling movie-actress smile. "We must circulate. Mingle. Charm the locals. That is why we are here, after all. We celebrities must play our appointed role."

Craig nodded to Lara. "Great to have met you." He looked at me. "We'll catch up later, I hope." He moved off into the crowd, with Alessandra on his arm. Andrej trailed behind.

As soon as they were out of earshot, Lara turned to me. "That was hilarious. Wasn't she the one in that sex video you told me about? The video you and Craig broke up over?"

"That's right. Craig must have talked to her about me. How else would she recognize my name? You saw it. She was perfectly pleasant until she heard my name. But then she went on the attack."

"Revealing herself as a grade-A bitch, with an ego larger than the known universe. You put her in her place, though," Lara said.

I sighed. "After that little scene, I need a drink. Not champagne. A real drink. Like a martini. And the ladies' room. Not in that order though."

"I'll get the martinis while you brave the line," Lara said. "Meet me by the bar, OK?"

I agreed.

14

I reached the ladies' room, and was grateful to find that there wasn't a line after all. By the time I finished washing and drying my hands, I stood alone at the row of sinks. I checked my face in one of the mirrors. My makeup was holding up just fine save for my lips, which needed a touch up. I dug around in my purse searching for my lipstick holder.

Just then, I heard the door open, and saw a flash of emerald green in the mirror. It was her, of course. Alessandra. She marched up to me, and tossed back her hair. She looked furious.

"Juliana West. You stupid, stupid little cunt. You and your moronic little wordplay. *Golden Showers*? Please. You think you know about Craig and me? I'm here to tell you that you don't."

I looked at her evenly. "Now that we've met, I know everything I need to know. Craig has way too much class to hang around with a ball-banging slut like you."

Alessandra threw back her head and laughed maniacally. The harsh sound of her laughter shattered and multiplied, echoing against the hard tile and gleaming mirrors that surrounded us.

"Oh my dear," she said, her voice dripping with sarcasm as she stabbed a finger into my chest. "My poor little lost lamb. Let me paint a picture for you. Together, Craig and I have experienced heights you cannot begin to imagine. We've gone places you'll never dare to go."

She put her fucking hands on me? My anger went through the roof. There was no turning back now. I slapped her hand away.

"Don't touch me again, bitch, or you'll regret it. You say you've gone places I don't dare to go? No, no, no, you psycho. You've gone places that I would never *want* to go. Maybe degradation is a turn-on for you. Maybe playing the whore to four men at once gives you a thrill. That and being pissed on. But that's your business. I truly couldn't care less. What I know is this, Alessandra—I have a healthy amount of self-respect. You, obviously, do not. Tell me, Alessandra, why do you hate yourself so much?"

Enraged, she screamed at me. "You fucking idiot! You understand nothing about men and women! You call me a whore, but I'm the one with the power. I'm the one in control." Lowering her voice, she hissed, "Listen to me, stupid girl. I'm the one who ruined it for you. I destroyed you and Craig without lifting a finger."

I couldn't believe what I was hearing. Who did this crazy woman think she was? Her delusions of grandeur obviously verged on megalomania, and I wasn't about to let her get away with it.

"What I see in you isn't power. A hot mess of complete disillusionment, that's more like it. You didn't destroy us. You don't have that kind of control over anyone. No one does, you malevolent harpy. Yes, Craig and I broke up because of his attraction to your fucked-up world, but you and he hadn't been together for over a year."

I stopped, took a deep breath, and told myself to calm down. There was no use arguing with a maniac. I needed to end it, to finish with her once and for all.

"This conversation is over," I said, my voice as calm as I could make it. "Please do me—and Craig—the courtesy of staying away from me for the remainder of the evening. My relationship with Craig is in the past, and no part of it, including our breakup, had anything whatsoever to do with you."

Alessandra's expression was triumphant. "So you tell yourself, because you are naïve. And unsophisticated. A silly little slop of a girl with a trivial mind that's too afraid to face the truth. Who do you think made that video? Who do you think sent it to him?"

"Why, *you* did, I suppose," I replied. "Which does explain both the slutty female lead and the lousy production values."

She shot me a condescending look. "That video is a treasure. I recorded the two of us without Craig's knowledge. Then I sent it to him on DVD so he would remember what we had together."

She'd recorded Craig without his knowledge? How unethical was this deranged woman, anyway? Was there any limit to how far she would go to get what she wanted? I was outraged for Craig. This bitch was definitely capable of blackmail, or outright revenge.

I looked Alessandra in the eye. "I suppose he didn't know you were filming the second video, then, either."

She looked at me scornfully. "Why would I? It's not as if he was in it. Isn't it obvious? I'm not a naïve girl, like you. I'm fully aware of my power as a woman, and I know how to use it. I know how to make him jealous, so that he will run back to me. One day, he will beg on his knees for the privilege of being with me again."

Now she had me totally confused. The gold-masked man in the group sex video wasn't Craig?

"So who was he then? The man in the gold mask, in the second video?"

"Oh, so you appreciated Tomás! Perhaps there is some hope for you after all." She laughed at me. "Oh, I see it now. You thought Tomás was Craig. It's written all over your face. What a shame. Although I do have to say that he does resemble Craig somewhat, doesn't he? His height, his coloring. But Tomás is... how shall I put it? More adventurous. But not rich enough, unfortunately." She smirked. "I am not, as you Americans call it, a cheap date."

"Tomás?" I felt sick to my stomach. That she would do this to Craig infuriated me.

"Big porn star in Czech Republic." She smiled suggestively. "Very big. Unfortunately for you, you're not his type. You're not Craig's type, either. You must know that Craig will always return to me, if only to experience the pleasures that I know how to give." She leaned closer, so close that I could smell the alcohol on her breath, and poked my chest with her outstretched finger. "If you know what's good for you, cunt, stay away from Craig. He's mine."

I'd told her not to touch me, and she'd ignored my warning. I took a step forward, grabbed a fistful of her hair with one hand, and slapped her hard across the face with the other, simultaneously releasing her hair.

"Barbarian!" she screamed, staggering from my slap. "How dare you?!"

She teetered precariously on her four-inch spikes, and tottered backward away from me and toward the row of stalls.

I seized the opportunity.

I charged toward her and delivered a solid, two-handed push that sent her off her feet and reeling through the stall's open door behind her. She landed in a sitting position on the open toilet seat, with a sizable portion of her dress floating in the dirty toilet water.

"You're nothing but a bully, Alessandra. I warned you not to put your claws on me again, but you just had to go there, didn't you?"

She cowered against the back of the toilet, clutching the back of her dress, and pulling it out of the toilet, where it dripped on the floor.

"Looks like someone's ready for her close-up," I said.

"Stay away from me!" she screeched. "You've ruined my dress!"

"Stop whining," I said. "A ruined dress is the least of what you deserve. And you're the one who needs to stay away from me, you insane bitch. Come after me again, and your whole head will end up in that toilet."

I turned my back on her and stalked out of the bathroom. I had to find Craig. I owed him an apology. Not to mention an explanation of why I'd just shoved his girlfriend—or whatever she was to him at the moment—into a toilet.

15

Upon exiting the ladies' room, I spotted Lara.

"There you are! Finally. The line must have been brutal. Here's your drink." She handed it to me.

I swallowed a large gulp of martini. "Thank you so much. You have no idea how much I needed that."

"Are you OK?" She looked concerned. "You're bright red."

"I'm fine," I reassured her. "Just furious. Alessandra came after me in the ladies' room."

"She what?"

I sighed. "She made the mistake of putting her hands on me—twice—and I shoved her crazy ass into a toilet."

"Oh no you didn't."

"Oh yes I did. I'll tell you all the details later; I promise. Right now, I need to find Craig. He deserves an explanation about why his date has vanished."

"The last time I saw him, he was near the windows on the harbor side," Lara said. "By the way, Connor and Duncan finally arrived. They're over by the bar."

"Why don't you catch up with them? What I have to say to Craig won't take more than a few minutes."

Lara headed for Duncan and Connor, and I made my way toward the harbor side. Thankfully, Craig was still there, chatting with Andrej. Feelings of guilt and remorse overwhelmed me as I approached him. What had I done? Craig had been nothing but good to me, and in return, I'd misjudged him. I'd made an unforgivable mistake. Maybe the biggest mistake of my entire life.

"Excuse me," I said, forcing a polite smile. "Craig, could I have a word with you? In private?"

"Of course," he said. He nodded to Andrej. "Please excuse me."

He took my arm and guided me out of the crowd.

"Let's take the elevator to the galleries. The party's at its height, so no one will be looking at the art right now."

When we reached the gallery level, it was deserted, as Craig had predicted. He led me through a couple of brightly lit spaces, and into a darkened room, with a video projected on one wall. Craig gestured toward a long leather bench that faced the video projection.

"Have a seat," he said. "We're unlikely to be interrupted in here."

I sank onto the bench, grateful to get off my feet. Craig sat down next to me.

"What's going on? By the way, I apologize for what happened earlier with Alessandra."

"You're not the one who needs to apologize." I took a deep breath. "Alessandra spilled her guts about the sex videos, and I'm the one who owes you an apology. I know the whole story now, and I feel terrible. I've been so unfair to you. There's no excuse for how I've behaved, but I'm truly sorry."

"Thank you," Craig said quietly. "I'm glad you finally know the truth."

"There's more. Alessandra told me about the videos—after she verbally attacked me in the ladies' room. Then she put her hands on me. I warned her not to do it again, but listening doesn't appear to be part of her skill set. The second time she stuck her finger in my chest, I slapped her across the face, and gave her a good shove. When I left your date, she was on her ass, halfway down a toilet. She's probably still hiding out in the bathroom, wringing out her dress under a hand dryer."

"So the only damage was to her dress?" Craig asked.

I shrugged. "And her oversized ego, I suppose."

He laughed heartily. "Fortunately, Alessandra isn't my date. I came by myself. Sounds like she got exactly what she deserved."

I felt a tremendous sense of relief wash over me. I had apologized to Craig, and he seemed to have accepted my apology. But I was still concerned for him. What if Alessandra went public with one of her home videos?

"Alessandra worries me, Craig. She strikes me as a loose cannon, to say the least. Could she create problems for you, by putting one of those sex videos on the Internet, for example?"

Craig looked at me, and his expression softened. "Don't worry about me, Juliana. After you discovered that DVD in my suite, I took immediate action to protect myself. I put a team of private investigators on Alessandra for several months. I have more than enough information and influence to ruin her movie career, and she knows it. Could she damage me? Perhaps. But she's not likely to go there, because she knows that if she did, I would destroy her. Completely and permanently."

"I'm relieved that you don't consider her a threat. Assuming she's sane, she'll probably behave. Although I'm not so sure about the sane part." I sighed. "I'm so sorry, Craig. I rushed to judgment without getting the facts straight. I wish I could make it up to you."

"What's done can't be undone. But you can make it up to me—if that's what you want." His expression became intense. "Come back to me, Juliana. I don't know what you have with this guy Jake, but it can't possibly be as amazing as what we have together. Break it off with him. Come back to me. We're meant to be together. I know it, and so do you."

I couldn't answer him. Craig had been my first love, and he'd always have a special place in my heart, but my feelings for Jake were strong. I could see myself building a life with him, something I couldn't quite imagine doing with Craig. Certainly not as equal partners.

Just then, I heard his cell phone vibrate.

"Don't you need to get that?" I asked.

"No. Whoever it is, you're more important."

I could hardly believe what I'd just heard. When Craig and I had been together, he'd always checked to see who was calling him, and he'd nearly always interrupted whatever we were doing to answer. At times, I'd felt that our relationship would always take second place to the demands of his work. What had changed? Was what he'd just said to me true? Was he really in love with me? Right now, I had to believe that he was, which just confused me even more.

He leaned toward me, and took my hand, circling my palm with his thumb. "Until you left, I didn't really understand what you mean to me. I love you, Juliana. You've been in my thoughts every moment of every day for the past eight months. I know I made mistakes, and I'm truly sorry. I should have opened up to you more about my past, especially my history with Alessandra. If I'd been more open about my past, maybe we'd be together today."

"I guess we both made mistakes," I said.

"Remember our weekend on the Cape? Those couple of days with you—walking on the beach, making love, watching you paint? I've never been so happy. Not with anyone." His expression was wistful. "I never thought I wanted marriage, or a family. My own family was pretty dysfunctional. A stepfather who beat me. A stepbrother who hated me. A mother who couldn't protect me because she was too ill. These are things I should have told you about, but I didn't because it's still too raw for me to go there. But you changed all that. I want it all, Juliana, and I want it with you. Marriage. Family. A little girl with your hair and eyes."

I couldn't believe it. Craig Manning? Talking about marriage and children? Not answering his phone? My mind went back to that romantic weekend on Cape Cod, and I recalled his tenderness toward me. His passion. His thoughtfulness—he'd set up an entire painting studio for me, complete with paints, brushes, and canvases.

"I can't listen to this right now, Craig. It's just too much, all at once. I've had a hellish evening, and I'm beyond overwhelmed."

His cell vibrated again, but he didn't break eye contact with me. If anything, the connection between us became more intense.

"Come back to me, Juliana. I'm a different man because of you, and I hope you'll give me the chance to prove that I've changed."

Reeling from the shock of what I'd just heard, I pulled my hand away.

"I can't do this, Craig. I'm with Jake now."

"Please, Juliana. Just one kiss. That's all I ask. One kiss."

I opened my mouth to refuse, but he pulled me to him and captured my lips with a rough, hungry kiss that seared through me. Every cell in my body awoke to his touch. I willed myself to pull away, and after a long moment, I finally regained enough self-control to do so. My heart pounded. My head spun. I'd never felt more alive—or more confused.

"Please, Craig. I really can't do this."

He looked at me, and his gaze penetrated me to my soul. "You belong to me, Juliana, just as I belong to you. You know in your heart that we're made for each other. Think about it. You just admitted that breaking up with me was a mistake. Well, I also screwed up by letting you go. Trust me, I won't make that mistake again."

I turned away, desperately grappling with a surge of conflicting emotions. In that moment, I realized that there was no easy answer, no simple way out. I would have to make a difficult decision, and no matter what I decided, someone I cared for deeply would be disappointed and hurt, and it was crushing for me.

"I have to be honest, Craig. We have a history together, and I do have feelings for you. Maybe I always will. But I'm in a committed relationship with Jake, and I have strong feelings for him, too."

Craig gently turned my face toward his, tracing my jawline with his fingers.

"I respect you for refusing to cheat on Jake. I really do. But I meant what I said. I'm not letting you go this time."

"Juliana?"

Recognizing Lara's voice, I turned. She stood, silhouetted in the entrance to the darkened gallery.

"Are you ready to leave yet? The party's shutting down." Her voice was cool. How long had she been standing there? How much had she seen and heard?

I got up from the bench, then turned back to Craig. "I need to go. My friends are waiting."

"I'll be in touch," he said.

16

After the elevator doors closed behind us, Lara looked me in the eye.

"You need to tell me what the hell is going on. Believe me, I don't want to think that my best friend is two-timing my brother, but what I just saw sure looked like it."

"I haven't cheated on Jake, and I never would. You know me, Lara. You know I'm not that kind of person."

Lara threw up her hands. "I'd like to believe you, but I just saw you kissing that man."

The elevator doors opened, and I grabbed Lara's arm.

"Around the corner. Now. I'll explain everything."

We went into the stairwell, which was thankfully empty.

I took a deep breath. "OK. You saw Craig kiss me. Then you saw me stop that kiss. You heard me tell Craig that I'm in a committed relationship with Jake."

"That's not really the point, though, is it? I'm not blind, Juliana. You're still attracted to Craig. Meanwhile, you're carrying on a relationship with my brother, who's head over heels for you, blissfully ignorant that you're hot for this other guy." She shook her head. "Jake needs to know the truth."

"Believe me, I've been nothing but truthful with Jake from the beginning. He knows all about Craig. I told him everything."

Her eyebrows rose in disbelief. "Including why you broke up with Craig? The sex videos you found?"

"Yes. Although it turns out that Craig wasn't the guy in the orgy video after all. It was some Czech porn star named Tomás. Alessandra told me the truth after she came after me in the ladies' room. Apparently, Craig wasn't adventurous enough for her, though she certainly liked his money."

"You broke up with Craig because he was in that video. Now, you're saying it wasn't him, it was some Czech guy. What's wrong with you, Juliana? You told me you loved Craig. Now you're saying you ditched him for something he didn't even do? Couldn't you at least get your fucking facts straight? But your irresponsibility isn't my problem. My problem is that you're about to break my brother's heart." She looked coldly at me. "You have the rest of the weekend to tell Jake whatever you want about what happened tonight. On Monday, I'm telling him exactly what I saw and heard. If he has any sense, he'll dump you before you have the chance to hurt him more than you already have."

"I never intended to hurt Jake, or anyone else—"

She raised her hand and cut me off.

"Going out for drinks tonight is off. Now that I've found out the hard way how fucked up you are, I can't be your friend. Regardless of what my brother decides, I'm done with you. I'll be professional at the office, because that's who I am, but our friendship is over."

"Lara—"

She left, slamming the door behind her.

I stood alone in the sterile concrete space of the stairwell. Tears filled my eyes. I couldn't believe what was happening. In a mere couple of hours, my whole world had imploded. My relationship with Jake was at risk. My friendship with Lara was in tatters. Even my job, which I loved and knew I did well, was no longer secure. How could I continue working closely with Lara if she despised me?

And it was all my fault. I couldn't blame anyone else for breaking up with Craig, or getting involved with Jake. Under the circumstances, I couldn't even blame Lara for ending our friendship. Sure, I'd meant well. I'd tried to do the right thing, but what did that matter? End results. That's what counted in life, and despite my good intentions, my results sucked.

I didn't know what to do. I didn't know what I wanted, except for the insanity to end. I wasn't even sure who I was anymore.

17

Just then, the door opened and Duncan entered.

"Jules! Where have you been?" Then he saw my expression and stopped. "What's wrong?"

"Everything. I'm so glad you're here." I threw my arms around him and held him tight. Thank God for Duncan. He was the one person in my life who never judged me. "How did you know where to find me?"

"I asked Lara where you were, and she said the last time she saw you, you were in the stairwell. Then she took off. Said she was putting an end to a bad evening before it got worse. So I guess it's just you, Connor, and me going out for drinks. If you're still up for it?"

"Hardly. Wait until you hear what happened, Dunc. Lara's furious with me. I'm afraid my friendship with her is over. And very possibly my relationship with Jake as well." My eyes started to well with tears.

Duncan grasped my shoulders and gave me a searching look. "Tell me exactly what happened."

"Did you see Alessandra d'Acosta? It started when we were introduced. As soon as she realized who I was, she went all catty on me. I gave it back to her, of course. Finally, Craig managed to drag her away." I took a breath. "Later, she followed me to the ladies' room. Went off about Craig. In the middle of her rant, she informed me that Craig wasn't the guy in the video. You know, the video that drove my decision to break up with Craig."

Duncan furrowed his brow. "So it wasn't Craig after all?"

"No. Apparently, the guy in the video was one of Alessandra's Czech fuck buddies. The video was dark and I never saw his face. His build and coloring were similar to Craig, and I jumped to the wrong conclusion. But there's more. Alessandra's crazy, Dunc. She threatened me. Then, she more or less threatened Craig."

"What did you do? How did you respond?"

"Well, she made the mistake of putting her hands on me—twice. The first time, I warned her not to do it again. The second time, I shoved her into a toilet."

Duncan threw back his head and laughed. "Sounds like you won that round." His expression sobered. "But where's Lara in all this? I'm still not getting why she's upset with you."

"I'm getting to that. After my run-in with Alessandra, I went to find Craig. I wanted to apologize to him, and to warn him about Alessandra. That bitch is out for blood, and she definitely regards Craig as her property. I wouldn't put anything past her."

"So you found Craig and told him what happened?"

"Yes. Craig said he was glad that I knew the truth, and that he wasn't worried about Alessandra. Then he asked me to come back to him."

"What did you say?"

"I told him the truth. That I'm in a committed relationship with Jake. That I have feelings for him, but I also have feelings for Jake. Then he kissed me. Somewhere in the middle of all this, Lara showed up, and saw Craig kissing me. She flew to the conclusion that I've been cheating on Jake despite the fact that she also saw me end the kiss, and tell Craig that I couldn't go there. I would never cheat on Jake. I would never cheat, period—you know that's not who I am."

Duncan shook his head. "What a mess."

"Tell me about it. Why do I keep fucking up, Dunc? I've tried so hard to get my life on track, but everything's completely screwed up —again. Craig's determined to win me back, and you know what he's like. He'll pull out all the stops. He'll repeat that he's changed, that he wants me to marry him and to have his children. Believe me, I can't even begin to process that. Things have been going great with Jake, but who knows what he will think of me after Lara tells him her version of tonight's events. You should have seen the look on her face, Duncan. She hates me. I'm probably going to have to find a new job—"

Duncan interrupted me. "Stop. Just answer one question for me."

"What?"

"Have you lied to any of these people? Have you been deceitful, or manipulative?"

"Of course not! You know me, Dunc. I've been completely honest. Not that it's done me any good."

"Then no one has the right to judge you. Life happens, Jules. Even good people make mistakes. You made an honest mistake with Craig, you apologized, and he accepted your apology. As for you and Jake, you're both adults. You'll tell him what happened, and whatever the two of you decide is no one else's business. Do you hear me? No one else's business."

"What about Lara?"

Duncan sighed. "You know Lara's got a temper. But her bark is much worse than her bite. Give it a few days. Give her time to calm down. Connor's told me how much your friendship means to her, and I think she'll come around once she's had time to process what she saw and heard. If I know Lara, part of her anger is coming from the fact that she played a role in getting you and Jake together. On some level, she probably feels bad about her own part in this, and she's taking it out on you. Meanwhile, as far as I know, you and Jake haven't made any long-term promises to each other. Maybe the two of you will come out of this stronger than ever. Maybe you'll go your separate ways. One way or another, this will be a turning point in your relationship."

As always, Duncan's thoughtful perspective made sense. Jumping to conclusions was part of what had gotten me into this mess in the first place. I didn't want to make that mistake again. This time around, I would not allow life to push me into a reactive, emotional, fear-driven place.

Duncan looked at me. "One more piece of advice. Try to stay calm when you talk to Jake. Focus on just telling him exactly what happened. I know you, Juliana. When you're stressed and emotional, you tend to shut down. And when you tell Jake about this evening, you need to be fully present."

He knew me so well.

"Duncan—I love you, and I'm so grateful to have you in my life. Your friendship means the world to me. I needed to clear my head, and you've helped."

Duncan smiled. "That's what friends are for, right? Now, are you coming with Connor and me for drinks?"

I shook my head. "Thank you for asking, but no. I'm going to text Jake that I'll be at his condo. Hopefully we can talk tonight after he gets back from his business dinner. Give my best to Connor, OK?"

"Will do." Duncan glanced at his watch. "Speaking of Connor, I'd better go find him. The party's breaking up, and he's probably wondering where I am."

He opened the door and we left the stairwell.

"Call me if you need me," Duncan said.

I kissed him on both cheeks. "Go find your boyfriend before he files a missing persons report."

After Duncan and I parted, I left the Institute for Contemporary Art and hailed a cab. As the driver pulled away from the Institute, heading toward the Back Bay, I thought about seeing Jake. I would be completely honest with him, and we would decide what to do—or not do—together. As for Lara, I'd keep my distance from her for the moment. After what she'd said to me, it wasn't as if I had other options.

None of this would be easy, and there was no telling what was ahead of me. Jake and Lara might both hate me before this was over. I could be looking for a new job before the week was out. But at least I would know that I had done my best to face my problems. This time I wasn't running away.

18

Later, in the living room of Jake's Marlborough Street condo, I was pacing back and forth.

Any minute, he would walk through the door. How would he respond to hearing that Craig had kissed me, and that Lara had walked in on us? I hadn't invited the kiss, and I'd ended it quickly, but would Jake believe me, especially after he heard Lara's version of events?

The waiting was killing me.

I'd never intended to end up here, but life had thrown me one mother of a curveball. Eight months before, I'd fallen in love with Craig Manning. But we'd only had a few weeks together before I came upon that video. I'd been outraged—and heartbroken. I'd broken up with him immediately, and refused any further contact with him.

Six months after breaking up with Craig, I'd met Jake. While it wasn't love at first sight, as I'd experienced with Craig, my relationship with Jake had developed and intensified over time. Now, after two months together, I knew Jake better than I'd ever known Craig. And I liked what I knew—a lot.

Jake and I were strongly attracted to each other, but beyond that, we were friends. We laughed together. We talked late into the night about anything and everything.

Then there was Craig. My first love. Our breakup had happened because I'd jumped to conclusions, and I felt truly remorseful for my actions. There was no question that I'd been terribly unfair to Craig. Now he'd asked me for a second chance. A few months earlier, I probably would have given him one on the spot.

But being with Jake had changed my perspective on love and partnership. With Jake, I'd experienced a completely different kind of relationship. I felt that Jake and I were equal partners, friends as well as lovers. Because of my past, trust was difficult for me. I tended to doubt the sincerity of others, and often second-guessed myself as well. But Jake's openness and honesty made me feel safe, and increasingly, I trusted him to the point that I was falling for him. I couldn't say the same for Craig.

Brilliant and driven, with a magnetic personality, Craig was a force. But on so many levels, he remained an enigma. In the past, I would have said that with him, true partnership wasn't possible. But after his declarations earlier this evening, I wasn't so sure anymore. Tonight, he'd revealed a different, more vulnerable side of himself. Maybe I'd misjudged him in more ways than one. He'd seemed sincere. Maybe he had changed, as he claimed. I had no way of knowing for sure.

The evening had left me shaken. I desperately needed time to calm down, and time to process the muddle of scattered, contradictory thoughts that rattled in my head. Regardless of Craig's desire for a second chance, I wasn't prepared to break up with Jake. But after I told Jake what had happened tonight, would he even want anything to do with me?

I heard footsteps on the stairs, then a key in the door. Jake was home. I took a breath, then walked to the door to meet him.

"Juliana! Wait until you hear. I have the most amazing news." He grinned, his happiness evident. He leaned down for a quick kiss; then pulled a bottle of Veuve Clicquot from the brown bag under his arm. "Just let me open this; then I'll tell you the whole story." He disappeared into the kitchen, and I heard the sound of a cork popping.

I didn't want to spoil the moment for him. My not-so-exciting news would just have to wait. I sat down on the couch, wondering what Jake's big news would be. Maybe he'd scored a new account? Or received a promotion?

When he reappeared, he held two glasses of champagne. He handed one to me before sitting down next to me on the couch. His eyes were bright with excitement.

"You're not going to believe this, Juliana, but it's for real. I've been offered the opportunity to head the London office."

"As in London, England?"

"That's right. London's an amazing city, and this is a great career opportunity. Our London office is smaller than the one here, but I'd be running the show. I haven't accepted the position yet, but that's only because I wanted to talk to you first." He paused. "I want this job, Juliana, and I want you to come to London with me. We could move together, find an apartment in the city—we're all but living together already—and I'm sure Uncle Edward could be persuaded to transfer you to the London office of Barlow Interactive. You'll love the London art scene, too—it's one of the best in the world. Much more going on there than in Boston. I did a semester abroad at Cambridge during my junior year, and I spent a fair amount of time in London then. It's an amazing city."

This was happening way too fast. I struggled to take it in. Jake wanted to take a job in London, and he wanted me to go with him. He had it all worked out.

"So what do you think?" he asked, smiling. "Are you up for an adventure—in one of the greatest cities on the planet?"

I tried to be happy for him. Jake worked hard, and he deserved this. I mustered the best smile I could and clinked my glass against his. "To you, Jake. Heading the London office is a great opportunity and a big promotion. I'm so proud of you."

He grinned. "This means partner level, Juliana. Maybe all those late nights at the office have finally paid off."

Partner level? This would put Jake in line—at least potentially—for the CEO position when his father retired. I sipped my champagne. "This is only the beginning, Jake. With your business acumen and work ethic, you'll be CEO of Barlow Financial someday."

"I don't know about that. Assuming Dad retires and turns over the reins sometime in the next five to ten years, I'd still be relatively young for the CEO position. Don't get me wrong. Running Barlow Financial is my dream. But I have to be realistic. The other partners are older and more experienced, and when the time comes to choose a new CEO, it will be a group decision. Although Dad owns a controlling interest, he would never force the partners to choose me. And frankly, I agree with him. The right decision is always to choose the best man—or woman—for the job."

I smiled at him. "I'm still betting on you."

"Thank you for the vote of confidence." His expression turned serious. "I don't mean to push you, and I know we agreed to take things slowly, but this opportunity changes things." He met my eyes. "I want you to come to London with me, and before you make any decisions, I need to tell you how I feel. I love you, Juliana. From the moment we met, I knew you were the one. The woman I've been waiting for all my life. If you don't want to go to London, I can always turn down the job."

I was blown away. Jake was in love with me? And willing to sacrifice the opportunity of a lifetime to be with me? How could I be so lucky, and so unfortunate, all at once? I'd thought that this night couldn't possibly screw with my head more than it already had, but life had now dealt me a royal flush of pure fuckery.

In the past, had my feelings for Craig really been love, or infatuation? In the present, I was with Jake, and my feelings for him had grown with time, but was I in love with him?

The whole damnable situation made my head spin. It was all so completely unexpected, and coming off this crazy evening, I hadn't had any time to process how I felt, let alone consider major life commitments.

As I struggled to regain focus, a feeling of guilt overcame me. Jake was the innocent in all of this. His love, not to mention his generosity, were so much more than I deserved. I couldn't hold back any longer. I had to come clean before he went any further. The last thing I wanted was for him to feel humiliated or rejected.

"Jake—before we continue talking about London, there's something I have to tell you."

I walked him through the events of the evening. Alessandra's verbal and physical attacks. My discovery that Craig hadn't been the man in the video. My apology to Craig for misjudging him, and Craig's pushing me to get back together with him. The kiss that Lara walked in on. The fact that I hadn't initiated the kiss, and had ended it quickly. Lara accusing me of cheating and ending our friendship.

Jake listened intently to the whole story. After I finished, he shook his head. "What an evening. Sounds like you had it coming from all directions." He leaned toward me and took my hands in his. "Juliana, you've never lied to me, or deceived me in any way. I trust you and I believe your account of what happened. You haven't done anything wrong, but we do need to talk about this."

I sighed. "After tonight, you have no idea how much I appreciate your trust. By the way, based on Lara's final words to me, she'll probably call you on Monday to tell you I'm a cheating slut who isn't worthy of you. Or something along those lines."

"Don't worry about Lara. Believe me, I'm fully capable of dealing with my sister. Lara has a big heart, and an even bigger temper. This isn't the first time she's gone overboard, and it's probably not the last. The real question here, Juliana, is about how you feel. About me—and about Craig Manning."

He released my hands and leaned back against the couch, his gaze focused on me as he awaited my response.

Several seconds ticked by as I struggled to find the right words. "I'm stunned, Jake. You've said that you love me. You want to go to London, and you've asked me to come with you. This is all happening really fast, and coming at the end of an insanely awful evening. I know I'm a mess, and I'm terrified of making decisions right now. I need time to calm down and think things through."

Jake's expression was grave. "Do you still have feelings for Craig?"

"My feelings about him don't add up. Maybe they never did. And then there's us, Jake. Nothing that happened tonight changes what we have, but I need time to think about London, all right? I mean, I don't even have a passport."

For a long moment, Jake was silent. I could see the disappointment on his face, and knowing that I'd hurt him crushed me. My heart ached, and my eyes welled with tears.

Finally, Jake broke the silence. "Look, Juliana. Moving to London together would be a big step. We shouldn't take that step until we're both ready. By ready, I mean ready to move forward wholeheartedly, with no regrets or reservations on either side." He paused. "Maybe it'll be best if we take some time off from each other."

"What do you mean?" I asked, blinking away tears.

"I mean that I'll take the London job, and you'll stay here in Boston. At least for the next month or two, until your passport comes through. Don't take this the wrong way. I love you, I want you to be happy, and I know we could have a great life together. But I'm well aware that Craig wasn't just another boyfriend. He was your first real love, and that's a powerful connection. At a minimum, you have unfinished business with him. Maybe he's the one, though I hope that I'll be the lucky man. Either way, Juliana, you have to sort this out for yourself. I'll leave for London at the end of next week, but let me make one thing clear. We agreed to be exclusive, and I'll continue to assume we still are—until you tell me that we're not. I hope you'll join me in London once you get your passport, but that's up to you."

The reality sunk in. I'd already lost Lara, and now I was on the verge of losing Jake as well. But if anyone was at fault, it certainly wasn't Jake, and I had to respect his decision.

After all that had happened that evening, in my current condition —exhausted and overwhelmed—I couldn't even come close to offering the certainty that he deserved. Over the past few hours, I'd reeled from outright shock to emotional devastation to a sort of numbness. At this point, nothing felt real anymore.

Jake was putting his own disappointment aside and was giving me time to think things through. He was giving me time and space to reflect, but was leaving the door open for me to join him in London. His generosity amazed me. Would Craig have been so unselfish? I wasn't sure.

"I'm really going to miss you," I said, wiping my eyes. "I can't imagine not having you in my life."

He released a sigh. "Believe me, I'll miss you, too. I hope with all my heart that you'll come to me in London. But you know the old saying, right? If you love someone..."

"You set them free." I looked into his eyes, and was devastated to see that he looked as despondent as I felt. Jake deserved better than this. He deserved better than me.

I put my hand on his knee. "I'm sorry for being such an emotional wreck. I'll sort myself out. I promise—I just need a little more time."

ON THE BRINK, VOL. 3

1

Boston
One week later

Somehow, I survived the week after Jake accepted his new job in London, but it wasn't easy.

At the office, I had difficulty focusing on my work, and Lara avoided me. Jake worked late every evening on projects that he needed to complete before his departure. The little time we managed together was strained and imbued with our mutual knowledge that within days, an ocean and five time zones would separate us.

On Thursday, I met Duncan for lunch at 29 Newbury. After we ordered, Duncan looked at me. I knew what was coming.

"Connor tells me that Jake's taken the London job. Does this mean that you'll be moving to London in the near future?"

"Not necessarily."

"What do you mean?"

"Jake told me that he's in love with me, but he thinks that spending some time apart is a good idea."

"Is this about last weekend, when Craig kissed you?"

"Not exactly. It's more than that. Jake thinks I still have feelings for Craig. He's called it 'unfinished business'."

"Well, is he right? Do you still have feelings for Craig?"

"It's complicated. Craig was my first love, and he'll always have a special place in my heart. I'll never forget our time together. But that's over now. I'm in love with Jake."

"Have you told Jake that?"

"There's no point in telling him."

"I don't understand."

"He wouldn't believe me. Not now."

"Why not?"

"Because I fucked everything up the night Craig kissed me."

"That was when Jake dropped his London news on you?"

"That very night. Of course, he knew nothing about my mindfuck of an evening. So there I am, trying to decide how to tell him that my ex-boyfriend kissed me without consent and that his sister now hates me because she misinterpreted what she saw, when Jake walks in with a smile on his face and a bottle of champagne under his arm, all excited to tell me about London."

"What did you do?"

"I didn't want to spoil his moment, so I listened. He told me about the London job, and that he wanted to take it. Then he told me that he loved me, and in the same breath, he asked me to move to London with him."

"Your head must have been spinning."

"It was. I didn't know what to say, but I had to say something. Unfortunately, what I said ruined everything."

"What did you say?"

"I told Jake that there was something I needed to tell him, and then I told him about my conversation with Craig. I told him about Craig kissing me, that I didn't initiate it, and that I ended it."

"So you told him everything," Duncan said. "Did he believe you?"

"He said that he believed me, but then he asked me how I felt about Craig."

"What did you say?"

"I was honest. I said that my feelings for Craig didn't add up, and that nothing that happened that night changed what Jake and I have together. I asked for time to think about London. Obviously, that wasn't what he wanted to hear. That's when he decided that we needed to spend time apart."

"Did you break up?"

"No, and that's my one ray of hope. But we haven't had a real conversation since that night, let alone made love. I know he's maxed out between finishing projects at the office and preparing to leave the country, so I haven't pushed. I don't know what to do, Dunc, and it's tearing me up inside. I don't know what to say—or not to say—to Jake right now. And no matter what I do or say, he's still going to get on a plane in two days, and I can't go with him because I don't have a passport."

"How did the two of you leave things?" Duncan asked.

"Jake said that he hopes I'll choose him over Craig, and that I'll come to London after my passport arrives. But it's all too obvious that he's not counting on it. I feel like an idiot, Dunc. I totally blew it. Can you blame Jake for wanting to get the hell away from me?"

"Don't think that way," Duncan said. "Maybe he's just trying to do the right thing for both of you. If you love him, then you need to see this through."

"How?" I asked.

"Ride out the storm. Respect and support his decision to take the London job. Tell Craig that it's over between the two of you."

"It has been over—for months. While Craig has made it clear that he wants me back, I've never encouraged him to think that could ever happen. In fact, I don't want it to happen. I want to be with Jake."

"Then put yourself in Jake's shoes. Try to see what happened from his perspective. He loves you, but he's questioning whether you'll return his love."

"But I *do* love him. You know I do."

"Then prove it to him. With actions, not just with words. Words are cheap. Actions say everything. I know this is hard to hear, but as your friend, I have to tell you the truth as I see it. Your relationship with Jake is on the line. What you do in the next two days could save your relationship—or destroy it once and for all."

"What do you think I should do?" I asked.

"Be supportive. Be there for him. Help him pack. Make sure you're both set up with Skype so that the two of you can stay in touch without enormous phone bills. And before Jake gets on that plane, find the right moment to tell him that you love him."

"That can't be enough."

"It isn't. You need to let him know that you'll come to London as soon as your passport arrives."

2

On Friday, I left work at a quarter past five and hurried several blocks to the supermarket. It was Jake's last night in Boston, and I wanted to make dinner for him. I'd decided on a green salad and spicy lasagna, which was one of his favorites.

I found the ingredients I needed, and headed for the wine section, where I selected a Syrah/Malbec blend. I paid for my purchases, left the supermarket with two large bags of groceries, and caught a cab back to Jake's condo, where I carried the groceries upstairs and unlocked the door, before texting Jake.

Spicy lasagna for dinner? I'm making it right now.

He responded quickly.

That sounds great, but I won't be able to leave work until 8 or so. And I still have to finish packing.

Dinner at 9, then? I can help you pack.

OK. See you then.

I breathed a sigh of relief. Throughout the week, Jake had stayed late at the office every night, which wasn't like him. I knew he had work to finish and projects to turn over before his departure. Still, part of me worried. Maybe working late was a convenient excuse to avoid me. I'd missed him terribly, which only made me realize just how much more I would miss him when he was half a world away.

As I browned the sausage, onion, and garlic for the lasagna, I felt more optimistic than I had all week. Maybe tonight would be different. Jake and I would have dinner together, I'd help him pack, and perhaps I'd find the right moment of truth to say what I needed to say to him if I was going to keep him in my life.

When Jake arrived, I was in the kitchen, checking the lasagna. He came into the kitchen, and stood behind me, put his arms around my waist, and kissed the top of my head. I leaned back into him and enjoyed the feeling of him holding me. His arms tightened around me.

"Thank you for making dinner," he said. "This week has been exhausting—and I'm starving."

"Maybe you'd like to change into something comfortable?" I asked. "Dinner will be ready in a few minutes."

"I'm down for that." He released me and walked toward the bedroom.

By the time he returned, dressed in jeans and a charcoal gray T-shirt, I had the food on the table. I poured us each a glass of wine, and we sat down to eat. Jake ate his lasagna with relish, and then he polished off his salad. To my delight, he helped himself to a second serving of lasagna.

"I forgot to eat lunch today," he said between mouthfuls.

"You forgot to eat?"

He nodded. "It was that kind of day."

As he continued to eat, I sipped my wine and picked at my food. I didn't have much of an appetite.

I was all too aware that this was our last evening together for a long time—maybe even forever—and I caught myself examining every detail of him. His tanned, strong hands that had held me so many times. The small scar on his chin, which I knew was a souvenir from playing rugby in college. The way his hair sexily curled at the back of his neck, one of my favorite spots to kiss him.

In that moment, I realized that I was trying to memorize Jake, trying to fix his image in my mind's eye, trying to hold on to him in the only way I could. I didn't want this to be goodbye, but after the past week, I feared that it might be. In fact, I knew that it could be—and the thought of that made me sick at heart.

After he finished eating, Jake leaned back in his chair and looked at me.

"I'm sorry that we haven't had more time together this week," he said. "I knew it was going to be a rough week at the office, but I didn't expect it to be quite so crazy."

"I'd hoped for more time with you too, but I do understand about your work. We'll just have to make up for it tonight." I paused. "There's something I need to say to you. I've just been waiting for the right moment."

"OK..."

"Last weekend, when you told me about your new job, I was in a horrible place emotionally. You know why, so there's no need to go over that again. But since then, I've had time to reflect. I love you, Jake. I love you more than you know or could possibly realize. I want to be with you. And as soon as my passport arrives, I'm going to come to London—if that's what you still want."

He was silent for a moment before he spoke. "My feelings for you haven't changed. I hope you come to London. Believe me—I hope it with all my heart. But I refuse to let myself count on it. I hope you understand that I really need to protect myself right now. And I think you understand why."

∽

Later that night, Jake made slow, passionate love to me. He worshipped every inch of my body, and I was ravenous to see, touch, and taste every part of his. Compelled by a relentless hunger for each other, we drove each other to climax repeatedly, each time more powerful than the last, until finally collapsing against each other, and falling asleep, our exhausted bodies intertwined. The tenderness of our lovemaking had communicated everything that neither of us had been able to put into words.

Our love for each other was real. Our passion for each other was tangible. But Craig's badly timed reappearance had compromised Jake's belief in the strength of our relationship. I knew that Craig and I weren't right for each other, but clearly Jake didn't share my certainty.

He was afraid that I would break his heart, and I was worried that he would never allow himself to believe in us again. Could we ever get back to where we had been before Craig Manning reentered my life? After the way Jake had made love to me, I felt hopeful. Maybe, in time, we could recapture what we'd once had.

Or maybe we couldn't.

3

On Saturday evening, Jake and I took a cab to Terminal E of Logan Airport. His overnight flight on British Airways would put him in London the next morning. The London office of Barlow Financial had booked a suite for him at the Andaz London, conveniently located in the financial and historic center of the city, where he would stay until he found a suitable apartment.

Our cab pulled up beside the terminal, and we got out. Jake paid the driver and retrieved his luggage from the trunk. I helped him wheel his bags inside, and we moved toward the British Airways counter, navigating around clusters of travelers.

"We're in luck," Jake said. "Look, that kiosk is open." He pulled out his bankcard, swiped it through the touchscreen kiosk, and tapped through a series of screens. "I'm just going to check the suitcases."

The kiosk emitted a series of cranky digital noises, before abruptly spitting out a limp piece of paper. The ink looked dangerously damp.

"My boarding pass," Jake said, taking it gingerly by one corner. "Now we can check the suitcases."

A customer service representative approached, scanned Jake's boarding pass, tagged his suitcases, and took them away.

"There." Jake put his boarding pass in his briefcase, and glanced at his watch. "We have a little time before I need to go through security. How about a cup of coffee?"

I forced a smile and nodded. "Coffee would be perfect."

We walked across the terminal to an area with a half dozen shops and restaurants.

"On second thought," Jake said. "Maybe I'll have a vodka tonic instead. I'd like to sleep during the flight, and coffee's not going to help."

"I'll join you." I looked around us. "There's a bar over there."

We sat down at the bar and Jake ordered two vodka tonics with lime.

"It's odd, you know?" he said quietly. "I'm psyched about the job, and you know I've wanted to live in London for awhile. But now that it's actually happening, I can't quite believe it. It just doesn't feel real."

"That's understandable. It's a big change, right? New job, new city, new colleagues. It must be difficult to imagine."

"Maybe that's it. I really don't know. I just feel disoriented, I guess. I know I'm going to miss my family and friends. And then there's you. I'm really going to miss you, Juliana."

It felt as if he was saying goodbye to me.

Feeling myself tear up, I blinked furiously to keep the tears at bay. I was too proud to let myself cry, and I didn't want to burden Jake with my tears. It would only make this parting harder for both of us. I had to pull myself together and do my best to stay strong. I mustered the best smile I could manage, and looked at him.

"Don't think for a minute that you've seen the last of me, Jake Barlow. I sent in my passport application several days ago. And since I paid for expedited service, I'll have my passport within two weeks. I'm warning you, it's just a matter of time before I show up on your doorstep."

He gave me a half-hearted smile. "If it happens, I look forward to that moment." Then his expression turned serious. "But don't forget what I said before. I don't want you to come to London out of a misplaced sense of obligation or loyalty."

At that, I couldn't help but take offense. I'd gone to a great deal of trouble to make sure that my passport arrived quickly. Did he think that I wasn't serious about this?

I leaned toward him. "Here's what you need to know about me, Jake. If I wanted to be with Craig right now, I'd be with him. And I'd be clear with you about it. But that's not what I want. I'm here today because I want to be with you. If you don't know that by now, I don't know what to say to you. If you want me to come to London when I receive my passport, I will. I want our relationship to continue, but only if you do too. If you don't—don't you dare lead me on. If you have any reservations about me or about us, I need you to tell me now."

He looked surprised. "That's not at all what I meant."

"Isn't it? Because that's how you've been acting, and how I've been feeling. Craig made a move on *me* that night—I did nothing. I've told you that. I'm also here with you now, not with him. Don't overlook that. Why would I waste my time if I didn't want to be with you? Answer that for me. Do you think this is a game?"

He looked shocked by my sudden outburst, and he didn't answer.

"I didn't come here on some whim, Jake. I'm here because I want what we have to continue. For a week now, I've walked your tightrope, and I'm about to fall off of it. Either you want me to join you in London, or you don't. So why don't you do us both a favor and tell me if I'm wasting my time. Do you want me to come to London or not?"

"Of course, I want you to come."

"Then start acting like it."

"I want it more than anything. You know that."

"Actually, when you say things like 'if it happens,' I have to wonder if you even believe that I want to come. And I find that insulting."

"I apologize. We've had a difficult time of it lately."

"I'll repeat—I've done nothing. Craig kissed me, not the other way around. I've been nothing but honest with you. In body and spirit, I'm here with you now, and I'm trying to make this work. Are you paying attention to that? I need to know now if you're also making an effort, or if all of this is senseless. Neither of us is here to bullshit each other. I'm certainly not."

"Juliana, I'm sorry. I want you to come to London. I want to be with you."

"If you want that, then we need to move beyond what happened with Craig. If we can't get beyond it, there's no need for us to go any further."

"We can get beyond it—of course we can."

"I guess we'll see." I looked at my watch. "We should get going."

He motioned the bartender over and paid our check.

We got up from the bar and walked toward the security area. Cordoned into a maze-like queue, several hundred travelers shuffled through three parallel security lines, each leading to a conveyor belt that fed an X-ray machine. Among these machines, people padded around in stocking feet, placing purses, shoes, and assorted belongings in gray plastic bins. The conveyor belts feeding the machines whined and jerked, stopping and starting, as each bin's content was inspected.

When we reached the security area, Jake turned to me. "Come to London, Juliana."

"I plan to, unless I feel a shift between us over the next two weeks. I guess we'll need to wait and see if there is. I'm hoping there won't be, but I won't come, Jake, if I don't feel certain that you want me there."

"I'm sorry if I treated you poorly—if I doubted you. That was never my intent. I do want you there."

"Apology accepted. Now, you should probably get in line." I took him in my arms, and I could feel him tense up. I leaned in to kiss him, but he turned his head and my lips brushed his cheek. When I released him, I saw emotions on his face that I'd never seen there before—sadness and resignation. He looked at me, and I glimpsed the pain in his eyes. "Goodbye, Juliana."

This is over, I thought. "Text me once you've landed at Heathrow?"

"I'll text you." He turned and walked toward the security queue.

As I watched him move into the crowd of travellers, I waited. I expected him to turn around, look back at me, maybe wave—but he didn't look back. Not once. He just kept walking, steadfast in his resolve to put distance between us—or at least that was how I interpreted it. When he eventually disappeared from view, my eyes filled with tears that I no longer had the will to hold back.

Jake's refusal to look back had confirmed my worst fears. I'd pushed him too hard. He no longer believed in me. He no longer believed in us.

I crossed the terminal, went into the ladies room, and locked myself in a stall. Alone and unobserved, I finally could release the torrent of emotion that had been building inside me all week. My shoulders shook and tears flowed down my cheeks as I cried as quietly as possible.

Jake was gone. He was on his way to a new country, a new job, and a new life. Perhaps without me—but at least he knew where I stood. At least he knew that he couldn't treat me like that anymore when I had done nothing to provoke what happened that night with Craig. But still, I wanted Jake. As for him wanting me right now? After that little exchange? That was in question. By turning his cheek away when I tried to kiss him, and by not looking back when he walked away from me, he had just confirmed my worst fears.

Today he was making a fresh start, and he wasn't looking back.

4

I spent the rest of the weekend alone in the Davis Square apartment that I shared with Duncan. He had gone to Maine for the weekend with Connor—and Barkley, Jake's dog, who was staying with Connor until the necessary paperwork could be processed for Jake to bring him to London.

At work on Monday morning, I'd been at my desk for about an hour when I heard a light knock on the open door. I looked up and saw that it was Lara.

"Mind if I come in?" she asked. "We need to talk."

I nodded. "Sure. Have a seat."

She sat down across from me. "I'm here to apologize—for what I said to you that night. I feel terrible about my behavior."

I looked at her. "Why are you apologizing now? Isn't it a little late for this?"

"You have every right to hate me."

"I don't hate you, Lara. After what I've been through in the past week, I don't have the energy. But that night, when I told you what happened, why didn't you believe me? We've been so close. Why didn't you trust me?"

"It wasn't about you—it was about me. I feel responsible for getting you and Jake together. I thought the two of you would be perfect for each other. I shouldn't have pushed, but I thought I knew what I was doing, and now two people I love have been hurt. That night, when I saw it all going wrong, I reacted without thinking, and I projected all my anger onto you." She sighed. "What I said was unforgivable, and there's probably no way I can ever make it up to you, but I have to at least try."

I sat in silence for a moment, and then came to a decision. With the exception of that one night, Lara had been a wonderful friend to me.

"I accept your apology."

"You do?"

"I'm not about to throw away our friendship over one crazy night. You've admitted that you messed up and you've apologized. As for making it up to me, I'd just like to get back to being friends and hanging out together."

"That's more than I deserve," Lara said. "I have to be honest, though. I can't help hoping that you and Jake work things out. The two of you are so perfect for each other."

I looked her in the eye. "Jake and I didn't exactly have the best farewell at the airport. But I love him, and as soon as my passport arrives, I plan to be on the next available plane to London, and we'll see what happens there. Your support means a lot to me, but after what happened, we need to get one thing clear."

"What's that?"

"Our friendship needs to stay separate from my relationship with your brother. Please don't try to fight Jake's battles, or mine. Jake and I are both adults, and you have to trust us both to treat each other fairly—and take care of ourselves."

"No more interference," Lara said. "I swear."

"Then we're good." I smiled at her.

She got up, walked around my desk, and hugged me. "You have no idea how much I've missed you. I feel like such an idiot."

I hugged her back. "I've missed you, too."
"Want to go out for drinks after work?"
"Is that even a question?"

5

After work, Lara and I walked several blocks to Newbury Street. It was a perfect evening to enjoy a drink and people-watch at one of the street's sidewalk cafés.

At first glance, Sonsie's outdoor seating appeared full, but just as we arrived, a table opened up, and we promptly grabbed it.

"Score!" Lara said. She waved a waiter over and ordered two martinis. "I'm on a vodka-and-salad diet."

"Sounds like a book title," I said. "*The Vodka and Salad Diet*. Now there's a book I'd read with interest."

"Have you read anything good lately? I'm in the mood for a good drama. Clearly, I'm suffering from a lack of drama in my own life."

"Count your blessings, girl. Too much drama is even worse."

"Speaking of drama, I'd love to hear the details of how you shoved that bitch Alessandra into a toilet."

I told Lara the story.

She shook her head. "That woman is deranged."

"Bonkers."

"Unhinged."

"Batshit."

Just then, our martinis arrived.

I lifted my glass and toasted "To visions of Alessandra dripping dirty toilet water." After we both sipped, I said, "You know, whenever I remember Alessandra in that toilet, clutching her dress and screeching like a banshee, I just want to laugh."

"I hope her dress has permanent shit stains," Lara said.

"I hope her soul does, too."

"Soul? Why credit her with something she obviously lacks? The bitch screams fembot. Just consider her big fake tits."

"You think she had a boob job?"

"Please. Even the most advanced push-up bra can only do so much. Nothing but a cheap boob job could produce the unnatural geometry that was showcased on her chest. But what really made me think fembot was her dead eyes. They make her look like a RealDoll."

"RealDoll? What's a RealDoll?"

"The things you need to learn…"

"Come on—what is it?"

"A highly realistic, life-size sex doll with ultra-flexible joints."

"How do you even know about that?"

"Surfing the web at midnight with a martini can be dangerous to your health. You never know what you might find."

We giggled until I needed to wipe tears from my eyes.

"God, I needed that," I said. "This week hasn't exactly been filled with humor. And I really need to get my shit together."

"Regarding Jake?"

"Yes. I need to catch up with him. He texted me when his flight landed yesterday, just as he promised me he would, but I haven't heard from him since. I told you that we had an awkward parting at the airport. I'm going to get up early tomorrow and try to Skype him."

"What about Craig?" Lara asked.

"I need to talk to Craig, too. The sooner, the better. I have to make it clear that I'm in love with Jake. I hope that he'll take it well, but after the past week, I'm not feeling very lucky."

"My crystal ball says that your luck's about to change for the better."

"I hope your crystal ball is more reliable than my Magic 8 Ball. That dumb hunk of plastic always tells me the same thing."

"What does it tell you?"

"*Ask again later*, or *Cannot predict now*."

"Well, that's just plain cruel."

"Lately, I've had thoughts of hurling it into the Charles River."

"You can't throw anything that toxic into the river. It would only float into the ocean and poison a pod of dolphins. Besides, you'd be destroying the hard work of some six-year-old Chinese kid."

"Wait a minute. Doesn't the state of Massachusetts recommend tetanus shots for anyone who falls into the Charles? That river would probably poison the Ball."

"And perhaps improve its predictive powers," Lara said.

"Maybe a little more alcohol poisoning would improve ours."

"Second martini?"

"Definitely."

6

The next morning, my alarm clock woke me at 6 a.m. I got up, made coffee, and drank a cup before I showered and dressed. By the time I poured myself a second cup, it was nearly 7 a.m.

I sat down at the desk in my bedroom, set my coffee down, and opened my laptop. The previous night, I had emailed Jake that I would try to Skype him at 7 a.m. my time, which was noon for him. I checked my email, saw that I had a reply from him, and crossed my fingers. Hopefully he would confirm our Skype time. I opened the email.

Hi Juliana,

I wish I could Skype today, but I can't. Work is impossible, and I have to look at several apartments later today. Let's catch up sometime over the weekend, OK?

xo Jake

Disappointed, I leaned back in my chair and sipped my coffee. Was

Jake avoiding me? After the way we left things at the airport, he certainly could be. Aside from sending a single text when he first arrived in London, he hadn't made any effort to communicate. Still, I wanted Jake Barlow, and I wasn't about to give up easily. I replied to his email.

Hi Jake,

Sorry to hear that we can't Skype this time, but I wish you good luck in finding the perfect apartment. Lara and I are back on solid ground. We went out for martinis at Sonsie last night, and ripped through our share of them.

Let me know when would be a good time to Skype this weekend. I can't wait to see your face and hear your voice. I miss you.

Love,

Juliana

I read over my reply, and then clicked the Send button. At that moment, a thought occurred to me. I needed to talk with Craig. I still had half an hour before I needed to leave for work. Better get that ball rolling. I typed a second email.

Hi Craig,

I apologize for not getting in touch sooner. It's been a crazy week.

The last time we met, our conversation was interrupted, and there wasn't time to say all that we needed to say to each other. I'd like to get together so that we can talk without interruption, which might give us both some closure.

I'm free in the evenings, and I'll be around this weekend as well. Perhaps we could meet for dinner or a cup of coffee?

Best wishes,

Juliana

I hit the Send button and felt a sense of relief. I'd taken the first step toward reconciliation with Jake, and after a long week of feeling cornered and insecure, it felt great to take action.

Perhaps Jake had lost faith. Maybe he didn't think that our relationship could be saved. But I believed that we were meant to be together, and I was ready to be strong enough for both of us.

What I couldn't know then was just how much my strength was about to be tested.

7

Throughout the day, I waited impatiently to hear from Jake—and Craig. Unfortunately for me, the hours passed without any response from either. At noon, I left work to pick up takeout salad for Lara and me. We ate lunch together in Lara's office, and when we finished, I sprinted back to my office and checked my personal email again. Nothing.

Finally, around 4 p.m., I received an email from Craig.

Hi Juliana,

No apologies necessary. I'd meant to contact you before now, but I've been in NYC on business for the past week, and it doesn't look like I'll be able to leave for another day or two.

I'll be in touch as soon as I get back to Boston. Looking forward to seeing you.

Love,
Craig

I read Craig's email a second time and tried to be optimistic. Today was Tuesday. A day or two—surely that meant that he'd be back in Boston by Thursday at the latest.

But by noon on Thursday, I hadn't heard from Craig. I hadn't heard from Jake, either, which especially concerned me because of what had happened between us at the airport. When Lara and I left the office for lunch, I vented my frustration.

"Lara, I take back my advice to you. I couldn't have been more wrong."

"What advice?"

"I advised you to date businessmen. As it turns out, I couldn't have been more wrong."

"Why? If I dated a businessman, at least we'd have one interest in common."

"Unfortunately, the biz in business means *busy*. As in perpetually busy. As in too busy to reply to email, or Skype, or whatever."

"In that case, who should I date? Maybe a hunky construction worker? I can see him now—shirtless, sunburnt, all ripped muscles and torn jeans, posed against a steel girder."

I shook my head. "You're asking the wrong woman. I only wish that I understood men. The fact is, I don't. They're an alien species. The mating rituals of insects make more sense."

"So you're frustrated with Jake? Or Craig?"

"Both. Jake is supposed to let me know when we can Skype this weekend. Craig needs to give me an update on when he'll be back in Boston."

"How long have they kept you waiting?"

"Since Tuesday."

"That's a drag."

"Tell me about it."

"What's going on?"

"Jake needs to find an apartment, and he's slammed with work at his new job. Plus I think he doesn't want to talk to me for reasons you already know."

"The scene at the airport?"

"That's right."

"Don't worry about Jake," Lara said. "He'll come around as soon as he settles in and you get your ass to London."

"I hope you're right."

"What about Craig? What's happening with him?"

"He's in New York for work. Who knows when he'll return? He said he'd get back to me in a day or two. But it's been two days, and I still haven't heard from him. With my luck, he's probably stuck in New York through the weekend and into next week."

"I have an idea."

"Tell me."

"It's beyond amazing," Lara said. "I can't believe I didn't think of it before."

"What is it?"

"We could kill two birds with one stone. Maybe even three."

"Stop being mysterious. The last thing I need now is more suspense."

"I'll give you a hint. Three words. The first is *shopping*."

"And the other two?"

"New York."

"Go on...."

"If Craig is still in New York this weekend, we can take the train there early Saturday morning, shop until we drop, and then spend the night. Surely Craig can manage to meet you for dinner or a drink Saturday night. Or brunch Sunday morning. Even billionaires have to eat. After you see him, we could catch a train back to Boston anytime Sunday afternoon or evening."

"You're a genius."

"No, just a girl in need of a shopping fix."

"What kind of shopping fix?"

"The kind that only Fifth Avenue can provide. If I'm going to reenter the dating scene, I need Bergdorf's. And then there's you. You need a new wardrobe for London."

"From Bergdorf's? It would take all of ten minutes to blow my entire annual income."

"We won't limit ourselves to Bergdorf's. We'll hit Saks hard too—the third floor has amazing sales. And anywhere else you want to go."

"I'm sold. Let's do it."

8

The remainder of the week crawled by without any word from Jake. On Friday morning, Craig emailed me that he would indeed be in New York through the weekend. Apparently his lawsuit with Syngenomics had heated up, and he needed to stay close to his New York-based legal team. We arranged to meet for drinks Saturday evening at the Waldorf, and Lara and I finalized our New York plans.

On Saturday, we took an early morning train from Boston to New York. When we arrived at Penn Station, we disembarked, wheeled our luggage through the busy concourse, and took the escalator up to the street level.

We took a taxi to the Pierre Hotel, where Lara had booked a suite for us. As our driver skillfully navigated the New York traffic, Lara turned to me.

"You're going to love the Pierre," she said. "It's very old New York. The lobby is classic—all black and white marble—and the rooms have amazing views of Central Park. Then there's the rotunda, which has a gorgeous curved staircase and these crazy trompe-l'oeil murals."

Our cab pulled up at the curbside in front of the hotel, and we got out. A white-gloved doorman greeted us and gestured to a bellman to take our bags.

After checking in and reaching our suite, I pulled out my phone and checked my email.

"Anything from Jake?" Lara asked.

"Yes. Finally." I opened the email and scanned it. "He wants me to Skype him Monday morning, 7 a.m. our time. He's busy all weekend—apartment hunting."

"And you're meeting Craig for drinks tonight."

"Yes—at ten o'clock, at the Waldorf."

"Let's get a quick lunch. Something low-cal. Maybe leafy greens. Or frozen yogurt. We have shopping to do, and I can't afford the risk of bloating myself with real food."

"Perfect. But after we finish shopping, let's ditch our low-cal ambitions in favor of the pleasures of fine dining. New York is a restaurant mecca, after all."

"Post-shopping? Put your fears to rest. I'm way ahead of you. Didn't I tell you? I've reserved a table for us tonight at La Masseria. Bring on the calories."

Ninety minutes, a spinach salad, and a cab ride later, we arrived at Saks. When we walked through the doors, we stepped into a seemingly endless array of cosmetic counters, but we dodged around the chaos of noise and activity that surrounded them to a massive bank of brass elevators at the rear of the space. We took one to the third floor, where Lara threw herself into shopping with vigor. She had already made one trip to the fitting room—and was ready for a second round—when I spotted the cocktail dress of my dreams.

Beaded in wide bands of silver and champagne, separated by narrower strips of glittering black, the dress combined a scoop neckline and a clean, fitted silhouette with the retro glam that I adored. I crossed my fingers for luck, and then looked for the price tag. When I found it, I couldn't believe my luck.

"Lara!" I said. "Just look at this dress. It's perfect, and it's under three hundred dollars."

Lara looked it over. "It's gorgeous, and it's going to look fabulous on you. Get your ass to the fitting room and try it on."

We headed for the fitting rooms, took stalls next to each other, and began to try on our potential purchases. After a minute, I heard a giggle through the wall.

"Lara?" I said.

"This blouse does terrible things to my neck. I know I have a long neck, but seriously? I look like a fucking giraffe in a blonde wig."

"Your neck is *not* too long. What about the Armani suit?" I asked.

"Give me a minute. I need to put on a different blouse, take a deep breath, and banish that giraffe image from my head."

I managed the contortions required to zip my dress in the back, and stepped out of my stall. A moment later, Lara emerged, looking svelte in a beautifully cut near-black Armani suit. She quickly appraised my dress.

"Buy it," she said. "It looks great, and it's totally you."

"I love your suit."

Lara turned in front of the mirrors. "I think I'll be very happy with this suit—once I find the perfect shoes to go with it. You're also going to need shoes, of course. You can't wear just any shoes with *that* dress. And earrings—I see citrine, or yellow sapphire. And a bracelet. Something chunky and retro."

After changing into our own clothes and leaving the dressing room, we headed for the jewelry section. Lara marched me past counter after counter, her eyes darting from one display to the next.

Suddenly, she stopped.

"Look at those crystal teardrop earrings," she said. "They're lovely, and they'll look amazing with your dress."

I looked at the price tag and suppressed a gasp. The earrings cost more than the dress. Then, at the next counter, I spotted a display of cuff bracelets that looked promising. One of them was pale gold and irregularly shaped, with a scattering of Swarovski crystals. It was ultra modern, but it would work well with my new dress.

"What do you think of this bracelet?" I said.

"Not at all what I'd imagined, but it's fabulous."

I did the mental math. The bracelet wasn't expensive. I could splurge on the earrings Lara had found, and still have enough cash left for a pair of shoes.

"I'll get this bracelet and the earrings that you found. Shoes next?"

Lara's face brightened. "I was beginning to think you'd never ask."

9

After selecting Prada ankle-strap sandals for me and Jimmy Choo pumps for Lara, we paid for our purchases, left Saks, and proceeded toward Bergdorf's, where Lara was certain she would find the ideal dress.

"Bergdorf's is the answer," she said. "They never fail me. But we need to make a stop at Prada on the way. My inner shoe whore is in top form."

After Lara chose a second pair of shoes at Prada, we walked to Bergdorf's. When we entered, a polished, middle-aged sales associate greeted us. She introduced herself as Dahlia, and sussed out Lara's taste within minutes.

"I have just the dress for you," she said. "We only got it in last week."

When she showed us the dress, my jaw nearly dropped. It was stunning. Lines of tiny beads traced ray patterns that spread and curved over the nude-colored fabric beneath. An illusion neckline created the effect of a wide collar necklace.

"It's exquisite," Lara said. Her fingers traced a line of beads, and her voice took on a tone of reverence. "This might be the one."

We headed for the fitting room, and Lara went into one of the changing rooms. Arranged in a circle around the perimeter of the fitting room, the changing room doors were mirrored. A low, round pedestal sat in the center of the floor. I stepped onto the pedestal, and realized that I could see myself from a myriad of angles reflected in the mirrored doors. I stepped down and looked around the space for a few moments.

Lara came out of her changing room and stepped onto the pedestal. She twirled around.

"What do you think?"

"It's fabulous. If you added a tiara, you'd look like an Art Deco princess."

Lara considered her reflection and struck a pose. "I feel like I need a cigarette holder. Too bad I don't smoke."

"You could always vape," I said.

"Vamp? I'm already a vamp. Just look at me in this dress."

"I said 'vape'."

"What's a vape?"

"An electronic cigarette. Supposedly, you get all the nicotine but none of the lung cancer."

"The last thing I need is nicotine. On top of all the coffee I drink? I'd be so tightly wound, I'd probably implode from the excess energy."

She went back into the changing room. A few minutes later, she reemerged with her new dress over one arm.

Just then, one of the changing room doors opened, and I was surprised—and dismayed—to recognize Alessandra d'Acosta. She wore a red halter-top evening gown that exposed much of her sides and back, and gold-sequined stiletto heels.

"What are *you* doing here?" she said haughtily.

"Ignoring the obvious, Alessandra?" I said. "Let me map it out for you. We're in a shop and we're—wait for it—shopping. Does that compute?"

Lara turned toward Alessandra and gave her a hard look.

"Let's go," she said to me. "Apparently, Bergdorf's is slipping. Someone's forgotten to take out the trash."

Alessandra took a step closer to us.

"You desperate, stupid girl," she said, trying to stare me down. "You chased Craig to New York, didn't you?"

"Your B-movie mind would craft such a scenario," I said. "But chasing a man is so much more your style. Of course, when chasing doesn't work, you just move on to blackmail. But I guess that's just the sort of person you are, Alessandra."

Alessandra took another step forward. "You ignorant cunt. Stay away from Craig Manning, or you'll regret it."

"You stay away from me, you crazy bitch," I said. "Did ending up in a toilet teach you nothing?"

Lara stepped between Alessandra and me. "While we're here, Alessandra, I feel I should tell you that you should rethink showing so much side boob. Fresh surgical scars *and* stretch marks? I smell a whiff of desperation around you. It clouds the air like the stink of your rotten breath. But I have to ask—where *did* you get the girls amped up? Mexico? The Ukraine? Boobs-R-Us?"

"Who the fuck are you?" Alessandra hissed. She tried to move past Lara, but Lara blocked her.

"I hear that Boobs-R-Us can get you in and out in ten minutes," Lara said cheerfully. "And by the looks of it, if they're the ones who worked on you, they beat their best time when they did yours."

Alessandra's face distorted into a sneer. "I don't know who you are, girl, but I already know this—you're just as stupid as your imbecile friend over there, who runs to New York to chase a man who will never love her."

"What do you know about love?" I said. "You don't care about Craig. If you did, you never would have made those videos without his knowledge, let alone schemed to blackmail him. No, you misguided piece of washed-up Eurotrash with a flailing B-movie career—you don't give a damn about anyone but yourself."

"You don't know me," Alessandra hissed.

"And I don't want to. Come on, Lara. Let's get out of here."

"Watch your back, ghetto girl," Alessandra said. Her voice turned taunting. "Little girls like you have no business playing in the big leagues. You'd better watch yourself. Because if you don't, you just might get hurt."

"No one threatens my friend," Lara said. "You want to see why? Here's why." And with that, she pulled back her hand and slapped Alessandra across the face. The blow was hard enough to make Alessandra stagger back, with one hand pressed against her cheek.

"Help!" she screeched. "I'm being attacked!"

"Back the fuck off," Lara said. "If you know what's good for you, stay away from Juliana. And stay the hell away from me."

Lara gave Alessandra a shove, and as she went down, her heel caught the skirt of her floor-length evening gown, tearing it badly. She hit the floor so hard, her breasts jolted out of the sides of her dress.

"Oh my God," Lara said. "I know a botched boob job when I see one, but I've never seen anything like this. Look! Her nipples point the wrong way. They're like googly eyes."

I whipped out my phone and took a photo. I then held up the screen in front of Alessandra's face. "See that? Here's a piece of blackmail for you, bitch. If you ever bother me—or Lara—again, this picture of your cross-eyed boob job will be all over the Internet faster than you can pay a street bum to take a piss on you."

We left the fitting room and headed toward the cash register. As we left, Alessandra continued to scream at the top of her lungs. "Police!" she bellowed. "Someone get the fuck in here *now*! I'm a celebrity, I've been attacked, and I demand the police!"

We were nearly at the cash register when I turned back and saw two female sales associates run into the fitting room. Three men who looked like security followed close behind, and positioned themselves just outside the entrance.

"Security just arrived," I said quietly.

Lara looked over her shoulder. "We'd better get out of here, before that lunatic gets Bergdorf's to send those security guys after us. The dress can wait." She quickly hung her dress on the nearest rack, and we headed for the doors.

We exited Bergdorf's, took a left into the teeming crowds on Fifth

Avenue, and disappeared within them. I glanced back to see if anyone had followed us. Fortunately, it didn't appear that anyone had. We continued to walk up Fifth toward our hotel.

"Now that we're out of there, thank you," I said. "That was one hell of a slap."

"It was, wasn't it? I opened my palm, pulled my arm all the way back, and gave Alessandra what she so richly deserved. Of course, now I wish that I'd ripped the rest of her torn-up dress off her body. Who knows what additional horrors we might have discovered? Ass implants? Evidence of liposuction?"

"My one regret is that we had to leave your dress behind."

"That's easy enough to fix. As soon as we get back to the Pierre, I'll call Bergdorf's, buy the dress over the phone, and have it delivered to our hotel room."

"That's a great idea. Maybe it will arrive in time for you to wear it tonight."

"Believe me, I'm counting on it."

10

Two hours later, we were ready for a night on the town. Lara's dress had been delivered in the nick of time, and she looked stunning.

"That dress is perfect on you," I said. "Prepare yourself—guys will be hitting on you like crazy tonight."

"Highly unlikely," Lara said. "Don't forget, I'm taller than most men, and in heels? I tower over them. I can scare away most men just by standing up."

"We're in New York, remember? New York has more of everything. Including tall men."

We left our suite, took the elevator to the lobby, and exited the hotel. The doorman hailed a cab for us, we got in, and Lara gave the driver our destination.

"Please take us to La Masseria on West Forty-Eighth Street."

A short cab ride later, we arrived at the restaurant. When we entered, we found it packed with people and abuzz with activity. Wooden beams, stone arches, and stuccoed walls gave the space a rustic Italian ambience, and the scent of freshly baked bread wafted through the air.

After we were seated at our table, Lara ordered a bottle of red wine, and then began scanning the menu.

"Tonight is a night of sin," she said. "We deserve it. I exposed the ugly truth about Alessandra, and you snapped a photo that proves it."

"When you sin, sin big. I'm thinking fried calamari to start, followed by ravioli."

"Good choice. All the pasta served here is freshly made onsite. I'm thinking carpaccio, followed by tagliatelle alla Bolognese."

"Followed by dessert."

"Definitely dessert. The tiramisu will make you think you've died and gone to heaven."

"Hell's probably a better fit right now," I said. "I did kind of blackmail Alessandra with that photo."

"I'd love to post that photo on the Internet. Get out your phone. I need to see it again."

I pulled out my phone and brought up the photo. If anything, it was worse than I'd remembered. "It's tempting. Part of me does want to post it." I handed the phone to Lara.

Lara studied the photo for a moment, and then handed the phone back to me. "So why don't you? This is a once-in-a-lifetime opportunity. Just title the post 'celebrity googly-eyed boob job.' It'll go viral in seconds."

"Alessandra's insane, and this photo is my one piece of leverage. I really just want her to stay away from me. I hate that woman, but I don't want to be responsible for destroying anyone's career—even hers."

"Her plastic surgery scars were fresh," Lara said. "That boob job is recent, and I bet she's already booked a second round of surgery to try to repair the damage. There are limits to what body makeup can conceal, and there's no way Alessandra could pull off a topless scene right now—unless the movie was set in a circus, and she was cast as one of the sideshow freaks."

Just then, our wine arrived, and as our waiter filled our glasses, my phone dinged. It was a text from Craig.

Unfortunately, I won't be able to make it tonight. I'm in conference now regarding the Syngenomics lawsuit. How about brunch tomorrow at the Waldorf? 1 p.m.?

As I stared at the screen, I heard Lara order her meal. When she completed her order, I gave the waiter mine, and then looked at Lara after he left.

"Craig just canceled."

"What? You came all the way to New York to see him, and he cancels just like that?"

"He wants me to meet him tomorrow for brunch instead, which is fine. I just hope that he doesn't cancel again."

"I don't get it, Juliana. How can he be stuck at work at ten o'clock on Saturday night? It's his company, and he's the one in charge. He's the one who tells everyone else what to do and when to do it."

I sighed. "This is Craig's life. And this is what my life would be like, if I'd agreed to get back together with him."

"What do you mean?"

"Phone calls that interrupt every conversation. Last-minute cancelations. Always taking second place. Here's the reality, Lara. Craig's amazing. He's a wonderful person, and a real, honest-to-God business genius. He built a multi-billion dollar business from the ground up, and that business is his baby. When I was in love with him, I didn't want to see the truth, though it was always there to be seen."

"What truth?" Lara said.

"The truth that Craig already is married—to his business. Whoever marries him will take the only position that's available—that of his mistress."

Lara nodded. "I understand. It's one thing to take a back seat to your partner's work sometimes—but all the time? I don't think I could take that."

"I know I couldn't."

"So will you meet him tomorrow for brunch?"

"Of course I will—I want this over with. There's no point in getting angry with him for canceling tonight—it's just who he is. Besides, I need to tell him face-to-face that it's over between us, completely and finally. I'll text him back right now."

While I texted Craig to confirm brunch at the Waldorf, our appetizers arrived. I sent the text and put my phone away.

"Let's forget about men for tonight," I said. "It's a beautiful summer evening, and we're in New York. Let the wine flow. Bring on the tiramisu. And after dinner, let's take a walk—in the general direction of our hotel."

"We could stop for a martini along the way," Lara said. "I know just the place."

11

After we left La Masseria, Lara and I walked east on Forty-Eighth Street, and then up Fifth Avenue in the direction of our hotel. It was a balmy summer night, and the streets were busy. Clusters of people strolled along the sidewalks, and taxis dodged and zipped through the evening traffic.

"So, about that martini," I said.

"Are you up for one?"

"Need you ask? The night is young."

"Perfect. Let's go to the King Cole Bar at the St. Regis. There's a huge Art Nouveau mural behind the bar that you'll appreciate. And the bartenders make a perfect martini."

When we reached the entrance of the St. Regis, we walked up a half-dozen red-carpeted steps and passed through ornate brass doors into the lobby, which was dominated by marble and brass details that looked original. The bar was just off the lobby. Chandeliers hung from the high ceiling, which was painted to resemble blue sky and puffy white clouds, and edged with gilded molding. Brightly colored and flawlessly lit, the mural that Lara had mentioned ran the full length of the wall behind the bar.

I looked down the rectangular space in search of an open table. "Looks like all the tables are occupied."

"I see a few open seats at the bar," Lara said. We walked to the bar and sat down.

"I think we just got lucky," I said.

"We did. It's a gorgeous summer night, and all of New York has come out to enjoy it."

We ordered two martinis, and I looked around. "This place is amazing."

"It's a slice of New York history. Supposedly, the Bloody Mary cocktail was invented at this very bar."

"Thank God someone invented it—I may need one tomorrow morning."

Our martinis arrived, and we each took one.

"To the best New York weekend ever," Lara said. "I'm with my best friend in my favorite city—what could be better?"

As Lara brought her full glass to her lips, a man walking past us bumped against her leg. The impact caused her drink to spill down the front of her new dress.

"I'm so sorry," he said to Lara. "I hope my clumsiness hasn't ruined your dress. At least let me buy you a fresh drink."

Their eyes met, and I saw Lara's face flush. And why not? He was devastatingly good-looking. "It's really not a big deal," she said, dabbing her dress with a napkin. "It's just vodka—it won't stain."

"I'm glad to hear that. But please allow me to replace your drink. What would you like?"

"A Belvedere martini with a twist would be perfect. Thank you."

He headed for the other end of the bar to order the drink, and I nudged Lara.

"He's gorgeous, Lara. Did you see how tall he is? And he's built like a tank. Six feet and four or five inches of solid muscle—and no wedding ring."

"He's just being polite. I'm the one who should buy *him* a drink. It's my fault that he bumped into me, after all. When I sat down and crossed my legs, I knew my big feet were sticking out too far past my chair. I just thought it wouldn't matter here at the end of the bar."

"He's scorching hot, and he totally checked you out."

"Probably evaluating the damage he mistakenly thought that he had caused."

"No, that was the look of a man who liked what he saw."

Just then, he returned with two martinis. His dark gray suit was perfectly fitted, and his thick, wavy hair was swept back from his strong, clean-cut features. In contrast to his dark hair and olive skin, his eyes were a striking gray-blue color, and he radiated self-confidence.

"Here," he said to Lara, handing her one of the martinis. He looked at both of us. "Mind if I take the chair next to you? I promise not to knock over any more drinks."

"Of course we don't mind," I said. "Please join us." He took the open seat on the other side of Lara. "By the way, I'm Juliana West, and this is my friend Lara Barlow."

"Cole Hunter," he said. "I'm actually from Boston, but I had business in New York this past week and decided to stay in town through the weekend."

"You're kidding! Now there's a coincidence," I said. "We're from Boston as well."

"So what brings the two of you to New York? Business or pleasure?" Cole asked.

"Shopping," Lara said. "And if you do it right, that sort of business *is* pleasure."

He smiled at her. "I did a little shopping earlier today myself. If you saw a tall guy walking down Fifth with a stuffed tiger sticking out of an F.A.O. Schwartz shopping bag, it was me."

"Shopping for your kid's birthday?" Lara asked. I knew exactly what she was digging for—was Cole married but allergic to jewelry? Or recently divorced, and on the rebound?

"My nephew. My sister's kid. He'll be four years old next week, and right now, he's all about dangerous carnivores."

I decided on the spot that Cole was one of the good guys. Any man with enough heart to carry a stuffed animal down Fifth Avenue—and all the way back to Boston—was probably a decent human being.

"Excuse me," I said to Lara and Cole. "I need to go to the ladies' room."

Lara gave her 'I'll-deal-with-you-later' look. I smiled at her, turned away, and headed for the ladies' room. With me out of the picture, the two of them would just have to talk to each other.

After fifteen minutes had passed, I returned to the bar, and when I reentered, I was delighted to see Lara throwing back her head, laughing, apparently at something Cole had just said. It appeared that they'd hit it off. They looked good together, and their rapport seemed natural. I wished that I could leave them alone for the rest of the evening, but since that wasn't happening, I returned to my seat at the bar. Lara gave me a radiant smile, and I knew I'd been forgiven for leaving her alone with Cole.

"You're not going to believe this," she said. "Jake and Cole are practically next-door neighbors. Cole lives in the Back Bay, on Beacon Street."

"Small world, right?" Cole said. "And my offices are just a few blocks from yours. You're in the Prudential, and I'm on Newbury Street."

"You lucky man!" I said. "A ten-minute walk between home and work? Now that's the perfect commute."

"Cole has his own public relations firm," Lara said. "Cole Hunter Communications."

"I started the company a few years ago," Cole said. I heard the pride in his voice, which I thought was sweet. Launching your own company was no minor feat. "We're small, but growing fast."

"What's your niche?" I asked.

"We do a lot of work with restaurants and hotels," he said. "Launches, promotional events, social media campaigns, et cetera."

As the evening went on, the connections continued to add up. Lara and Cole were both runners. They both loved sushi. And the incendiary looks they exchanged left little doubt of their mutual attraction.

When closing time arrived, Lara reluctantly got up from her seat at the bar.

"Time to call it a night," she said. "We should probably leave before the bartenders kick us out."

"Thank you both for a great evening," Cole said. "Any chance that you're free for brunch tomorrow? I'm staying here at the St. Regis, and the brunch here is excellent."

Perfect, I thought. "I have brunch plans with a friend, but Lara might be free."

"So, how about it?" he said to her. "Meet me for brunch tomorrow? It doesn't have to be here. We could go anywhere. It's New York, after all."

"I'd love to have brunch—and here is fine. Does noon work for you?" Her face glowed, but she managed to keep her voice steady. She was playing it cool, at least as cool as it could be between a man and a woman who clearly wanted to tear each other's clothes off.

"It's a date," he said. "I'll meet you in the lobby tomorrow at noon." He shot her a mischievous look. "I have to say that right now, I'm kind of glad that I spilled your martini."

"So am I," Lara said.

12

After our taxi accelerated away from the curb, Lara unleashed her excitement.

"A date! An honest-to-God date. Although I'm not sure if I can manage to eat while he's looking at me with those gorgeous gray eyes. I'll probably choke on a shrimp or something."

"Cole *is* yummy," I said. "And he seems perfect for you—tall, handsome, and confident. Not to mention ambitious. Did you see the look on his face when he talked about his work?"

Our cab reached the Pierre, and I paid the driver. We got out, walked into the hotel, and took the elevator to our suite. When we went inside, Lara threw her purse on a chair, removed her heels, and flopped on the couch.

"I have to watch myself," she said. Her expression was dreamy. "Cole seems too good to be true."

I took off my shoes and sat down next to her.

"Don't worry. He'll probably reveal a minor flaw or two over brunch that will ease your mind."

"Minor flaw? Like what?"

I shrugged. "Maybe he prefers his steak well-done instead of rare."

"Maybe he wears argyle socks," Lara giggled.

"Maybe he's afflicted with dandruff."

"Well, there are medicinal shampoos for that. Maybe he has goat breath in the morning."

"Who doesn't?"

"I don't," Lara said. "At least I don't think I do."

"Don't kid yourself. No one's immune."

"Maybe he wears tighty whities," Lara said.

"Definitely not tighty whities. Trust me, Cole's a boxers man."

"Where is this conversation going…?"

"Where do you think it's going?"

"I did *not* check out his package, if that's what you're asking."

"You should have, darling. What a missed opportunity. Quelle dommage."

Lara's eyes narrowed. "You went there?"

"Of course I did."

"Tell me what you saw."

"I will if you tell me how you managed to avoid seeing the obvious."

"Are you saying that he's hung?"

"Like Catherine of Russia's horse."

"You're evil."

"I just have a wandering, curious mind."

"I can't let myself get too excited. I've been disappointed too many times."

"Excuse me? Romantic Disappointment was my middle name—until I met Jake. Cole seems like a great guy. Maybe your luck's about to change."

13

At half past twelve the next day, I took a taxi to the Waldorf to meet Craig for brunch. Lara had left an hour earlier for the St. Regis and her date with Cole.

When my cab pulled next to the Waldorf, I paid the driver, got out, and closed the cab door. I turned and looked up at the imposing gray stone façade, and then glanced down at my watch. I was ten minutes early. I decided to go inside and find somewhere to sit down in the lobby, as my feet were still sore from all the walking Lara and I had done yesterday.

I entered through the heavy brass doors and went up the marble stairs to the second-floor lobby. Square, fluted columns surrounded the center of the space, where a large chandelier hung, sparkling with warm light. Beyond the columns, around the perimeter of the space, clusters of chairs were arranged around small tables. I walked to a chair and sat down, grateful to relieve my aching feet.

When one o'clock arrived with no sign of Craig, it occurred to me that perhaps we'd missed each other. Maybe he was already in the restaurant, and waiting for me there. I got up from my chair, picked up my purse, and crossed the lobby to the restaurant's entrance.

But when I looked around the space, Craig was nowhere to be seen.

Just then, my phone dinged. I pulled it from my purse. Sure enough, it was a text from Craig.

Sorry I'm running a little late, see you around 1:20.

I stuffed the phone back into my purse. Last-minute delays weren't unusual for Craig, and I felt relieved that he hadn't canceled.

"Table for one?" I looked up and saw the maître d'.

"No, table for two. My friend will arrive in twenty minutes."

The maître d' led me to a table and pulled out a chair for me. I sat down, and a waiter came over immediately. He carried a tray with a glass of water and a glass of orange juice.

"Would you like water and freshly squeezed orange juice?" he asked.

"Yes, please."

He placed the two glasses on the table. "Can I also bring you a glass of champagne?"

"Not now, thanks. I'll wait on the champagne until my friend arrives."

After the waiter left, I pulled out my phone and texted Craig.

I'm at a table in the restaurant. See you soon.

As I waited for Craig to arrive, I sipped my orange juice and looked around. While the brunch was a buffet, it was a buffet like no other that I'd ever seen. Men in white chef's jackets and hats stood beside platters and towers of beautifully arranged food. I noted smoked fish and meat, a raw bar with caviar and shellfish, and an incredible variety of desserts surrounding a fondue fountain. Enormous black marble columns and gilded Art Deco details gave the space a luxurious 1930s ambience. The well-dressed crowd around the food and the near absence of empty tables testified to the excellence of the Waldorf's famed Sunday brunch.

At about half past one, I saw Craig enter the restaurant. More than a few female heads turned, and I didn't blame them for looking. Even in this enclave of wealth and privilege, he stood out. His striking good looks and poise would turn heads anywhere.

When he spotted me, his face lit up. He crossed the room and sat down across from me.

"Sorry to be late," he said. "It's been a crazy week."

"You mentioned the Syngenomics lawsuit in your email. Is everything OK?"

"Better than OK. I've proven that Syngenomics stole my company's research, and they've agreed to settle out of court. We're still hammering out the details, but the gist of it is that I own the drug under dispute, and Syngenomics has to write me a big check."

"Congratulations," I said, delighted that Craig had won his legal battle. "You must be relieved."

"You don't even know."

"I have a good idea."

Just then, our waiter appeared with water and orange juice for Craig. I looked at him. "How about a glass of champagne? We'll drink to your victory."

He smiled at me, then turned to the waiter. "We'll both have champagne."

When the waiter left, Craig said, "How have you been? What did you and Lara end up doing yesterday?"

"That's a long story. How about if we get some food first? Lara and I ended our day in New York with late-night martinis, so I'm ravenous."

After we returned from the buffet with plates full of food, we sat down and resumed our conversation. We drank to Craig's legal victory, and I related the events of the previous day, concluding with a description of Alessandra's recent botched plastic surgery.

Craig shook his head. "It's a shame. Alessandra's a talented actress, but she's really gone off the rails since her career took off, and her drug habit's taken off with it."

"I didn't realize she was into drugs, but that explains a lot."

Just then, Craig's phone dinged. He looked at the screen. Then at me.

"I'm going to have to take this," he said. "I'll just be a few minutes." He got up and walked out of the restaurant, his phone at his ear.

I felt a wave of irritation. Couldn't his business have waited for once? I'd traveled to New York to talk with him face-to-face, yet he nevertheless canceled our Saturday evening plans. Today, he'd arrived half an hour late for brunch. And now here I was again, waiting for him while he took another call. The underlying message was crystal clear. With Craig, work came first. Personal relationships—even his relationship with me, the woman he'd purportedly loved and whom he'd asked to marry—were a distant second.

I didn't want to get angry—what was the point? I had already made up my mind, after all. Craig's behavior only reinforced my certainty that I had made the right decision.

At that moment, I felt oddly calm. I picked up my fork and enjoyed my meal, which was delicious.

Fifteen minutes later, Craig returned and sat down across from me.

I raised my eyebrows at him. "Is everything OK?" I asked.

"It's fine now. Everything is under control. But we've spent more than enough time talking about my legal issues." He looked at me, and his expression turned serious. "I hope you've had time to think about what I said to you the last time we met."

"I have had time, and I've thought about every word you said."

"And?"

"And while I'll always love you, and I hope that we can remain friends, I can't marry you. We're just not right for each other. It's not about you—you've been nothing but wonderful to me. It's about me, and what makes me happy. It's about the kind of life I want."

His eyes darkened, and his lips became set in a firm line. "Nothing would make me happier than to give you everything that you want, Juliana."

"Except yourself, Craig, which is all I ever wanted. You know that I never gave a damn about your money, let alone your celebrity. I wanted you, and only you. But you're not available to me. Look at this weekend for instance—canceling on me last night, late for brunch today, and then taking a phone call because whoever was on the other line was far more important than this very moment. I'm sorry, but your life would directly and negatively affect mine. You're already married—to Manning International."

At that, he put down his champagne glass. His eyes burned into mine, and his voice vibrated with intensity.

"Look, Juliana—the stress of this lawsuit has really weighed on me. Now that it's over, things will be different."

I shook my head. "Let's be real. There will always be another lawsuit, or some other business situation that demands your full attention. Your heart belongs to the company that you've spent your life building. I'm not criticizing or judging you for the way you are—if I'd built anything like Manning International, maybe I'd be married to it, too—"

"I can change," he said. "I love you, and I'll do anything to be with you." He looked crestfallen to me, but his voice was steely with determination.

I looked him in the eye. "Given your business and the stresses that go with it, how could those changes possibly last? How long would it take for you to resent me for demanding more than you truly want to give to me?"

"There's so much love between us, Juliana. How can you just throw that away?"

My eyes widened. "Throw it away? Are you suggesting that I haven't thought about this? Do you think this is easy for me? This is the hardest choice I've ever had to make. I can assure you, Craig—I've given it a great deal of thought."

"I'm just trying to understand." His voice was tense with frustration.

"What's not to understand? I just laid it out for you. So, let's just admit it, Craig. I've always come second with you. When we were together, I tried to ignore that reality. I did my best to deny it. But your actions constantly threw the truth in my face."

"I didn't mean to upset you," he said.

"This is an upsetting situation. There's no getting around it. You know, before Alessandra—and that damn video of hers—I was so in love with you that I would have done anything to be with you. When we broke up, I was devastated. I couldn't imagine that I'd ever be able to love another man. But life was kinder than I could have expected or hoped. As time passed, I gained clarity about what our relationship had been, and what it would always be. Fundamental things that I felt certain would never change."

"You mean me being married to my business, as you put it."

"That's right. Then I was lucky enough to meet Jake, and we fell in love. Someday, I hope that he'll ask me to marry him."

"What if he doesn't?"

"Even if Jake and I don't make it, that wouldn't change my decision. I hope you understand, Craig—I don't want a life in which I always come second with the man I love. That's the root of all this. That's what this comes down to. I hope you can respect that."

"I've respected you enough to ask you to marry me."

I just looked at him. I'd said enough.

Craig looked down for a long moment. I saw grief on his face, but also resignation. After a few seconds, he raised his eyes to meet mine. "I do respect you, and you deserve to be happy."

"You deserve happiness too, and I hope that you find the right woman someday."

"You're the perfect woman for me. Isn't there anything I can do to convince you to reconsider? To give me one more chance?" His voice was pleading, and it pained me to hurt him, but he deserved the truth.

"I'm not the right woman for you, Craig. The right woman won't try to change you. She'll embrace your entire life and love you for everything that you are. I'm just not the one."

He pushed his plate away, and then looked at me. "I'm finished. We can leave whenever you're ready."

I looked at my half-eaten food and realized that I'd lost my appetite. "I'm done, too."

Craig motioned to our waiter, who promptly came over. "Check, please."

We sat in silence until the waiter returned with the check, which Craig paid. Then we left the restaurant together, walked across the lobby, and went down the stairs toward the Park Avenue entrance.

The moment we exited the Waldorf, we found ourselves suddenly surrounded by a horde of photographers. Cameras flashed. Bright spots flickered in my eyes. The crowd milled around us and jostled against us. I felt surrounded—and terrified.

Craig gripped my right arm and began to push through the crowd toward the curb, where his limousine was idling. He leaned toward me and spoke into my right ear. "I'll give you a ride. It's the fastest way to get you out of here."

As we approached Craig's limo, the heel of my left shoe caught on the pavement just as one of the photographers bumped against me. My ankle turned and I nearly fell, but Craig sensed my imbalance and quickly caught me in his arms. As he did so, his right hand landed on my left breast, and the flashes intensified. An overwhelming sense of claustrophobia gripped me. I struggled to regain my balance and attempted to shield my face with one hand. As Craig helped me into the car, the crowd pressed around us and the cameras continued to flash with a vigor that was relentless in its intensity.

Craig got into the car after me. He closed the door firmly, and then leaned forward.

"Get us out of here," he said to the driver, who promptly stepped on the gas. The car pulled away from the curb and sped into Park Avenue traffic.

I took a breath and felt a momentary sense of relief. This aspect of Craig's world—life in the public eye—was something with which I'd never been comfortable. And now that I'd had a taste of how brutal it could be, I couldn't be more certain that this wasn't how I wanted to live.

Then I thought of the photos that had just been shot, and of Jake's reaction should he see them. Our relationship was already under strain, and this was the last thing we needed. What would Jake think when photos of me—in Craig Manning's arms, with his hand on my breast—flooded the Internet?

I turned to Craig, "I'm not blaming you, but how the hell did they find us? Who told them that you were at the Waldorf?"

Craig pressed a button to close the privacy barrier, and then spoke quietly. His voice had an undertone of frustration and exhaustion. "Some jerk at the Waldorf must have recognized me and made a few phone calls. Where would you like to be dropped? Your hotel?"

"That would be kind of you."

Craig pressed the intercom button and spoke to his driver. "Take us to the Pierre Hotel on Sixty-First Street."

After that brief exchange, we lapsed into silence again. The atmosphere between us was tense, and the short drive up Park Avenue seemed to take forever. The divide between us felt as wide as the median on Park. As I looked out the car window at the buildings going by, memories of the intimacy Craig and I had once shared flooded through me, and contrasted with the painful distance that was now cemented between us. A sense of loss overwhelmed me, and tears crept into my eyes.

As the car turned left onto East Sixty-First Street and approached the Pierre, Craig took my hand in his. His eyes were bright with emotion. "Goodbye, Juliana."

I squeezed his hand. "Goodbye. And thank you."

When the car pulled in front of the hotel, the doorman opened the car door and helped me out. I turned back and looked at Craig one last time. The devastation I saw on his face cut through me, but I knew that I'd made the right decision—for both of us. I gave him a little wave and tried to smile through my tears.

Then the door closed, the limousine jetted away from the curb, and that was the last I saw of Craig Manning.

14

After Craig's limo disappeared from sight, I turned and walked into the Pierre. I crossed the lobby and stepped into an open elevator. When the doors closed behind me, I pulled a fresh Kleenex from my purse and dabbed my eyes. I felt emotionally drained, and I still had to explain the photos of me in Craig's arms to Lara, and after that, to Jake. I hoped that both of them would believe me, but what if they didn't?

I left the elevator, walked down the hall, and slid my keycard into the door of our suite. As I opened the door, I wondered if Lara was back from her brunch date with Cole.

"Lara?"

"In my room," Lara called. "Packing."

I walked into her room. Neatly folded clothing rested on the bed in several piles, and Lara's open suitcase was half full.

"How was brunch with Cole?" I asked.

"Fabulous. We talked about literally everything. He made me laugh until I cried. I had a wonderful time, and we made plans to go out for dinner later this week." She looked up from her packing and saw my face. "Are you all right? What you just had to say to Craig can't have been easy."

I sat on the bed next to a stack of clothing. "You don't even know."

"What do you mean? How did Craig take it?"

"As well as could be expected, I guess, given that what I had to say wasn't what he'd hoped to hear. But that's not all. When we left the Waldorf, a horde of photographers attacked us."

"Oh no. Some creep must have spotted Craig and tipped them off."

I held up my hand. "It gets worse. As we walked to Craig's car, my heel caught on the pavement and I started to fall. He caught me by my left boob, which probably has its own Internet address by now. Jake and I have a Skype date tomorrow, and instead of talking about me coming to London and how he likes his new job, what will we talk about? These bullshit photos, that's what."

"Just call Jake right now and tell him what happened," Lara said. "You'll feel better after you've talked to him."

"You're right, but my cell isn't on an international plan."

"Neither is mine, but we can use the room's landline."

Lara walked to the bedside table, picked up the phone, and punched in Jake's number. We waited several long seconds before Lara shook her head, hung up the phone, and looked at me. "I just called his hotel room. He's not there, and I don't think he has a UK cell phone yet. Email?"

"I guess that's my only option. I'll write Jake a quick email asking him to call me."

"If we finish packing and leave the hotel soon, we can make the five o'clock train back to Boston. It's eight-thirty in London right now. Jake's probably out getting dinner somewhere. He'll call you back soon."

"OK. Let's do it."

After our train back to Boston arrived at South Station, Lara and I parted ways and headed for our respective apartments. Jake still hadn't called, which frustrated me.

By the time I reached home, it was a quarter to eleven. I let myself into the apartment I shared with Duncan. He wasn't home, but there were several pieces of mail stacked on the coffee table. I put down my suitcase, walked to the couch, and sat down.

I flipped through the stack of mail. Two bills and a brown padded envelope. I picked up the envelope and tore one end of it open, and then slipped my fingers inside and pulled out the contents, which turned out to be a small booklet with a dark blue cover and gold lettering. I stared at my new passport in near disbelief, and a thrill rushed over me.

I opened the passport, inspected my name and photo, and flipped through the empty pages. Soon there would be a UK entry stamp on one of them. There was so much riding on my trip to London. I clutched the passport to my chest. Soon I would be with Jake again. But after our time apart and what had happened at the airport when he left, would he welcome me back into his arms? I didn't know, and it sickened me.

Had he called or emailed? I pulled my phone out of my purse and checked. Once again, nothing. I was dying to share my news with him, but it was too late to call. With the time difference, it was nearly 4:00 a.m. in London. No doubt he was asleep. Between his new job and his apartment search, he was probably exhausted and hadn't checked his email.

Now that I had my passport, I wanted to be with Jake as soon as possible and I wanted to make things right between us again. I wasn't sure how he felt about us right now, and I was concerned that the photos of me with Craig might make things worse. I had no idea if our relationship was still alive—Jake and I needed time together to work things out, preferably without the constant pressure that had dominated the week before his departure.

Tomorrow morning, I would ask Lara just how soon I could schedule a vacation.

15

When I arrived at work the next morning, I went straight to Lara's office. The morning sunlight played across the papers that were spread across her desk, where she sat, sipping a cup of coffee.

As I entered, she looked up. "Juliana! Get in here and join me. I finally got a voicemail from Jake. He's just gotten a UK cell phone, and he said that he'd try calling again later today. He said he'd tried to reach you too, but you didn't pick up."

"Damn it. I hate phone tag. He must have called while I was in the subway. I called his hotel room earlier this morning, but the line was busy."

"Now that he has a cell, at least the phone tag will move faster," Lara said.

"Speaking of Jake, look at this," I said. I reached into my purse and pulled out my passport. "When I came home last night, it was in my mail. I'm going to surprise Jake by showing it to him later today when we Skype."

"Then we have travel plans to make," Lara said.

"We do."

"When would you like to go to London?"

"The sooner the better."

"For how long?"

I hesitated. "Would a week or so be OK? I don't want to cause problems for the team."

"Want to really surprise Jake?" Lara asked. Her expression was mischievous. "You know how I love to shock."

"I do, which is why I need to know what you're thinking before I agree to it."

"It will add drama to your Skype conversation."

"Drama? Now I'm frightened."

"You shouldn't be. It's a fabulous idea, if I do say so myself."

"You're teasing me."

"Of course I am. What are best friends for?"

I rolled my eyes. "Just tell me, OK?"

"Why don't we buy your airline tickets before you Skype? That way, you can wave both the passport and the tickets in front of Jake's face. That should melt his heart."

"I love it," I said, and then I put my palms together in front of my chest and did a little Japanese-style bow. "Look. I'm bowing to your genius."

Lara giggled. "You're ridiculous. Go and get a cup of coffee—bring me a fresh cup, too—while I scour the Internet for the best price on a round-trip ticket to London."

"Fabulous. I'll be back with coffee in a minute."

I left Lara's office, walked down the hall to the office kitchenette, and made two cups of coffee. As I waited for the coffee to brew, my excitement intensified. It was really happening. I was going to London. Soon I would be there, with Jake Barlow, the man of my dreams.

I just hoped that I was still within his dreams…

When I returned to Lara's office with two coffee cups in my hands, Lara motioned for me to come around her desk. I handed her a cup, then walked around the side of the desk and stood next to her. She sipped her coffee, and then pointed at her screen with her free hand.

"Check this out. For just over twelve hundred dollars, we can get you on a British Airways flight that leaves late tonight. It's a direct flight, and you'd arrive at London Heathrow tomorrow morning."

"Tonight?" I almost couldn't believe it. "That's even sooner than I'd imagined. I need time to pack, for God's sake!"

"Here's how we do it. You leave the office before traffic starts to pick up—you know, around three o'clock—and take a cab to your apartment. You'll have between three and four hours to pack, so you'll need to write a list now and be brisk when you get home. Then, I'll pick you up at seven and drive you to the airport."

I looked at the dates Lara had entered. "You've set my return for three weeks from now. There's no way I have more than two weeks of vacation time."

Lara smiled. "That extra week is my little gift to you and Jake."

"I appreciate that, but what if it's a disaster? You know how it ended between us when he left for London. And now those ridiculous photos of me with Craig. What if it all falls apart? What if he's already moved on?"

"I don't think he has."

"But how do you know?"

"I don't. I can't promise you anything. But I can say this with conviction—I know my brother very well. I think just seeing you again will get him back on track."

"What if it doesn't?"

"Juliana, come on. You need to start focusing on if it does, OK? Jesus. You're a total downer."

"Sorry.... I'm just concerned. Jake and I have barely spoken. You know that."

"When you arrive in London, you'll have plenty of time to speak. And once you do, you need to break that passport in properly. With three full weekends, you and Jake could use one weekend to go to Paris or Amsterdam."

"You're such a good friend, Lara."

"And so are you. We have each other's backs, right?"

"Absolutely." I reached into my purse, took out my bankcard, and handed it to Lara. "Let's buy that ticket. Let's just throw caution to the wind. London, here I come."

She sighed as she started entering my information into the computer. "I'm going to miss you. We both know that you won't be coming back to Boston, at least not on a permanent basis."

"If I do end up moving to London, we'll just have to Skype frequently and rack up tons of frequent-flier miles. Best friends forever, right?"

Lara smiled at me, but it was a wistful, bittersweet smile. "Best friends forever," she said. "And forever after that."

16

Two hours later, I sat at my desk and prepared to Skype Jake. My passport and e-ticket rested on the desk next to my keyboard. I was excited, but nervous. Before he'd left, things had been tense between us. He hadn't exactly left me on a positive note, which concerned me since we'd barely spoken since. And now he was in a new city with new ideas, a fresh scene, and new women whom I knew would go after him in a hot second.

Jake had said that he wanted me to come to London, but our parting had been so strained that we'd hadn't had a real conversation since he'd left Boston. I hoped that he hadn't changed his mind about us, but I had to be prepared for it. He very well might have. I just hoped that he still wanted me to come to London.

When noon arrived, I opened Skype and clicked on Jake's name, and then Video Call. After two rings, he answered.

"Juliana," he said.

My heart quickened when I saw his face. I didn't know how this would go. Would this be it? I wasn't sure. I felt sick inside.

"You're a sight for sore eyes," he said.

"Am I?"

"Of course you are."

As his video image flickered into focus on my screen, I could hardly restrain my excitement. I'd missed him terribly, and the sight of his familiar face thrilled me. But it was the expression on his face that really made my day. He appeared happy to see me. The expression he'd left with at the airport wasn't here. This was the Jake I knew and had fallen in love with.

"It's so great to finally see you," I said. "I can't tell you how I've missed seeing you. And being with you."

On my screen, I could see Jake from his chest upward. He sat in an office chair in front of large windows with the blinds down, no doubt to allow him to see his own screen clearly. He looked handsome in a dark jacket and a white button-front shirt with the top buttons undone—but I saw fatigue in his eyes. Obviously, his first week at his new job had been demanding.

"I'm sorry that it's been so difficult to reach me," he said. "The London office set me up with a Blackberry smartphone, but I hated it so much that after a day, I turned the damned thing in and demanded an iPhone." He reached off-screen, and then held up a new iPhone for me to see. "As of today, you should be able to reach me anytime. I called you this morning, so my number should already be in your phone."

I stilled my anxiety, and just went for it. "I also have something to show you," I said.

He furrowed his brow at me. "What's that?"

I picked up my passport and airline tickets, and held them in front of me.

His eyes lit up. "Is that what I think it is?"

"It is."

"So when are you coming? Soon, I hope."

"Surprisingly soon."

"Like this week?"

"Like tonight. Lara's given me an extra week of vacation, so we'll have three weeks together."

Jake leaned back in his chair and did a double fist pump. "Yes!" He leaned in toward the camera. "When will your flight arrive?"

"At 11:35 tomorrow morning, at Heathrow Airport. I'll be on British Airways."

"I'll meet you at the airport. I still haven't found an apartment, but my suite at the Andaz is nice, and it's central."

"I couldn't care less where we stay, as long as you're there. Jake, I'm so sorry about how we left things at the airport in Boston. It's worried me for days. I thought for sure that I'd lost you."

"Are you serious?"

"The mood had darkened when you left me. I kept waiting for you to turn around and wave at me when you left. When you didn't, I thought that was it. I thought that I'd pushed too hard."

"I didn't turn back because I was crushed that I was leaving you. I needed to focus on what was ahead of me. This has been a big step for me—I was just trying to process it. That, and leaving you. I've never doubted you."

"So, I misinterpreted?"

"You did."

"Why haven't you returned my texts, emails, calls?"

"The only reason is that it's been insane this week. I hope you didn't think that I'd lost interest in you within a mere week, Juliana. Come on—I'm a better man than that. Right? Well, I try to be. I'm just still getting acclimated here, which is challenging in a thousand small ways. You'll see! Tomorrow can't come soon enough for me. I can't wait to see you, to hold you and to kiss you, and to show you all around the few areas of London that I know at this point."

He was telling the truth. I could feel it. The sense of relief that shot through me at that moment was incredible. I hadn't blown it—we were still a couple!

"There's something I need to tell you. I met Craig Manning at the Waldorf to tell him once and for all that I want to be with you. We had that conversation, but afterward, when we left the hotel—"

Jake made a dismissive gesture with one hand. "Do you mean the photos of you with Craig outside the Waldorf? If so, don't give it another thought. One of my Boston colleagues emailed me a link, and I checked out a few of the images for myself."

"You did? Did my left boob have it's own URL?"

"Umm, no."

"Well, that's a relief! I haven't worked up the courage to go online yet to see them for myself."

"You have nothing to worry about. The photos show exactly what happened. You tripped, Craig caught you, and thank goodness he did. You could have sprained your ankle."

Gratitude and anticipation washed over me and cleansed me. Within hours, I would be on a plane to London—and to Jake. The love of my life. I'd be with him again, perhaps forever. And I could tell by his voice—Jake was eager for my arrival.

For the first time since that mess in the airport, I felt wholeheartedly optimistic about the future of our relationship.

17

At eleven o'clock that evening, my flight took off. From my window seat in the British Airways 767, I looked out at the clear night sky and the city below. Viewed from above, the geometric lines of streetlights and the shadowed forms of buildings resembled the motherboard of an enormous computer. The engines thrummed, the aircraft gained altitude, and I watched the lights of Boston gradually fade into the distance.

I leaned back in my seat and relaxed. Despite three hours of frantic, last-minute packing, it couldn't have been a better day. Lara had picked me up at my apartment and driven me to the airport, where Duncan and Connor had met us to see me off. As they each gave me a kiss out of their support for Jake and me, I knew that I truly was with my family.

Surrounded by the love of my dearest friends, I had felt incredibly fortunate. Whatever struggles I had survived, and whatever the future might bring, I was lucky to have true friends who wanted the best for me—and who always had my back. And thanks to Lara's generosity, I was about to enjoy what would hopefully be three fabulous weeks with the man that I loved.

When the flight reached cruising altitude, I put my seat back, arranged my pillow, unwrapped my blanket, and tucked it around my shoulders. It had been a long day, and I needed to try to get some sleep, if only so that I didn't look like a total wreck when Jake met me at Heathrow. I set my watch to UK time—five hours forward—and then, after a strong cocktail, drifted to sleep.

～

Seven hours later, after landing at Heathrow, I got my passport stamped, which was like a badge of honor for me at this point, and took my luggage through the customs check. I walked down a short hallway toward a pair of doors. As they swung open, I saw Jake. He was turned slightly away from me, and he hadn't spotted me yet. I stepped through the doors and paused for a second to enjoy the moment.

Jake looked as handsome as ever in a dark green T-shirt that was snug across his muscular chest and 501s that hugged his ass perfectly. He stood about thirty feet away from me, on the other side of the cordon that separated arriving travelers from the friends and family members waiting to meet them. His casual clothing told me that he'd taken the day off from work, which meant the world to me since I knew how busy he was.

Craig wouldn't have done this. Craig would have sent a car for me.

When he turned, our eyes met.

Jake's face broke into a joyous grin, which was all I needed to see in that moment. I dropped my bags and ran across the remaining space between us. We fell into each other's arms, my body curved into his, and he met my lips with a deep, sensuous kiss that almost made me want to cry.

"I've missed you," he said into my ear. I felt him begin to harden against my thigh, and my core tightened in response.

I leaned back, cupped his face in my hands, and kissed him deeply. "Mmmm. I can feel just how much you've missed me. I've missed you too. More than you know."

He appraised me. "You look beautiful. How was your flight?"

"Long, but I might have had a drink first thing and slept for much of it."

"Have you eaten?"

"I had a breakfast sandwich on the flight, so I'm fine for now." I looked at him. "What about you?"

"I had breakfast at the hotel, so I'm good if you are."

"I know you're good, but can you walk in your current, uh, situation?" I put my hand on his upper thigh.

He gave me a look. "Putting your hand there isn't helpful, you know. People are staring."

"I thought you liked being watched. And some of them were staring already anyway. It's not as though your jeans are up to the task of concealing what you're packing in them."

He moved my hand firmly away from his package. "Give me a minute. I'm bringing up the image of my fifth-grade math teacher. Horrible person. She never fails me."

"What was her name?"

"Mrs. Snowdon. Morbidly obese, with half a dozen facial moles and a glint of pure evil in her eyes." He adjusted himself, and then grabbed the handle of my suitcase. "Let's get out of here and find a taxi before you have a chance to crotch me again. Don't think that you'll get away with it twice."

I smiled at him. "Who said that I want to get away with it?"

18

An hour and a taxi ride later, we reached Jake's suite at the Andaz London. He swiped his keycard, and then opened the door for me.

"Take a look. I wish I'd been able to find an apartment before you got here, but at least it's comfortable, and there's plenty of space."

While Jake brought my luggage in and closed the door, I looked around. The large, open space was decorated in a contemporary, Japanese-inspired style and was separated into two rooms by a wall that ran two-thirds of the suite's width. The first room was furnished with bright red lounge chairs, and a matching chaise longue. Jake's laptop rested on the desk, next to an assortment of paperwork. One end of the second room held a bright red throw rug, two red armchairs, a beige sofa and a curved-glass coffee table. A king-size bed with a white duvet and an assortment of red, dark brown, and gold-green pillows occupied the other end. A pale wooden work desk sat in front of the expansive windows, together with an Eames chair.

"It's beautiful." I put my arms around Jake's waist. "After eight hours on a plane, I'm feeling more than a little grimy. Can I take a shower?"

He kissed the top of my head. "Not unless I can join you."

"I was hoping you'd say that." I took his hand and pulled him toward the bathroom, which was decorated in black-and-white and featured his-and-hers sinks, a built-in marble tub that looked large enough for two, and a spacious walk-in shower.

I shed my clothes, turned on the water, and stepped into the shower. The hot water cascaded over me, and I sighed blissfully. After removing his own clothes, Jake joined me under the hot spray.

"Here," he said, turning me so that my back was against his front. "Let me wash your hair."

Was he serious?

Apparently, he was. He squeezed shampoo into one hand and began to knead it gently through my hair. When he was finished, he brought his hands up to my hairline and began to massage my scalp with his strong fingers. I leaned back into his muscular body and felt the tension of the past twenty-four hours leave my body.

After Jake rinsed my hair, I reached for the body wash, but he stopped me.

"I've got this," he said.

He took the body wash, poured some into his left hand, and began to work his way down my body. His hands circled slowly over my breasts, then moved down and around to caress my buttocks—and my sex, almost making me lose it. He reached up and kneaded my shoulders, then slid his hands around my waist and lightly circled my navel. My nerves were on fire, my core throbbed with anticipation, and I could feel Jake's hard length against my back. We both were beyond ready.

"Jake—" I said.

"I'm not finished yet."

He washed me gently between my legs, and as his wet fingers slid lightly over my most sensitive parts, I shivered with desire. He carefully rinsed the soap from my body with long, slow, deliberate strokes of his hands, and then turned me to face him. He pulled me against his body, and captured my lips in a slow, searing kiss that made me wet for him. I reached down to caress him, but once again, he pushed my hand away.

"Not yet," he said softly.

He dropped his head to my breasts, circled their hardened tips with his tongue, and wrapped his arms around my hips. Then he knelt, parted my delicate folds with his fingers, and started to suck on my clit. He penetrated me with one finger, then two. His fingers sunk into my wetness while his tongue circled my clit and flicked it. As my excitement built, I gripped his muscular shoulders. Waves of sensation rippled through me as he drove me relentlessly toward climax.

When I shuddered my release around his hand, he pulled me closer and pressed his lips against my sex. I caressed his head before he rose to his feet. Overwhelmed with love for him, I traced his handsome features, and then moved my hands downward to stroke his thick erection. He groaned softly as I touched the length of him and pulled on his swollen balls. Every cell in my body quivered with lust and anticipation.

I looked into his eyes. "I need you inside me."

Jake's gaze was heated. He positioned me against the wall under the shower's spray, supported my left leg in the crook of his right arm, and entered me with an exquisite slowness that made me feel every silky inch of him. As the hot water cascaded over our bodies, he kissed my lips, my neck, and the tips of my breasts. His hands caressed my hips, and then he gripped them. We moved together in a rhythm that began as a sensuous dance, but quickly flamed into raw passion. Nothing existed except the two of us, and our hunger for each other. I raked my fingers down his back, and he buried himself in me, again and again to a point that was almost violent in his claiming of me.

My last boundaries melted away, consumed by the heat of our passion. Any lingering doubts drifted away like scraps of paper in the wind.

This was right. *We* were right.

Thank God for this moment.

With a final powerful stroke, Jake drove me over the edge, and we came together in a transcendent moment of shared ecstasy. Afterward, we wrapped our arms around each other, looked into each other's eyes, and a kind of wordless communication passed between us. What I read into it was this:

Nothing and no one will ever separate us again.

19

I opened my eyes, and for a brief moment, I felt disoriented. A very good kind of disoriented. Jake and I were in his suite at the Andaz London and we were ensconced in the king-size bed. We were facing each other. His left arm was wrapped around my waist, and our legs were intertwined. Last night, we'd christened the bed thoroughly, and then fallen asleep, in a contented tangle of bodies and bedding.

He traced the side of my face with his fingers. "You're awake."

"How long did I sleep?"

"About three hours. I've been awake for the past hour or so."

I kissed him on the lips. "Bored?"

"Not at all. I like watching you sleep." He brushed a finger against my lower lip. "Are you hungry yet?"

"Ravenous. I didn't eat much on the plane."

"Would you rather go out, or eat in?"

I looked at him. "Maybe eat in—you know, after I take care of a pressing issue."

He raised an eyebrow. "A pressing issue? Is something wrong?"

"Oh, no. There's obviously nothing wrong with it, and it's *pressing* against my thigh right now."

He smiled at that. "And what do you plan to do about it?"

"I'm considering my options."

"Which are?"

I blinked at him. "Too many to count."

"Bankers are great at counting, you know. Can I be of service?"

"Why, yes. I'm about to take advantage of *all* your services. The full menu. A la carte. The room service menu isn't going to satisfy what I have planned, so it'll just have to wait until I'm finished."

Afterward, while Jake ordered a small feast from room service, I got up, stretched languorously, and put on a robe. He'd pulled on a pair of black button-fly boxer shorts that rode deliciously low on his hips and showcased every contour of what was beneath them, and his tanned, muscled torso had a light sheen from our recent activities. When he put down the phone, I walked over to him and wrapped my arms around his waist, and reached up on my tiptoes to kiss him.

I looked into his eyes. "I think you know this already, but I need to say it out loud. I love you, Jake. I'm in love with you."

He took me in his arms. "I fell in love with you the first day we met. Remember when we went kayaking in Harpswell?"

"I'll remember that day for the rest of my life. It changed everything for me." I squeezed his hand, and we sat down on the couch together.

"Would you consider moving to London, or would you like me to request a transfer back to Boston?" Jake asked.

My heart swelled with love for him. I would never ask Jake to give up his dream job, but his offering to meant the world to me. Also, I knew that in the London office of Barlow, I could find and grow into my own dream job.

"Your job here is too good to pass up. I'll request a transfer." I smiled at him. "We'll be Londoners together."

Jake leaned over and kissed me. "Thank you."

"I'm not being totally unselfish—I'll find a job of my own here.

Through Barlow. And I'll bust my ass to move up through the ranks. I've never lived anywhere outside of New England. It'll be an adventure."

He put his arm around me, and I leaned my head against his shoulder. "We'll visit Boston often, and our friends and family can always visit us here. With our combined incomes, we can afford a larger place than I had in Boston, with extra space for guests and a big, sunny room that we can turn into a painting studio."

"Over the next couple of weeks, we can look for an apartment—"

"Flat." He grinned at me. "If you're going to be a Londoner, you need to learn the lingo."

"I know some British slang from watching *Masterpiece*."

"Such as?"

"Lots of great four-letter words. Snog. Shag. Boff. Bonk."

"You've got a one-track mind today."

"And you've been on that track with me—all the way." I snapped the waistband of his boxers.

Just then, we heard a knock on the door.

"Room service," Jake said. "I'll put a shirt on and get it."

He stood up, pulled his dark green T-shirt over his head, and then tugged it down over his torso. He walked into the lounge area and opened the door. I heard the clatter of plates and cutlery, followed by low voices.

After I heard the door close, I joined Jake in the lounge area for brunch. He'd ordered a delicious assortment of Asian food, which he knew I loved. Steaming bowls of miso soup, a variety of sashimi, and a savory beef curry. A bottle of Dom Perignon rested in an ice bucket, and two filled glasses sat on the table.

"There's dessert too," Jake said. "But that's a surprise. I hope you'll like it."

"If I don't, my dessert will be ravishing you again."

He gave me a look. "Then I hope you hate it."

"Now you're talking."

20

The next morning, after we enjoyed coffee and croissants together, Jake prepared to leave for work. He looked handsome in a dark gray business suit and a white button-front shirt.

I was headed out for a day of sight-seeing, and had decided on khaki capris, a white camisole tank top, and a lightweight blouse with a geometric pattern of blues and greens.

Jake finished putting on his tie, which was a subtly textured gold color that brought out the flecks of gold in his green eyes. He rummaged in a drawer. "Better bring this," he said, handing me a mini umbrella. "You never know when it will rain here."

I gave him a quick kiss on the lips, and tucked the umbrella into my shoulder bag. "I never would have thought of that. Thank you."

He'd already supplied me with a pre-paid cell phone, a keycard for the hotel suite, a street map with a subway map on the reverse side, and £100 in ten and twenty-pound notes. I hadn't wanted to accept the money, but he'd insisted that he'd feel safer if I had some cash and didn't have to immediately search for an ATM.

"I should get going," he said.

"So we'll meet back here at five-thirty?"

"Yes." He smiled. "I'll trade the business suit for something more casual, and we'll go out for a real British pub dinner."

"Perfect. I'm going to visit the Museum of London, and then I'm going to check out the Oxford Street shopping scene."

He embraced me and kissed me meaningfully on the lips. "Call me if you need anything."

I cupped his face in my hands. "You've thought of everything. Go to work. I'll be fine."

He released me and walked to the door. "See you later."

"Oh, you'll definitely see me later."

I spent the morning at the Museum of London, and then took the subway to Oxford Street, a busy, colorful street with shops that ranged from posh to touristy. I stepped into a shop filled with London-themed T-shirts, with the thought of buying a couple for Lara and Duncan, but stopped when I saw a display of novelty boxer shorts.

One pair featured two arrows, titled THE LEGEND and THE MAN. The arrow for THE MAN pointed up, while the arrow for THE LEGEND pointed to the crotch. I couldn't help but giggle. Maybe I should buy them for Jake. After all, what he had down there *was* legendary. Then I spotted another pair, with a packing theme and the words LARGE PACKAGE—HANDLE WITH CARE.

A young woman with a bright pink chin-length bob sauntered over to me. "Looking for something fun?" she asked with a knowing smile.

I nodded. "Maybe. I'm just not sure which ones to choose. They're all pretty funny."

She pointed to a black pair with the words DANGER—CHOKING HAZARD. "I fancy those. Bought them for my bloke last Valentine's. The red devil pair with the flames on the crotch is brilliant, too."

Just then, the ring of my phone startled me out of my thoughts. I pulled the phone out of my shoulder bag. It was Jake.

"Hello?" I said.

"It's me. Where are you? Are you busy right now?"

"I'm on Oxford Street, doing a naughty bit of shopping."

"Goodness! I just got a call about an apartment that could be perfect for us, so I'm leaving work now to take a look at it. Want to meet me and see it together?"

"I'd love to. Where should I meet you?"

"Take a cab to 7 Shepherdess Place—it's in the Shoreditch area. I'll meet you outside the entrance. It's a warehouse loft conversion, and it's close enough to the Barlow offices that we could both walk to work, at least in good weather. Shoreditch is a great neighborhood, too—plenty of hip restaurants and nightlife."

A tingle of excitement raced through me. "I can't wait to see it."

When my cab arrived at Shepherdess Place, I spotted Jake immediately. He walked over to the cab, opened the door, and helped me out after I paid the driver.

We walked to the entrance, where a slender blonde in a dark suit waited.

"Moira, this is my girlfriend, Juliana West. Juliana, meet Moira Allen. Moira's the agent for this building."

Moira and I nodded to each other, and then she led us into the building's entrance area.

"The conversion was just completed a few weeks ago," she said. "There's been a lot of interest, and all but two of the units are already taken. You're interested in the top floor unit, right?"

"That's correct," Jake said.

We followed Moira into the elevator, where she pressed the button for the fourth floor. When the elevator stopped, she led us down a wide hall that was illuminated by skylights and enormous, multi-paned windows. She unlocked and opened the door nearest to the end of the hall, and we stepped inside.

"Have a look around," she said. "There's no hurry. I'll be here if you have any questions."

I looked up, then around. The loft had been converted in a contemporary style—stainless steel kitchen, sleek spiral stairs to the mezzanine level—but the brick walls, original tin ceiling, hardwood floors, and multi-paned windows gave the space a texture and warmth that I liked. The main living area was the full height of the unit, which looked to be about twenty feet.

Jake turned to Moira. "Juliana and I are just going to walk the space alone. If we agree that it could work for us, I'm prepared to start the paperwork tomorrow morning."

"Of course," Moira said. "Here are the keys. Just lock up when you leave, and drop the keys in the building manager's box. It's in the entrance area, just to the right of the doors."

She left, and Jake turned to me. "Let's look around," he said. "Based on the photos Moira emailed me earlier, the room on the end might work as your painting studio."

We walked down the hall, and when we reached the room Jake had mentioned, my heart leapt. The room occupied the entire end of the building, and, with windows on three sides, it was filled with light.

Jake indicated the left side of the interior wall. "We could put in a sink here," he said. "And some drawers and shelves over on the right."

His concern for my happiness moved me. "It's perfect. I could spend the rest of my life painting in here."

"Wait until you see the master suite upstairs," he said. We looked at the other first floor room, which would be our guest bedroom, and checked out the downstairs bath, linen closet, and laundry room. Then we climbed the spiral staircase to the second floor mezzanine.

"We could use this front part as a sitting area, or turn it into a home office for both of us," Jake said.

We walked down a short hall. On the left, there was a walk-in closet and dressing area that was more than large enough for both of us, and on the right, a luxurious master bath. The master bedroom was at the end of the hall, and was similar in size to the first-floor room that Jake had suggested for my painting studio.

Jake looked at me. His excitement was palpable. "So. What do you think? Should we buy it?"

"Buy?" I was confused. "Just yesterday, you were talking about renting."

"That was before I saw this place. I really like it, it's a good investment, and we can afford it. But how do you feel about it?" He gave me a searching look. "Could you be happy here?"

I wrapped my arm low around his waist. "I'd be happy anywhere with you. But I'd like to know a bit more about the neighborhood before making any decisions. You mentioned restaurants and nightlife, but what about the practical day-to-day stuff? Who lives here? Is there a good grocery store nearby?"

"There's an organic grocery just a few blocks away. And Shoreditch is popular with young professionals like us, so we'll make friends here. It's up-and-coming, just like we are. The unit comes with two parking spaces in the underground garage, which is beyond rare for London. And everything we need is within walking distance."

I leaned over and kissed him on the lips. "Then I agree. This is the perfect place for us. We should put in an offer before someone else snaps it up. The location, the brick walls, the high ceilings, the big windows—it's gorgeous, and with enough space for a home office and a painting studio? I love it. And I love you."

21

The rest of the week flew by. Between work and arrangements for the purchase of our new loft, Jake was busy during the day, but we spent every evening together, just as we had in Boston. Meanwhile, I occupied my days with seeing more of London. On Thursday, I visited the Tower of London and the Design Museum. On Friday, I strolled through a dozen of London's best art galleries in the morning, and did a little shopping on Oxford Street in the afternoon.

When Saturday morning arrived, Jake suggested that we spend the day at Hyde Park, followed by dinner at the OXO Tower that evening.

"You'll love the restaurant," he said. "The view of London is spectacular, especially at sunset."

I smiled at him. "It sounds terribly romantic."

He kissed me lightly. "I'll call and reserve a window table right now. Then I'll call room service and have them put together a picnic basket for our lunch."

Two hours later, we were wandering hand-in-hand down one of the tree-shaded paths that wound through Hyde Park. It was a perfect summer day. Sunlight filtered through the treetops, casting delicate, green-tinged patterns of light on the path, reflections that moved and flickered in response to the gentle breeze that rippled through the leaves. Birds chirped and sang, and an occasional squirrel darted between the trees.

Jake carried our picnic basket on his other arm. "Want to rent a boat?" he asked. "We can row around a bit, and then find a quiet picnic spot by the edge of the lake, sort of like we did in Harpswell."

"What a lovely idea," I said.

We strolled to the boathouse, where Jake rented a boat for the afternoon. After we walked to the dock and found boat number twenty-nine, Jake stepped from the dock into the boat and stowed the picnic basket between the seats. Then he turned to me, held out his hand, and helped me into the boat. After I was seated in the bow, he sat down facing me and took the oars in his strong hands. With a few strokes of the oars, we moved away from the shore.

I leaned back and trailed the fingers of my right hand in the water. "This is perfect. It's just what we needed. It's a beautiful day, and after a week in the city, it feels wonderful to be outside—in nature. I'm a Maine girl, after all."

As Jake rowed our boat across the water, I reveled in the view. The lake was dotted with boats like ours, and light reflected off and sparkled against its smooth surface. Ducks and swans floated serenely along the banks. One swan came so close to our boat that I could nearly touch its snowy white feathers.

Watching Jake row was an experience in itself. His dark blue 501s and fitted gray T-shirt were sexy as hell, and his biceps and chest muscles flexed with each pull on the oars. The light breeze blew his thick, wavy hair back from his handsome face. Joy filled my heart. He'd planned this day for us, and the happiness that I felt when we were together was beyond anything I'd ever known.

We approached the shore, and Jake maneuvered the boat into a secluded nook along the water's edge.

He rested the oars and looked at me. "How's this for our picnic spot?"

"It's perfect," I said. And it was. The surrounding trees provided privacy and partial shade, and the grass-covered ground, dappled with sunlight, looked relatively flat.

Jake nudged the boat onto the shoreline, and then got to his feet and stepped onto dry ground. After helping me ashore, he retrieved the picnic basket, and set it down in the shade of one of the trees. He opened the basket, removed a folded picnic blanket, and handed it to me.

I spread the blanket on the grass and sat down upon it. Jake handed me wineglasses, plates, napkins, and cutlery, which I arranged while he continued to unpack an assortment of bags and boxes. After he had finished, he sat next to me and uncorked a bottle of Cabernet Sauvignon.

I glanced at the cloth napkins and the sparkling silverware. "This is quite the picnic," I said. "I feel like I'm in a five-star restaurant, but with birds singing and chirping all around."

"Never say things like that on a picnic," Jake said. "If you do, one of those birds will fly over and crap on your hair. It could happen. Birds are small, feathered dinosaurs, Juliana. They're predators. Just look at the jackdaw perched in the tree behind you."

I looked. Black-feathered with a silvery purple sheen on the crown of its head, the bird did appear to be eyeing our picnic arrangements.

"See those beady yellow eyes? That calculating expression? That bird is strategizing the perfect flight trajectory to crap on your head, so it can take advantage of the ensuing confusion to steal your lunch."

I laughed. "I hope to God you're wrong. If a bird shits on me *and* steals my lunch, I'll never live it down. And you'd never let me forget it."

"Of course not. A moment like that would be unforgettable. Though I might be persuaded not to tell Lara—for a price, of course."

I gave him a look. "I wonder what that price might be."

His smile widened. "I'm sure I could think of something appropriate." He handed me the two wineglasses. "Here—hold these."

He filled our glasses, and then stopped the wine bottle by pushing the cork in halfway. I handed him one of the filled glasses.

"To our first picnic in London," he said, lifting his glass.

I clinked my glass against his, and then leaned forward and kissed him. "And many more picnics to come."

We both drank, and then began to dig into the food. In addition to a delightful assortment of little sandwiches, we had a freshly baked baguette, a round of Brie, and a large bunch of green grapes.

For the next hour, we reclined on the picnic blanket, side-by-side. We fed each other bites of food, exchanged banter and kisses, and reveled in each other's company.

After we had finished eating, Jake got up and went over to the picnic basket.

"Time for dessert," he said.

I propped myself up on one elbow. "What's for dessert?"

"It's a surprise. I hope you like it."

His familiar words triggered a host of wonderful memories, and I smiled to myself. Jake was such a romantic. He loved to surprise me with unexpected gestures. Flowers. Cards. My favorite champagne-filled chocolate truffles. Thoughtful gifts that let me know I was always on his mind.

He returned with a white cardboard food box that he handed to me. I sat up, and opened the box. A single, perfect red rose rested across the top of two plastic-wrapped ramekins of crème brulée.

Between the ramekins was a small black velvet jewelry box. Time stood still, and my hands shook as I picked up the box.

When I opened it, my breath caught. The most stunning engagement ring I'd ever seen rested inside. A ring of small diamonds surrounded a large, cushion-cut diamond that was at least three carats in size. The setting was platinum. The diamonds caught the sunlight and glittered with inner fire.

I looked up at Jake, who had gone down on one knee. The intensity in his expression overwhelmed me. We gazed into each other's eyes for a long moment before he spoke.

"Juliana, I love you. The day we met, when we searched for Barkley on the beach, and went on our first kayak trip and picnic together, I had no idea that my life was about to change forever. But I'm so glad that it did. By the end of that day, I knew in my heart that you were the one. My soulmate. My true love. The one woman I've waited my whole life to meet."

My eyes filled with tears of joy, and Jake took my hands in his.

"That first day in Harpswell, I couldn't tear my eyes away from you, and every time that we're together, I know that I never want us to be apart. I love everything about you—your quirky sense of humor, the way your smile lights up your face when you're happy, the way you twirl your hair in your fingers when you're deep in thought. I can't imagine life without you, and I never want to. Will you marry me?"

I threw my arms around him and silenced him with a passionate kiss. When we finally came up for air, Jake looked at me.

"Can I take that as a yes?"

I looked at him and nodded, too overcome by emotion to speak.

He lifted the ring from the box in my hands. He then took my left hand in his and slid the ring onto my finger. We both admired the ring, and then he brought my hand to his lips and kissed it. "You've made me the happiest man alive."

I squeezed his hand. "No, you've made me the happiest woman."

Jake flopped onto his side and pulled me down beside him on the picnic blanket. He draped his arm over my hips.

"We can argue about who's happiest later," he said. "Right now, I just want to celebrate this moment—with my lovely fiancée."

And we proceeded to do exactly that.

22

Later that evening, Jake and I took a taxi to the OXO Tower Restaurant on the South Bank, where he had reserved a table for dinner. I'd worn the new cocktail dress that I'd purchased in New York the previous weekend, and the scorching head-to-toe look Jake had given me when I stepped out of the dressing room of our hotel suite left no doubt of his approval.

As our cab zipped through the busy streets of London, I looked down at the beautiful ring on my finger. I couldn't believe that I was engaged to the love of my life, and I was so happy that we were going to spend the rest of our lives together. I ran my fingers over the ring and wondered just how we would go about sharing the news of our engagement with our family and friends.

My family was straightforward enough. I was an only child, and I wasn't close to my parents or anyone in my extended family. While I sometimes wished that my family was closer, that particular cloud did have a silver lining, which was that no one questioned my decisions.

Jake's tight-knit family was another matter.

I'd met his parents—John and Fiona—only once, not long after we'd begun dating, at an opening reception at Connor's gallery. Our meeting had been pleasant but brief, and given that John and Fiona barely knew me, I had no idea how they would respond to the announcement that their treasured oldest son intended to marry me. On the bright side, I knew that Lara, Duncan, and Connor would be supportive, and felt optimistic that Nick, Jake's youngest brother, would be as well.

I leaned into Jake's side, and a wave of love for him washed over me. He'd proposed in such a beautiful, romantic way, and now we were on our way to dinner at one of London's most fabulous restaurants. Questions of who to tell, when, and how could wait. Tonight was about us.

Jake squeezed my hand. "Penny for your thoughts?" he asked.

"I was just wondering if you could pinch me. I'm having difficulty believing that this is real."

"Where would you like me to pinch you?"

"I'll let you figure that out later. But seriously, I feel so lucky. Not everyone has what we have."

He nodded in agreement and put his arm around my shoulders. "We're very fortunate to have found each other."

Our cab crossed the Thames to the South Bank and soon arrived at the OXO Tower. Jake paid the driver, and we went inside. We took the elevator to the eighth floor restaurant, which Jake had told me offered one of the city's best views.

Still, I wasn't prepared for what I saw when we entered the restaurant. The dining room faced the river, and its angled floor-to-ceiling windows provided a stunning view of the Thames and the city. The setting sun painted the sky with streaks of vivid color. Silhouetted against the sky, the London cityscape glittered and pulsed with life.

Inside the restaurant, the shuttered ceiling glowed with blue-tinted light that contrasted against the red hues of the floral arrangements and the red-tinted lighting at the base of the trees on the terrace outside.

After we were seated and Jake had ordered a bottle of Veuve Clicquot, he reached across the table and took my left hand. He'd traded his jeans and T-shirt for a fashion forward dark suit paired with a fitted white button-front shirt, worn tieless with the top two buttons undone. He looked hot enough to melt a North Atlantic iceberg, and more than a few female heads had turned when we'd entered the restaurant.

"What do you think of getting married on the beach in Harpswell?" he asked. "It's where we met and fell in love, and it's also my favorite place in the world."

I could picture it. A beautiful summer afternoon—hopefully sunny—with the stunning Maine coast as a backdrop. The wedding party, dressed in summer beige and white, with touches of gold.

"I love the idea of getting married where we first met," I said. "Do you think that your parents would be OK with it?"

Jake furrowed his brow. "I think so. Of course, if you'd rather have a big church wedding—"

Just then, our waiter arrived with the champagne and poured us both a glass.

After the waiter departed with our dinner order, I raised my glass and looked at Jake. "Here's to a small, intimate beach wedding."

He clinked his glass against mine. His relief was apparent. "I knew I was marrying the right woman."

"Seriously, the thought of that kind of three-ring circus—not to mention all the planning and expense involved—isn't even remotely appealing."

"Three-ring circus is a pretty good description of half the weddings I've attended."

"It goes on forever because it takes hours just to get everyone in and out of the church. And then there's the food. Invite two hundred people and by the time dinner hits the table, it's cold."

"Roast beef au jus," Jake said. "Which should really be called lukewarm meat in cold blood."

I laughed. "Congealed mashed potatoes."

Jake grinned. "Dry chicken in brown sludge."

"Stringy green beans."

"Rubbery pork in pink water."

"Wilted salad."

"Calcified bread rolls—so hard that they could function as a murder weapon."

"You're killing me," I said. "I'm so glad that you're not into the whole big white wedding extravaganza."

"Not at all. If we limit the guest list to close family and friends, maybe we could do a lobster bake on the beach. We could have a three-day weekend house party, with the wedding on the second day."

I smiled at him. "That's it. You've just described my dream wedding."

"Maybe Memorial Day weekend next year?"

"That would be perfect. Between your new job, me moving to London, and settling into our new condo, we'll be busy until the snow flies. And if you want to get married in the winter, we'll have to elope to Vegas, because despite my New England heritage, I refuse to get married in a snowbank."

"Elope to Vegas?" Jake grinned. "I'd elope with you right now, but my mother would kill me, and Lara would roast you over a slow fire."

Later, after our meal arrived, we continued to bounce wedding ideas back and forth, and by the time we finished our entrees, we'd agreed on an overall plan. The wedding would be the climax of a weekend-long house party with the friends and family who were dearest to us. It would be casual, intimate and fun. Lara would be the maid of honor, and Connor the best man.

When our waiter had cleared the table and handed us each a dessert menu, I looked over the top of my menu at Jake. The blue-tinted light caught the highlights in his hair and reflected off the planes of his cheekbones and jaw.

As I watched him peruse the menu, I could hardly believe that this beautiful, wonderful man was my fiancé. *My fiancé.* The words sent a shiver of excitement down my spine.

Until I'd met Jake, I hadn't truly known what love could be. At this point, we were so much more than the sexual chemistry that had drawn us together when we first met. Our relationship had been challenged, and we'd not only survived that challenge, but come out of it stronger and more committed to each other than before.

Every time that a decision needed to be made—where to live, what sort of wedding we wanted—talking it through with Jake only made me more aware of how similar our core values were. Like any couple, we occasionally disagreed, but our disagreements tended to be about small, unimportant things. When it came to the big stuff, we were totally in sync. I knew that Jake was my soulmate, and earlier today, he'd used the same word to describe how he felt about me.

He glanced up and caught me watching him. His lips quirked. "See anything you like?"

I gave him a look. "On or off the menu?"

"Let's start with the menu," he said. "We'll have plenty of time to go off-menu later."

23

When we returned to our hotel, Jake picked up a brown paper shopping bag at the front desk.

"What's that?" I asked.

"You'll see," he said. He folded the top of the bag over, and tucked it under his arm. I was consumed by curiosity, but restrained myself.

After we took the elevator to our floor and entered our suite, Jake suggested a hot bath, which sounded fabulous to me.

"I'll run the bath while you get undressed. Then I'll join you." He gave me a look that left no doubt about his intentions.

I went into the dressing area and began to remove and put away my clothes. As I did so, I smiled to myself in anticipation of a hot bath and sexy times with Jake. It had been a wonderful day—the best day of my life—and I didn't want it to end.

When I emerged from the dressing area and walked through the bedroom to the bath, I realized what had been inside Jake's shopping bag.

A profusion of rose petals were scattered around the built-in marble bath, where fragrant bubbles rose from the steaming water. A dozen lit candles illuminated the room, creating a warm, romantic atmosphere. I was moved that Jake had gone to so much trouble to make everything about our engagement day special.

I kissed him meaningfully on the lips. "I love this—and I love you."

"I hope the temperature is OK," he said.

I dipped a finger in the steaming water. "It's perfect." I stepped into the bath, eased myself to a sitting position, and leaned back languorously, releasing a little moan. The hot water felt amazing. "Oh, Jake. It's incredible. Get your clothes off and join me."

He leaned over the bath and kissed me. "Back in a flash," he said, and disappeared into the bedroom.

I slid downward and submerged myself completely for a moment. Then I raised my head above the water, pushed my dripping hair back from my face, leaned back, and closed my eyes. As the heat caressed my weary muscles, I felt myself relax completely.

When I heard footsteps, I opened my eyes, and saw Jake enter the room. In the candlelight, his tanned, muscular body reflected hues of bronze and gold. As he walked toward me in all his naked glory, I admired the beautiful proportions of his body. His broad, well-developed shoulders and chest narrowed to his waist and sculpted abs, where a light trail of hair ran down to his impressive package, which was clearly ready for action. His lean, muscular flanks flexed with each step as he approached the bath.

He reached for my shoulders and gently slid me forward just enough so that he could step into the bath behind me. After he sat down, I leaned back against his broad chest. His arms curved around me and his hands moved up to cup my breasts.

He released a contented sigh. "A perfect end to a perfect day."

"You made it perfect," I said. "You make me feel so loved…and treasured."

He began to play with my nipples, which quickly hardened in response to his touch. "I treasure you, and I treasure every moment we have together." He trailed kisses and love bites over my neck and shoulders, and continued to caress my breasts. Heat built and spread inside me, and I felt his arousal against my lower back.

His right hand dipped to my sensitive folds, and stroked me lightly. I gasped when his fingers went deeper and slipped inside me.

"I could make you come like this," he said. "But I have something better in mind. Get on your knees in front of me."

I did, and looked back over my shoulder just in time to see him raise his body out of the water and smooth lube onto himself. The sight of his strong hands moving over his thick girth inflamed my desire, and I shuddered with need for him. He slid back into the water, grasped my hips, and guided me onto his hard length.

As he entered me, my entire body quivered, and I knew I couldn't last long. He set a slow rhythm that drove me to the brink of climax, and then held me there for what seemed like forever. The room spun, and the flickering candles seemed to hover around us like so many stars that shattered into fireworks when we came together, calling each other's names.

Afterward, we lingered in the bath for several minutes before Jake roused himself.

"I'm turning into a prune," he said. "My skin feels like it's shrinking." He carefully untangled himself from me and climbed out of the bath.

Before he could step away, I reached my arm out and stroked my hand along his length. "Fortunately, this hasn't shrunk at all. If anything, it's grown."

He gave me a look. "You're welcome to continue checking me for signs of shrinkage—after we dry off."

He helped me out of the bath, handed me a towel, and began to dry himself with another. When he'd finished, he wrapped his towel loosely around his hips, where it hung deliciously low, tented by his erection. Then he grabbed a third towel and began to squeeze the water from my hair.

"There," he said, when he was finished. "Your hair is damp, but the rest of you should be warm and dry."

I stood on my tiptoes and kissed him. "I've never asked you—do you want a large family like the one you grew up in, or a small family?"

"Large."

I smiled at that. "Same here."

He looked at me. "But we'll wait for awhile. We're young, and we have plenty of time."

"Agreed. But if we're going to make babies together, we'll need to practice—a lot. Practice makes perfect, you know."

In a single smooth movement, he bent down, picked me up, and held me against his broad chest. He carried me into the bedroom and laid me gently on the bed, which was also strewn with rose petals. He removed first the towel wrapped around my body and then the one around his own, and flung both aside.

"Let's practice right now," he said.

And we did.

24

Less than a week later, Jake and I were on a plane headed for Portland, Maine. After much discussion, we'd decided to announce our engagement at the Barlow family's annual Fourth of July celebration in Harpswell.

I watched through the airplane window as the Portland harbor came into view. Aside from a brief layover in New York, we'd been sitting for hours, and I could hardly wait to stretch my legs.

Jake looked at me. "We'll be on the ground in ten minutes, and in Harpswell in an hour or so. Are you ready?"

"I'm ready," I said. "I just hope your parents approve."

Jake squeezed my hand. "They already know that you're moving to London and that we're getting a place together. Our engagement may come as a surprise, but once Mom and Dad get to know you, I'm sure they'll love you. And you know Lara will be over the moon, which will mean a lot to my parents."

I looked at the stunning diamond ring on my left hand, and it occurred to me that the ring was an announcement in its own right. I turned back to Jake. "I know you want to tell everyone at once, but won't my ring give us away?"

"I've already thought of that," he said. He reached into the pocket of his jeans and pulled out the black velvet box that the ring had come in. "We'll put the ring in its box, and I'll keep it in my pocket. After I announce our engagement, I'll put the ring back on your finger in front of everyone."

I leaned my head on his shoulder. "You think of everything."

"I just want the whole family to find out at the same time," Jake said. "If we tell some people before others, someone may feel hurt or offended that they weren't the first to get the news."

I looked down at my ring. "You know I'm going to go into mourning when you take this ring off my finger."

"It's just for a few hours," Jake said. "We'd better do it now, in case Lara or Connor has decided to surprise us by meeting our flight."

"You're right, but I've become very attached to it." I twisted the ring off my finger and gave it to him.

"It's in a good cause." He put the ring in its box, and then leaned over and kissed me. "I promise to put it back on your finger soon."

After we left the plane, we picked up our luggage and walked to the Avis counter to pick up the keys for our rental car. Jake signed the necessary paperwork and we headed for the parking lot.

It was a sunny July day, and I enjoyed the warmth of the late afternoon sun as we walked, each pulling a wheeled suitcase behind us. Jake looked handsome as ever in a gray T-shirt, 501s, and black Prada flip-flops. Not every man could pull off sandals, but Jake certainly could. His feet were as toned and as sexy as the rest of him. As we walked, I slung my right arm low around his hips, and he draped his left arm across my shoulders.

When we arrived at the lot, Jake pointed out a red BMW Z4 convertible. "There's our car. Since this is a short trip and we don't have much luggage, why not have a fun drive?"

"That car is almost as hot as you."

We piled our bags into the trunk and got into the car. Jake turned the key in the ignition, and the engine roared to life. He put the top down and then backed out of the parking space.

"Make sure your seatbelt's fastened," he said. "This baby's got plenty of horses, and I plan on using every one of them."

"So long as you keep us on the road, stud."

Forty-five minutes later, we were in Harpswell. Just after we turned onto the narrow road that led to the Barlow house, Jake pulled over and we reviewed our plan.

My ring was in its box in Jake's pocket so that no one would know anything until we broke the news to them. My finger felt oddly naked without it, but Jake would put it back on as soon as he announced our engagement.

"Whatever you do, don't look Lara in the eye," Jake said. "If you do, she'll know in a heartbeat. My sister is no fool, but there is one thing that will work in our favor. She's bringing Cole with her, which should distract some of her attention away from us."

"You're right. I'd better not look at Duncan, either. He can totally read my mind. You'd better tell everyone soon after we arrive, before Lara or Duncan susses it out."

"I'll work fast," Jake said. "You'll say that you need to freshen up, which will let you avoid immediate cross-examination. While you take a shower upstairs, I'll get everyone out on the deck. And when you come back downstairs, we'll do it."

I pulled my compact from my purse and checked my hair. "I *do* need to freshen up. Thank goodness I have a brush in my purse—my hair's totally out of control." I gave my wavy hair a quick brushing, put it up in a loose chignon, and then inspected myself in the mirror. "That's somewhat better."

"I don't know," Jake teased. "I kind of liked your windblown warrior princess look."

"Please. I looked like I had jammed my entire hand in an electrical outlet."

He eyed himself in the rear view mirror and rubbed his jaw. "I could use a shave, and my mother is guaranteed to call me out on it. Just wait and see."

I ran my fingers over his jawline. "I like your stubbly look."

"That's fortunate, because it's what you're going to see every morning from now on." He leaned over and kissed me. "Ready to get this show on the road?"

I smiled at him. "Let's go."

25

After Jake and I arrived at the Barlow house, we got out of the car and began to remove our luggage from the trunk. I heard a door slam, and Lara ran out to meet us. She threw her arms around me, and I hugged her back fiercely.

"I've missed you," she said. "I have so much to tell you. And I want to hear everything about London."

"I've missed you terribly," I said. "London is fabulous, but thanks to ten hours of air travel followed by an hour on the road, I feel horribly sticky and grimy. Mind if I take a quick shower? Then we can catch up over a glass of wine."

"Of course," Lara said. "Go rinse off your travel grime. You're in the same upstairs room as the last time you were here."

I looked around, but didn't see Duncan and Connor.

"Where's Duncan?" I asked.

"And Connor?" Jake said. "Did they go into Brunswick or something?"

Lara shook her head. "They left to take a walk on the beach an hour ago. I expect them back any minute. Everyone else is out on the deck enjoying this perfect Fourth of July weather."

I looked at Jake, who cocked his head toward the house. His message was clear. I needed to get my ass in the shower before Duncan and Connor returned from their walk.

"Go take your shower," he said. "Don't worry about the bags. I'll bring them to our room."

"Back in a flash," I said, and headed toward the house. "I won't be long."

Half an hour later, clean and refreshed from my shower, I went downstairs, crossed the main living space, and stepped outside onto the deck. I walked over to Jake, who stood against the deck railing with Barkley at his side. The golden retriever sat next to Jake, contentedly thumping the deck with his tail.

I glanced around. It appeared that Jake had successfully maneuvered the entire party outside. People sat or stood in small clusters on the deck, which overlooked the beach and the ocean beyond. The sky was streaked with orange, pink, and gold, interspersed with patches of blue and purple, and the ocean waves reflected and scattered the vivid colors. Several bottles of Chateauneuf-du-Pape stood on the table, and everyone had a glass.

Jake's parents, John and Fiona, were seated in deck chairs next to Connor and Duncan. John was an older version of Jake, but dark-haired like Nick, with streaks of silver at his temples. Slender with blonde hair worn in a sleek chignon, Fiona was a good three or four inches shorter than Lara, but like Lara, she exuded a natural authority. Like everyone else, Fiona was dressed casually, but she'd accessorized her capri pants and T-shirt with a gorgeous string of pearls and matching earrings.

Nick and his girlfriend Ariel stood together, talking in low voices. Lara and Cole stood side by side, leaning on the railing of the deck, Lara's blonde head next to Cole's dark one. She threw her head back and laughed at something he'd said. I knew from Lara that she and Cole hadn't made love yet, but from the way those two were looking at each other, I didn't think that it would be long before they did.

Jake leaned over, and spoke into my ear. "Now that everyone's out here—it's time."

I nodded, and patted his shoulder. He cleared his throat, and then began to speak. "Hey everyone—while we're all here together, there's something I'd like to say."

Conversation halted, and heads turned toward Jake. He waited for a moment, and then spoke.

"All of you know that Juliana will be transferring to London so that we can be together. What you don't know—yet—is that six days ago, in Hyde Park, Juliana made me the happiest man in the world, when she agreed to marry me."

"Yes!" Lara shouted, as cheers and whistles broke out from the rest of the party. She pointed an accusing finger at us, "You two tricked me!"

"We *so* got you, girl," I said.

"No one ever pulls one over on me!"

"Well, you can't say that now, can you?"

We both laughed.

Jake held up a hand for silence. After the group quieted, he pulled the ring box from his pocket, opened it, and removed the ring, which he slid onto my finger.

He looked into my eyes. "Juliana—I love you more than words can say. The day you said yes—the day I put this ring on your finger—was the best day of my life. Today, here in Harpswell, where we first met and fell in love, I'm so happy—and so proud—to share our engagement with our closest family and friends."

Tears of joy welled in my eyes. Jake pulled me into his arms and kissed me, as the cheers and whistles started up again. Excited by the commotion, Barkley jumped on us, and Jake released me to settle him down. "That's right, buddy," he said to the dog as he scratched Barkley's ears affectionately. "You're coming to London, too, as soon as your doggy passport comes through."

Lara ran over and threw her arms around me.

"Now we're truly sisters," she said.

I hugged her fiercely. "Sisters—and best friends forever. Will you be my maid of honor? You introduced me and Jake, and it's really important to me that you be part of our wedding."

She hugged me again. "Of course! I'm thrilled that you want me to be part of your big day."

Duncan and Connor were close behind Lara.

Duncan hugged me. "I'm so happy for you," he said, and then shook Jake's hand. "Take good care of my best girl." He winked. "Or you'll have—"

"Two brilliant and resourceful queens wreaking vengeance on your sorry ass," Connor finished Duncan's sentence. "Condragulations, old man."

Jake looked at Connor. "Old man? I'm only two years older than you. And what the hell does condragulations mean, anyway?"

Connor shook his head. "What a pity. Such ignorance."

"Just think RuPaul," Duncan said.

"As in 'RuPaul's Drag Race'," I said.

"As in creative genius and epic hilarity," Connor said. "Juliana, you need to take charge of your fiancé's education, because obviously, I've failed."

Jake laughed. "I get the gist, OK? And I promise to take good care of Juliana. Which, by the way, begins with signing you on as best man, Connor. And Duncan and Nick as groomsmen. And you have to come visit us in London soon, once we're settled into our new place."

Connor hugged Jake. "Of course I'll be your best man. I love you, bro, and I wish you and Juliana all the happiness in the world."

Then Jake's parents approached. Fiona embraced me warmly, and John said, in a voice that was gruff with emotion, "I look forward to getting to know the lovely woman who's won my son's heart." He gripped my hand, and then kissed my cheek. "Welcome to the family."

Fiona smiled at us. "So when will the wedding be?"

Lara chimed in. "And where? We need to start making plans."

"We'd like to get married here in Harpswell, on the beach," Jake said. "We want to keep it intimate—just family and close friends."

"When?" Lara asked.

"Next year. Memorial Day weekend," I said. "We've talked about having a three-day house party, with the wedding on the second day."

Fiona nodded briskly, and I saw an echo of Lara in her expression. "We'll talk to your Uncle Edward and Aunt Anne. Between their house and ours, we can host about fifty people."

"Thanks, Mom," Jake said. He looked at me. "You remember Uncle Edward's house, right? It's similar in size to ours, and just down the beach from us."

I nodded, and Jake turned back to Fiona. "For our wedding dinner, we're thinking of having a lobster bake on the beach."

"And maybe fireworks after the sun goes down?" Lara asked. "Now that fireworks are legal in Maine, I've become an expert. Cole and I brought a trunkful to set off tonight."

Jake grinned at her. "Once a pyro, always a pyro." He turned to me. "Guess who nearly set this house on fire when we were kids."

"That's a lie," Lara said.

"The scorch mark on the kitchen counter doesn't lie," Jake said.

Lara rolled her eyes. "Once—and only once—I left a stick of incense burning. It fell out of the holder and scorched the counter, and Jake will never let me live it down."

"Why should I?" Jake said. "I'm your big brother, and teasing you is part of the job description. But I'm glad you brought fireworks. Need any help setting them off?"

Lara shook her head. "Cole and I have it covered."

Fiona clapped her hands together. "OK, everyone," she announced. "We'll eat dinner and afterward, Lara and Cole will set off the fireworks. Nick and Ariel, fire up the grill. Connor and Duncan will help me with the salad. And John, this occasion definitely calls for champagne. There should be a case of Veuve Clicquot in the basement—get half a dozen bottles and put them on ice for later. Jake and Juliana, you're in charge of setting up glasses, plates, and cutlery for ten on the table on the deck. Lara, you and Cole can light the deck lanterns."

"Aye-aye, Mom," Jake said. He kissed his mother on the cheek. "It's good to be home."

Fiona reached up to ruffle his hair. "I hope you shaved before you proposed to this beautiful young lady. You look like a porcupine."

Jake grinned down at his mother. "Fortunately for me, my fiancée likes porcupines. Hopefully, she likes interfering mother-in-laws too."

Fiona gave me an exasperated look. "Don't listen to him," she said. "I'm sure you know this by now, but my son is and always has been a terrible tease."

I smiled and reached for Jake's hand. "His sense of humor is a big part of why I fell in love with him."

Fiona looked at us, and her expression softened. "Never forget to laugh," she said. "As long as there's love and laughter between you, you'll be strong enough to handle whatever life throws at you."

Jake put his arm around her. "I love you, Mom."

She hugged him. "And I love you," she said. "Now go set the table before the food's ready and there are no plates to put it on."

After dinner, Connor and Duncan opened the now-chilled champagne and poured a glass for each of us. When everyone had a glass in hand, John pushed back his chair and stood up.

"This is a very special moment for Fiona and me," he said. "Thirty years ago, we were blessed with our first child, a beautiful baby boy who we named Jake. Over the years that followed, I watched him grow and become the man we all know and love today—a man who I couldn't be more proud to call my son."

He turned to Jake and me. "As the two of you begin your life together, I wish you all the best of what life has to offer. Cherish each other, cherish the love that you have for each other, and always be honest with each other. If you do these things, your love for each other will only grow as the years pass."

John reached down and took Fiona's hand, and she gave him a radiant smile. Then he raised his champagne glass. "To Jake and Juliana. May their life together be long and happy."

"To Jake and Juliana," the party echoed.

We all drank, and then Fiona took charge. "Nick and Ariel, help me move these chairs so that everyone will have a good view of the fireworks. Lara and Cole, you can go set them off now."

Within a few minutes, we sat facing the beach, our champagne glasses freshly filled. Jake and I had pushed our chairs together, and we sat in silence. My head rested on his shoulder, and his arm circled my waist. I touched the ring that he'd put back on my finger tonight, and my heart swelled with love for him. The way he had announced our engagement had been so romantic, like a second proposal. One proposal from the man of my dreams was amazing enough. But two? It was beyond anything I ever could have imagined.

The fireworks began with a pop, a crackle, and a series of Roman candles that rose and sparkled in the sky. I heard a low boom and a whistle when Lara and Cole set off the first aerial shell. Several more quickly followed. Explosions of color lit the night sky. The fireworks expanded and cascaded like giant sprays of flowers, which scattered reflections of light across the surface of the ocean beyond. For the next few minutes, Jake and I relaxed, sipped champagne and enjoyed the show.

He took my left hand, brought it to his lips, and kissed it. "What an evening," he said.

"Your parents are amazing," I said. "They made me feel so welcome."

"Mom and Dad have been in love with each other for over thirty years," Jake said. "They can tell that you and I are the real thing." He leaned back in his chair and continued to watch the fireworks explode over the water.

As I watched the vivid colors of the fireworks play across his handsome features, my thoughts returned to the day we first met, here in Harpswell, on the very deck where we now sat. From the moment I first saw Jake Barlow, I'd found him devastatingly attractive. Still, with my history, I'd never expected to find the kind of love that we had. I hadn't had a clue that such love existed.

Our first day together, when we'd chased Barkley on the beach and gone kayaking together, I'd begun to fall in love with him. The relationship that we'd kindled that day had only strengthened with time, and we'd overcome every obstacle that had threatened to separate us.

Jake had changed my world. He'd given me faith in love—and family. As I glanced around at the people who surrounded us, I felt overwhelmed by gratitude. Duncan. Lara. Connor. They were my closest and dearest friends. They were my family, and I was so fortunate to have them in my life. I'd just begun to get to know the rest of Jake's family, but they'd all been nothing but wonderful to me, and supportive of our engagement.

I leaned over, cupped Jake's face in my hands, and kissed him with everything I had in me. He pulled me into his arms and deepened the kiss.

After we came up for air, he looked into my eyes. "That was quite a kiss. What did I do to deserve it?" He traced my chin with his thumb.

I met his gaze. "I love you, Jake Barlow."

Reflections of the fireworks sparkled in his beautiful green eyes. "I can't wait to be able to call you Juliana Barlow."

I tried the name out. "Juliana Barlow." It sounded perfect. It felt even better to say it and know that one day soon, it would be real.

I slid onto his thigh and wrapped my arms around his neck. "Tonight begins the rest of our lives, and I can't wait to spend the rest of my life with you."

His smile broadened. "I can't wait to spend *tonight* with you. After Lara's fireworks end, let's make some fireworks of our own."

I kissed him. "I was hoping you'd suggest something along those lines."

He slipped an arm around my waist. I leaned against his broad chest and rested my head against his shoulder. As I watched the fireworks illuminate the night sky and reflect across the ocean waves, I could feel his heart beating next to mine.

My own heart was filled with love—and overwhelmed by joy. I felt incredibly fortunate, and grateful. Held in Jake's strong arms, I knew that nothing could ever part us. It was an incredible moment, and I looked forward to many more such moments with the man of my dreams, the love of my life—and now, my fiancé.

Our new life had begun.

AFTERWORD

Thank you for reading *On the Brink*! I know that your time is valuable and sincerely thank you for finishing this book! If you would take a brief moment to return to where you purchased the book and leave a review it would be much appreciated.

Reviews help new readers find my work and accurately decide if the book is for them, as well as provide valuable feedback for my future writing.

This page on my website contains a list of all my books, as well as links to all retailers who carry them, to save you from needing to search for the book's page in order to leave your review.

Thank you again, and be sure to check out my other books here!

Get the latest on new and upcoming releases!
Find me on Facebook at https://www.facebook.com/ErikaRhys.Author

I'm on Facebook often and enjoy chatting with my readers.

Join my mailing list at http://erikarhys.com/subscribe/. List members receive about one email a month featuring free ARC, giveaway, and book release announcements.

Your email will NOT be shared with anyone else, and you can unsubscribe from the list at any time—although I hope that you'll choose to stay!

Printed in Great Britain
by Amazon

20894012R00200